come back
for me

NEW YORK TIMES BESTSELLING AUTHOR
CORINNE MICHAELS

Come Back for Me

Cover Design:
Sommer Stein, Perfect Pear Creative

Editing:
Ashley Williams, AW Editing

Proofreading:
Michele Ficht
Janice Owen

Formatting:
Alyssa Garcia, Uplifting Author Services

Cover photo © Brian Kaminski

1048149

The Arrowood Brothers Series
Come Back for Me
Fight for Me
The One for Me
Lie for Me

To Melissa Saneholtz, thank you for your unending friendship, laughter, and love. Feel free to add this as reason number 2099485.

come back
for me

—

one

"Arrowood! Wake the fuck up!" Someone punches my arm, and I shoot out of my seat. My eyes dart around for whatever danger is present, but only find my buddy, Liam, next to me on the plane. "Man, you sure like to talk in your sleep."

I rub my hand over my face, trying to clear the cobwebs. "I have no idea what I was dreaming about."

"A woman."

Great. God only knows what I said. "Doubtful."

"Dude, you were totally talking in your sleep." His voice goes higher. "Oh, Connor, you're so sexy. Yes, give it to me like that." Then he returns his voice to normal. "I'm just saying that she was very animated."

I know exactly what I was dreaming of—an angel. A beautiful woman with dark brown hair and the bluest eyes I'd ever seen. It doesn't matter that I spent one night with her eight years ago, I remember her perfectly.

The way she smiled and crooked her finger at me to follow. How my legs moved without my brain ever giving them permission. It was as if she were sent from above to save me.

The night my father had gotten so drunk he sucker punched me as I walked out the door for boot camp, promising never to return.

She was perfect, and I don't even know her name.

I elbow him, knowing there isn't a chance in hell I'm about to confess any of that. "Thank God you're married. No woman would be stupid enough to ever go for you now. Your impressions suck and you're an asshole."

He grins, no doubt thinking of his wife. Some guys have it all—Liam Dempsey is one of them. He has a beautiful woman to come home to, kids, friends, and he had one of those picture-perfect childhoods.

Basically, his life is the opposite of mine.

Only things I have that are worth a damn are my brothers.

"What are you talking about? There's a reason they call me Dreamboat and call you Arrow. I'm a goddamn dream."

"Here we fucking go. They call me that because of my last name, asshole."

Liam chuckles and shrugs. "Maybe, but mine is because of my glowing personality."

Even though he's a total idiot, I'm going to miss him. I'm going to miss all of my team. I hate that this was my last deployment and I won't be a part of this brotherhood anymore. I've loved being a SEAL.

"Thankfully, you're so vain that I will see your glow anywhere I end up."

"Any idea where that's going to be or what you're going to do now?" Liam asks.

I lean back in the much too uncomfortable chair of this C-5 plane and push out a deep breath. "Not a clue."

"Glad to see you're on top of your life. You need to get your shit together, Arrowood. Life isn't going to hand you shit."

Liam has been my team leader for the last two deployments and is like a big brother to me, but right now, I'd like not to be lectured. I have three older brothers who do enough of that as it is.

Although, I guess that's what the SEAL team is ... brothers. Brothers who would do anything for each other, including help the other through a big transition, even if it's one that's been coming for a while. Three years ago, I was on deployment. It was a routine checkpoint and my leg was crushed when a car tried to run through. I had a few surgeries, all looked good, but I'm not healing right. This deployment, I was on light duty, which was basically admin. I fucking hate admin. I wanted to be out there, making sure my brothers were safe. Then the doc gave me the news that I'm going to be medically discharged.

I'm no longer fit to be a SEAL.

And if I can't do this, then I don't want any part of it.

"I have plans."

"Like?" he asks.

"Kicking your ass, for one."

"You could try, young buck, but I wouldn't put money on it."

"If my leg were a hundred percent ..."

Liam shakes his head. "I'd still kill you. But, all kidding aside, you can't sign the papers in two weeks and have no idea what to do."

My oldest brother Declan was up my ass and saying the same thing when I called him a month ago. Dec runs a huge corporation in New York City and said he was looking for a new head of security, but I'd rather ram my bad leg through a meat processor than work for him. He's a hothead, who knows everything, and he doesn't pay shit. I've already done eight years of that, so I'd like an upgrade in the financial department.

Still, he has a point. I can only survive on what little savings I have for so long, then I'll need to get a job.

"I'll figure it out," I tell him.

"Why not go back home to the farm?"

My eyes narrow, and I bite back the anger that fills me at the mention of that place. "Because the only way I'll step foot on that land is if I'm burying the man who resides there."

The Arrowood brothers made a vow to take care of each other, protect one another, and that was what each of us did until I could get out. Two weeks after graduation was the last time I touched that farmland in Pennsylvania. I'll live on the streets before I go back there.

He puts his hands up. "All right, brother, no need to look like you're about to slice me open. I get it. No going home. I'm just worried. I've seen a lot of guys get out and struggle to navigate civilian life. As much as we bitch about this life, it becomes us, you know?"

He's right. Hell, I've seen it too, but I wasn't ready for getting out to be my reality. I would've done twenty years with a smile because the navy saved my life. I was going to end up in jail if I hadn't enlisted. Then, when I was in, I got selected for BUDs and refused to ever be anything else. Now, it isn't my choice.

"I'm not sure what else I could even be at this point."

"My buddy Jackson has a company that takes broken SEALs, I'm sure he has room for one more."

I flip him off. "I'll show you broken."

Before we can get any further into a spat, the officers come around, letting us know we're preparing for landing and how they want the offload to go.

Homecomings are like nothing anyone can comprehend.

They are filled with emotions, balloons, fanfare, tears of happiness, and a lot of excitement. The wives are dressed up, and the kids look perfect and polished when we know that their lives the last nine months were anything but. You can see the families so ready for a glimpse of their loved one they would climb on top of each other.

Then there is how we feel.

Our nerves are different. We are ready to get home and see the people we love, but at the same time, we know that it won't be easy. Loving a man who is preparing to leave again can't be easy. It's why I'm grateful that love and marriage were never high up on my priority list.

I like knowing that there is no sacrifice made in order to love me.

The commander falls quiet, waiting for everyone's attention. "Patterson and Caldwell will go first since they had babies while we were gone. Then it'll be alphabetical to deplane. Once you've checked out with me, grab your gear and don't report back to base for two weeks, understand?"

"Aye." We all answer in unison.

He puts the clipboard down and eyes us all. "Don't make me have to explain to my wife why I have to leave home to come bail one of you idiots out."

A few of us laugh, but he isn't because it may have happened two deployments ago. Thankfully, it wasn't me.

The plane touches down, and I swear I can feel the energy shift. Since it's alphabetical, I'll be one of the first off, but our team is filled with guys who have kids. I'll wait until they're off, take the ass-chewing from Commander Hansen, and go on my merry way the same as the other single guys do.

Commander calls my name, but I stay rooted. His voice rises again. "Arrowood!" He glares at me, but I shrug. "Jesus, every damn deployment you morons do this. Fine, I'll call your name twice, and if you don't get up, you're moved to the back of the line. Idiots. I'm surrounded by them."

"See you in a few weeks," Liam says as his name is called.

"I'll be sure to say goodbye."

He slaps me on my chest. "You do that."

After the rest of the names are called, I hear mine again.

Commander doesn't look at all happy, but I see the hint of pride hidden behind his scowl. "You're a good man."

"Those kids want their fathers."

He nods. "Here's your paperwork. I'll see you back in fourteen days."

I nod, take the paper, and head off. The sun is shining, and the air smells clean. There's no dust or dirt clinging to my skin as I walk down the stairs.

"Yo, douchebag." I freeze for a second before turning to face my brother—who isn't supposed to be here.

"Sean?" He walks toward me, arms open and a huge smile on his lips.

"Good to see you home in one piece."

We give each other a hug, slamming our hands on each other's backs. "What the hell are you doing here?"

"I figured someone should see you home from your last deployment."

"Well, it's good to see you," I say with a smile.

"It's good to see you too, little brother."

I may be the youngest, but I'm not little. Sean is the shortest out of us, but he has the biggest heart. I sometimes wish I was more like him.

"You know, I can slice you from ass to cheek in about ten seconds, you really want to spar?"

He slaps me on the shoulder. "Not today, I'm here for something else."

"Yeah?"

"Yeah, we have to go meet Declan and Jacob . . ."

A sliver of worry fills me. We don't exactly have family reunions. In fact, I think the last time the four of us were together was the day I graduated from boot camp. My brothers and I are all one year apart going down the line. My poor mother had four kids in four years and then spent the next seven years raising four boys who weren't known for being easy kids. We banded together and were best friends—in all things mischievous.

Now, though, we're all scattered like the wind and only see each other separately for the most part.

"Meet them where."

Sean clenches his jaw and then releases a heavy sigh. "Sugarloaf. Our father is dead. It's time to go home."

two

"And now that's over," Declan says as he stares down at the hole in the ground where the casket rests. The graveyard is old with a few headstones that are still broken from the bonfire night where we all were idiots.

It's quiet, and the smell of farming fills the air. A bit of manure, a bit of smoke, and a lot of regrets. I thought I would feel better now that he's dead, but all I feel is anger.

"Not completely," Sean reminds us. "We still have to figure out what to do with the farm and the land."

"Burn it," I say without feeling. Being back here makes me itch. Even with him dead, I still feel as if he's watching, judging, and preparing to raise his fists. Hell, it still feels as if the secrets we've kept because of him are trying to choke me.

"Connor has a point. Although, it would make me feel better if the old man were still in it when we set it on fire," Jacob tacks on.

I agree. My father used to be a good man. He loved his

boys, his wife, and his farm, giving everything he was to each one. Then my mother died and we lost both parents.

Gone was the kind, fun, and hardworking man who taught me how to ride a bike and fish. Instead, he became a hollow drunk who used his fists to speak his rage.

And boy was he angry.

At everyone. At everything. Mostly, at my brothers and me for reminding him of the woman he loved and God took way too soon. As if we weren't grieving the loss of the most wonderful mother who ever drew breath.

Dec shakes his head. "This is the only thing the bastard left us, and it's worth millions. It's also where Mom's ashes are scattered. We're going to be patient, like we've been, and sell it. Unless one of you wants it?"

"Hell no." I don't want a damn thing to do with it. I want it out of my life so I never have to come back to Sugarloaf again.

Everyone else grunts in agreement.

"Well, we're all going to have to meet with the lawyer sometime this week, and then we sell the fucking thing."

I have no doubts Dec has already pulled strings to get us the hell out of here as quick as possible. Just like the rest of us, he has a lot he wants to avoid in this town, which won't be possible if we're here more than a day.

The four of us pile into Sean's car and head back to the house, but as soon as we get to the entrance, the car stops.

The wooden pillars with the sign overhead and our last name burned into the wood is aged, but still standing strong. I try not to remember my mother's voice, but the memory comes too strong and too fast and I'm eight years old again.

"Now, what is one truth about an arrow?"

I groan as her brow lifts and she waits for the answer. "Mom, the new Nintendo game is at home, and I want to play."

"Then you best answer me, Connor. What is one truth about an arrow?"

I saved money from my last birthday, but it wasn't enough so I had to borrow money from Jacob for the game. He's so mean, he made me do his chores for six months, but now I have the new Mario. All I want to do is play. I don't care about the arrow.

She puts the car in park and crosses her arms. Mom used to be my favorite.

"Why do we have to say this each time?" I ask.

"Because it's important. Family is what matters in this life, without that, you have nothing. When we cross this threshold, we're back home. We're with those who love us and this, my sweet boy, is where you will always belong."

My mama is the best person I know, and as much as I want my Nintendo game—and I really want it—I want to make her happy more. I like making Mama happy.

"You can't take a shot until you break your bow," I grumble, hating that this is one fact she makes me recite.

She smiles. "That's right. And why is that important?"

"Moooooom," I whine because the game is calling me.

"Don't, Mom me," she tsks. "Why is it important?"

"Because if you don't break the bow, you'll never go forward, and an arrow was meant to forge ahead."

Her eyes fill with love and happiness as she stares over at me. "That's right, and you were meant to go places. Now, let's go to the house to see if your brothers have left it standing."

"And I get to play my game."

Mom laughs. "Yes, and that—after your chores."

"I can't do it," Sean admits as he stares at the dirt driveway.

One by one, my brothers left this place, and each of them

took shifts coming back until I was old enough to leave as well. They protected me in a way I couldn't appreciate at the time. Jacob delayed going to college by a year to make sure Sean could play ball and I wasn't alone with Dad as much. Sean would take me to games, making sure I got out of the house once in a while after Jacob left. Declan went to college but spent his summers back at the farm, ensuring he could shield me from Dad's fists whenever possible.

He looks the most uncomfortable, but he's also the strongest willed of us all. "What is one truth about an arrow?" Dec chokes the words out, and I close my eyes.

Mom. What would she think of us now? Would she understand why we all left this place? Did she see the hell he put us through and what we became because of his choices?

Jacob answers. "Removing half the feather will make the arrow curve and alter its course, which is why sticking together matters."

"Mom would be disappointed in us," Declan says. "No women, no kids, nothing but jobs."

"We have each other," I pipe up. "We always have, and she would've wanted that."

Declan stares out the window. "She would've wanted us to have more . . ."

"Yeah, well, it's hard to have more when you grow up the way we did."

Jacob's voice is quiet and full of sadness. "We made a pact. No marriages, no kids, and never raise our fists in anger. She would've understood. She would've wanted us to stand by each other and be nothing like he was in the end."

Maybe she would, God knows that's what we hoped for. I like to believe that if she's watching, she has seen it all and would understand that her boys made this choice for a reason. I had her the least amount of time, but I think she would've respected the desire to protect others.

If we came from a man like that, surely it was inside us too.

Declan looks at Sean, the brother who was by far the closest to her. He has never forgiven himself for the night she died. "Drive, brother. It's time to go forward."

Sean slams his hand on the steering wheel before putting the car in drive and slowly accelerating down the path to hell.

None of us speak. I know that I can't gather a thought long enough to say a word. There are memories everywhere.

The fence that lines the driveway where my brothers and I would sit and watch the cows, dreaming about running way. I spot the tree that's on the left side of the property where we made a ladder with scraps of wood so we could climb into the branches, pretending we were hidden and safe.

Dad could never reach us up there.

He was always too drunk to get up more than two of the rungs.

Over to the right is the archery course where my brothers and I spent hours imagining we were Robin Hood or other great men who did right.

I can hear the four of us arguing over who shot better, all the while knowing it was Sean. The bastard always had the best form and aim.

And then what once was my home comes into view.

"It's like a fucking time warp," Dec comments. "Nothing has changed."

He's right. The house is exactly the same as it was when I left. It has two stories, and a big wrap-around porch with a swing. The white paint is faded and chipping, and the black shutters are missing on one of the windows and hanging off another. While it may be the same structurally, it's not the home the four of us remember.

I clear my throat. "Only now it's a damn mess."

"I don't think the old man did a damn thing after we left." One of my brothers says from behind me.

There's no way we'll sell this house for what it's worth. Although, the house has never been the prize, the land has been. Over three hundred acres of some of the best cattle land in Pennsylvania. A winding brook flows through it, the grass is premium for the cows, and it's picturesque.

"How could he?" Declan snorts. "He didn't have his work-horses to tend to things while he was drunk off his ass."

I nod, feeling a new type of anger toward him. At least he could've cared about the farm.

"What about the animals?" Sean asks.

"We'll need to do a full inventory and see what the hell we're walking into," I speak up.

My brothers agree, so we divvy up the tasks. It's time to see what else he destroyed.

The farm is a mess, that's all I keep saying to myself. It's a nightmare. He hadn't maintained a single thing other than the diary equipment, which he would've had to keep up and running if he wanted to make enough money to buy his liquor.

Still, the fact that he let the land go, is unbelievable. What could've been a ten million plus inheritance is worth half that at best. It's going to take a hell of a lot of work to get it close to what we'd want to sell it for.

I'm walking in the field out to the left of the creek, the place that I would come to hide. The first time my father drank himself into a rage, I was ten, and Declan took the beating, shielding all of us and telling us to run and hide.

I didn't fully understand what had happened, just that my brother, who I loved, was screaming for me to go.

So I did.

I ran. I ran so hard that I wasn't sure I'd ever stop. I ran until my lungs struggled to get air. I didn't stop until I was where I thought no one could ever find me because Declan had something in his eyes I had never seen—fear.

I'm standing here, on the edge of the creek, looking up at the platform I built in the tree where I spent so many days and nights hiding from the hell that was in my house.

What a fucking mess.

Being here is the last place I want to be, but there's nothing I have to hide from anymore. I'm no longer that scared little boy, and there are no more monsters hiding in the house. Yet, I can't help but feel the pit in my stomach.

The quiet is almost loud as I stand here listening to the creek that used to lull me to sleep. The farmland is beautiful. I can't help but see the lush greens and deep pink hue of the setting sun in the sky, illuminating the clouds and making them look like cotton candy.

I close my eyes, lifting my face to the sky, hearing the sound of my breathing.

And then a thump from above causes my senses to kick in.

I look around, trying to see what it was.

Then a sniffle.

"Hello?" I call out, turning to the tree and the platform high in its branches.

There's a scuffle, the sound of feet shuffling on the wood. Someone is up there. It has to be a kid because a grown adult wouldn't be hiding up on that platform. However, whoever it is doesn't answer.

"Hello? I know you're up there," I say a little softer because I'm trying to be less scary. "You don't have to be afraid."

Another bit of movement and then a cry that is clearly in pain.

I don't wait, I move up the tree, using the wood steps my brothers helped me build so I would always be able to come here.

"I'm coming up. Don't be scared," I instruct, not wanting whoever is up there to fall off the scrap of wood.

I make it to the platform and a little girl is huddled in the corner. Her eyes are wide and full of fear. She doesn't seem much older than I was the first time I headed up here, but I'm not really around kids much, so I have no clue how old she really is. I do know all about the apprehension and the tears running down her face. I used to wear a similar expression in this spot.

"I won't hurt you, are you okay? I heard you cry."

She nods quickly.

"Okay, are you hurt?"

A tear falls down her cheek and she nods again, clutching her arm.

"Is it your arm?" I ask, knowing that's what it is. When she still doesn't speak, I try to remember what it felt like to be hurt and alone, hiding in a tree. "I'm Connor, and I used to live here. This was my favorite place on this whole farm. What's your name?"

Her lip trembles, and she seems to wrestle with whether she can answer me. In the end, her green eyes watch me like a hawk as she clamps her lips tight, letting me know she has no intention of speaking to me.

I take another step up the ladder and lean on the platform. "It's okay, you don't have to tell me."

I'll stay up here for as long as it takes to get her down.

She sits up, her brown hair falling around her face, and she sniffs before pushing it back. "You're a stranger," the little girl says.

"I am. You're right not to talk to strangers. Would it help if I told you that I was also a sort of police officer in the navy?"

Her eyes narrow, assessing me. "Police officers have uniforms."

I grin, smart kid. "That's right. I wore one, but I'm not working now since I'm on the farm. Can you tell me how you hurt your arm?"

"I fell."

"How'd you climb up here?"

She shifts a bit. "I didn't want anyone to find me."

My gut tightens as a million answers as to why this little girl is hiding up here with her arm in pain instead of running home for help. I have to keep myself under control and remember not everyone has a shitty home life. It could be anything.

"Why not?"

She worries her bottom lip. "Daddy said I wasn't supposed to leave the house, and I didn't want him to be angry." Then she wipes her nose with her arm and another tear falls. "I came here so I could wait for Mommy to come home."

I give her a knowing nod. "Well, I'm sure your daddy is worried about you. We should get you back home and get your arm looked at."

"He's going to be so mad." Her lip quivers.

Poor thing is terrified. Of her father or because she broke the rules, I'm not sure. I don't know who she is or who her father is, but she can't stay up here injured and scared. She'll fall. "How about I don't tell him where I found you if he doesn't ask."

She eyes me curiously. "You mean lie?"

"No, I just think that friends keep secrets, and we're friends now, right?"

"I guess so."

"Well, friend, you know my name is Connor, but I still don't know yours."

Her lips purse. "I'm Hadley."

"It's nice to meet you, Hadley. Can I help you down since your arm is hurt?"

Hadley's head bobs quickly.

I instruct her how to get close, and then she wraps her arm around my neck, holding on tightly as I get us both down without jostling her too much. When we get to the ground, I set her on her feet and squat.

We're eye to eye, and there's something about the way she looks at me—as though I'm her savior—that makes my heart ache.

"Is your arm okay?"

"It hurts." Her voice is small and holds a quiet tremor of pain. She moves it across the front of her body, cradling it closely.

"Can I look at it?"

Hadley is a tiny thing. Although, I have no frame of reference on how old she is, if this is a normal height for a kid, or I'm an idiot.

"Okay."

I take a look and there's some bruising and it's swollen, but nothing glaringly obvious that she broke it.

"Well, it doesn't look terrible, but I think we need to get you home so they can make sure it's not broken. Where do you live?"

She points across the creek to where the Walcott farm is.

"Is your last name Walcott?"

"Yup."

I smile. It's good to know they didn't sell off their farm. The Walcott's were good people. My mother and Mrs. Walcott were close friends. When Mom died, Jeanie would bring us food and make sure we still had pie every now and then. I loved her and was sad when she passed. Tim died about a month after her, and my father would say it was from a broken heart. I wish my father loved my mother enough to go die alongside her, but I wasn't that lucky.

I had no idea if someone bought it or if the property was passed down to someone. They never had kids of their own, but it seems it's still in the family.

"I'll walk you home and make sure you don't get hurt again. Do you want to cut across or would you rather I drive you?"

I see her worry, but there's no way I'm letting this kid go off on her own when she's hurt.

"We can walk."

"All right." I stand, put my hand out, and smile when she takes it, knowing I earned a little of her trust.

We make our way to her house, neither of us saying much, but then I feel her start to tremble. I can remember all too well not wanting to go home because my parents were going to be mad at me. Too many times I had the wooden spoon to my hide because my mother said to be back before dark and I'd wandered off, lost in the vast lands that looked the same, and one of my brothers had to come find me.

"How long have you lived here?" I ask, wanting to take her attention off her impending punishment.

"I grew up here."

"Yeah, and how old are you?"

"I'm seven."

She must've moved in right after I left. "You live here with your parents?"

"My daddy runs the farm with my mommy. She's also a teacher."

"They sound like nice folks."

Hadley looks away, and that feeling niggles at me again. I've lived my entire life based on trusting my instincts. In the military, it's kill or be killed. I had to rely on myself to know when something was a threat or not. Something about her demeanor has red flags going up all over.

"My parents probably aren't home, so you won't meet them."

I nod as though I don't see through what she's doing. I grew up making excuses as to all the reasons my friends couldn't come or my teachers shouldn't call. My father was sleeping, he wasn't home, he was on the tractor, or he was out of town. Anything I could say to deter someone from seeing anything. From finding a reason to ask questions.

Hiding wasn't just for me, it was for everything about me.

"Well, if they're not, I'll at least know you got home safely."

"Do you think I can come over sometime to climb your tree? It has steps and mine doesn't."

I grin at her. "Anytime, kid. My tree is your tree. And if you come by in the next few days, I can show you two other hiding spots my brothers and I built."

"Really? Cool!" Hadley lights up.

"Really."

We get toward the drive and there's someone at the car. Her dark brown hair falls down her back in waves and she's lifting a paper bag from her trunk. When she turns, our eyes meet, and my heart stops.

Her lips part as the groceries tumble to the ground forgotten as I come face to face with the woman who has haunted my dreams.

My angel has returned, only she isn't mine.

three

It can't be.

This can't be happening.

It's been eight years since that night. Eight years of pretending that it was all a dream because it had to be.

I never saw him again. No matter how many days and nights I scanned crowds or looked at every driver—it was never him.

Partially, I was grateful because that night was one of the most heartbreaking and incredible nights of my life. I never should've given myself to him, but I was so unsure of where my life was going and if marrying Kevin was the right thing to do. I only knew that I needed to be loved and cherished, even if it was only for one night. I wanted to be held the way that this man held me when we danced.

The other part was the agony because I was getting married the next day, and God help me, I prayed that I would never see him again so I could find a way to forgive myself for the sins I committed.

I should've known that I couldn't ever atone for my sins to be forgiven and him being here is proof of that.

"Mommy!" Hadley rushes over, her eyes filled with terror at the groceries on the ground.

Shit. I let them fall.

I hate that she worries so much. "It's okay, baby. I'll get them."

Hadley turns to the man when she sees my eyes go back to him. "Connor, this is my mom."

Connor. I'd given him so many names, but Connor is fitting. The name is strong, like the man.

Time has done nothing to lessen how attractive he is. His eyes are a deep emerald green that makes me feel like I'm drifting. His hair is longer up top, pushed over to the side, giving him a bit of a boyish look, but it only adds to his appeal. Then there's his body. God, his body is sinful. His shirt is clinging to his arms, and there's no denying the muscles beneath it.

His chest is broader than I remember.

And I remember everything.

His touch, his scent, the sound of his voice as he made love to me in a way I didn't know existed.

I needed him and the memory of that night more than he can ever know. I've relived it so many times, clinging to those feelings that I was desperate for, loving how my world came alive and colors were brighter when I was with him. He was like a comet that set the sky on fire, and the tail has never faded for me.

But now, him being here? It threatens *everything*—including the life of the little girl he's standing next to.

I look to both of them as I crouch to try to pick up the stuff I dropped. "And how do you two know each other?"

He heads over as well, bending to help gather the items that are out of my reach. "I found Hadley in a tree, and I think her arm is pretty messed up. I wanted to make sure she got home okay."

Immediately, my attention shifts to her. I don't know how she hurt it or if someone hurt her. "Are you okay? What happened?"

She looks to him and then back to me. "I fell."

I close my eyes, willing that to be the truth. Kevin may hurt me, but he's never raised his hand to Hadley. "Let me see."

She tugs up her sleeve, and I touch the bruise marring her skin and hate that it looks swollen. "I need to get her checked out."

Connor lifts the bag of food into his arms and hands it over. "Can I help?"

I shake my head quickly. "No, no. I've got it all. My husband is working on the farm. I'll get this inside and then take her. Thank you."

I can't let Kevin see him. It will send him into a million questions about who he is, how I know him, why Hadley wasn't in the house where she was supposed to be, and what happened to her arm. Right now, my emotions are too unsettled to deal with any of it.

"Are you sure?"

"Very."

Connor gives a sad smile and then touches the top of Hadley's head. "You be careful, all right?"

Hadley smiles up at him. "You too."

He laughs. "I'm not the one who is hurt."

"You should still be careful because you're a soldier."

That's why I haven't seen him. He's been gone, but clearly, he's back. Only, I don't know what that means or if it means anything at all. I don't even know why I care what that means. I have my life here with Kevin and Hadley.

We can't leave, even if we wanted to. Kevin ensured that when he moved me here, away from anyone I might know.

Still, my lips part and I find myself asking, "You're in the military?

"I am, for another few weeks, at least. Then I'll be out."

I nod, thankful that he'll be leaving again. "Well, thank you for bringing Hadley home."

He takes a step closer, making my pulse spike. It takes every ounce of strength I have to stand my ground. "You're welcome . . ."

My insides battle over telling him my name. I don't want to lie, but giving him this is like relinquishing all the false pretenses. But I owe him. I owe him so much, so I stop fighting myself and tell him the truth. "Ellie."

Connor takes another step closer, his deep voice brushing over me as he says my name far more beautiful than I've ever heard it. "Ellie. You're welcome, and it was nice to meet you."

I smile tentatively. "Yes, same, Connor."

Saying his name feels like a piece of the puzzle fitting together.

Hadley takes my open hand, and we walk up the steps that lead to the falling-down house we call home, leaving him standing there and watching us, and I wonder if he could see what I've been ignoring for the last seven years—that Hadley has his eyes.

"It's not broken, but it is sprained," Dr. Langford says as he checks her arm. "Second sprain in the last two months."

"Yes, she's . . . she's so full of life and loves to run and climb. I can't keep her feet on the ground."

Dr. Langford nods. "I had a little one like that. Always covered in bruises and scrapes. It's also the farm life. Explains why you've had a bit of bad luck too, huh?"

I nod.

I hate the lies. I hate all of it, but I'm so afraid.

I know, and I have to leave because, while there's a fraction of truth that Hadley is rambunctious and always climbing, I'm not home all the time and I don't trust Kevin. She swears it's the fall, and I've never seen him physical with her, but can I really trust a man who is willing to unleash his anger on his wife not to do it to a child?

I would leave this very instant if I had a place to go, but I don't. My parents died the week before I married Kevin, and I have no money, no help, no family to take us in. When I leave him, it has to be planned.

That was why taking the teaching job was necessary.

"Now, you need to be more careful and stop climbing while your arm heals."

Hadley smiles. "I will. I made a new friend."

"You did?"

"His name is Connor. He owns the farm next to us."

The doctor's eyes widen. "Connor Arrowood?"

She shrugs. "He said he was in the navy and a police officer. He carried me with one arm."

"I've known the Arrowood boys for a long time, good kids, had a rough time once their mother died."

Of course he's an Arrowood. It didn't occur to me that he must be if he was on the farm next door. I've lived here eight years, and the only time any of them were mentioned was when someone told me they haven't stepped foot in this town in almost a decade.

"How long ago was that?" I ask.

Dr. Langford looks up, seeming to ponder. "Had to be when Connor was about eight. It was a shame, cancer came and took her fast. They must've come back because their father passed."

"Yes, I felt bad that I missed the funeral."

He nods. "I wasn't there either, but I wasn't a big fan of him. When his wife passed, it changed him. Anyway, makes sense the boys would come to bury him and sell off the farm."

"Sell it?" I ask.

He shrugs and then starts to fit Hadley with a sling. "Sure, they won't stay around here long, even if their father is gone." He gives me a look that tells me that the "rough time" they had after their mother died was more than grief and then continues, "Still, you made a good friend, Hadley. I always liked Connor."

She grins, clearly agreeing with the doctor's assessment, and a part of my fear breaks away. If he won't be around, then I don't have to worry. He'll sell it off, go back to wherever he's living, and I can avoid any . . . disruption in my plan to get away from here.

Now that I know his name, though, I can set things right once I'm away from here. Find out for sure if Hadley is his.

"All right, peanut. You're all set. Remember what I said about climbing and taking it easy until you're all healed. No horsing around too much."

"I promise," Hadley says with false promise. That kid doesn't know how to be careful.

"Good, now can you give your mama and me a few minutes to talk? I think Mrs. Mueller has some lollipops out there."

He doesn't need to say anything else, she's gone.

"How are you feeling?" he asks with a fatherly tone.

"I'm good."

"Ellie, I'm not trying to pry, but you've got a pretty ugly bruise on your arm here."

I pull my sleeve down, hating that it rode up enough for him to see the marks. "I hit the wall when I was getting all the supplies for the classroom out. I've always bruised easily."

And I've gotten really good at avoiding medical attention. The last time Kevin gripped my wrist, causing it to pop out of the joint, I set it myself and splinted it. Then, when he tripped me and my ankle sprained, I wore a brace for a month and tried to ignore the pain. There was no way I could go to the emergency room, so I'd found ways to hide injuries.

However, if he saw my side, he'd never believe that her fall, which I'm not even sure was a fall, was innocent, and that would be the last I saw of her. I can't let anyone take her away. I will protect her better. I'll do what I have to do to make sure we're gone in the next two months. I need time and provisions.

His eyes study me, and I can see that he isn't buying it. "No judgment here, I want to help."

Help with what? Kevin owns the farm, the car, the bank account, and I have nothing. Kevin is controlling, and when things don't go his way, he loses it. When we go, we have to end up so far away that he won't be able to find us, no matter how hard he looks. And he will look.

He'll want his daughter, and he will never let me go.

I attempt to give him my warmest smile. "There's nothing wrong, Dr. Langford. I promise."

He sighs, deducing that I won't say anything more. There is nothing that anyone can do to help. "All right, well, I'll see you back soon. Take care and don't hesitate to call if you need anything."

"I promise, I'll do that."

He leaves, and then Hadley comes running back into the room with a pocket full of lollipops and a smile on her face. She heads straight to me, wrapping her arms around my middle, causing me to wince.

"Sorry, Mommy! I forgot you had a bruise."

I always have bruises. "It's okay, baby."

"Did Daddy get mad again?" Hadley's eyes brim with concern. "He shouldn't hurt you like that."

God, this can't be the life I show her. "It was an accident," I lie. "I'm okay."

She shakes her head. "I don't like that you have another bruise."

Me either, and that's why I have to do this. For her, I will get her out of his home and I will protect her. I married a man who will ultimately destroy me and Hadley, unless I can get away first. Which is exactly what I plan to do.

four

"There's a lot of work we'll need to do if we want to sell it," I say as I grab the beer Declan brought to the table.

"No shit." Declan shakes his head. "At least the land is good. That's the real cash cow."

"Pun intended." Sean smirks while raising his beer.

Idiots.

At least my brothers and I are all in agreement. None of us want the place and all of us are ready to get out of Dodge.

Then I think about the woman living next door, the one who I've dreamed of for eight fucking years, who is now married and has a kid.

I can't stay around here. I'll want to see her again, to find out if everything I created in my mind is true.

Jacob leans back in his chair and points the bottle at me. His head is now shaved thanks to the new role he was cast for.

"You're the only one who's a wild card, Connor."

"Me?"

Jacob is the closest in age to me. He and I also look the most alike. So many times people thought we were twins. He and I are both six-foot-two, have dark brown hair, and green eyes. We're also both the biggest assholes in the group.

"Yeah, you have nothing to go back to, no offense, kid."

I really hate that they still see me as the little brother who is gullible and needs these three asshats to protect him. They don't see that I'm a fucking Navy SEAL or that I've fought in a war, been shot at, shot people, and could destroy all of them if I wanted to.

"I have plenty."

Sean shrugs. "You're getting out of the navy, you have nowhere to live and no job. I mean, maybe you should take the farm until you get on your feet."

"It's not a bad idea," Declan, the traitor, says.

"The fuck it's not!"

That would completely destroy my plan of getting out of this fucking town. Too many memories that I've worked so hard to forget have been rearing their ugly heads since I've been back.

"All we're saying is that it might give you something to have for a bit. We all know you're the handiest of us," Jacob tries to explain. "We all agree there's a ton of work that needs to be done, it makes sense. What about his leg, though?"

I huff and then chug my beer before answering. I'm full of anger and disgust that they'd suggest I stay in this house. Each time one of my brothers went off to live their life, my father grew worse. He drank more, punched harder, and I hated everything in this town a bit more.

My good times were almost nonexistent. The only memory I have that I hold on to is the night with my angel.

But, like all angels, she doesn't belong here anymore than I do. She is meant for more, and that more sure as fuck isn't some broken ex-SEAL who has been dreaming of a married woman. She had told me she wanted to fly, which was why we never even told each other our names.

She clearly didn't fly far, though. In fact, she got married and had a kid less than a year after our night together. Clearly, I held on to that memory far stronger than she did.

"His leg is fine, he's healed, just not fit enough for duty," Declan tacks on.

No, not fit for duty and definitely not staying here.

"Yo, are you listening?" Sean jabs me.

"Not to you idiots."

He releases a heavy sigh, looking away. "Jacob has a point, the farm needs work, you need a life, and all of us have things on our plates."

"Oh, so I'm just the one with nothing else to do?"

"Pretty much," Declan responds.

Now I remember why I hate being around the three of them.

"I'm not staying in this town."

Declan puts his beer down and turns to face me. "Why? He's dead. He can't hurt you."

No, but something else could—the possibility of more.

"Then why don't *you* want to be here?" I challenge. "We both know why, and it has nothing to do with our father."

It's a beautiful blonde who stood at my father's grave and then left before he could even speak to her.

"Fuck off, Connor."

"You fuck off, Dec. You want me to be here, dealing with it all, when you're unwilling to do the same damn thing?"

"Once we sell the farm, none of us have to ever be here again," Sean tries to mediate the situation. "It makes sense, Connor. If you stay, you can work on cleaning up the farm, you have no plans, while Jacob has to get back to Hollywood, Declan needs to get back to New York, and I'm in the middle of spring training and have to return to Tampa to meet with the team."

If I weren't so angry that they were making sense, I would keep fighting. But they're right. I have nothing to rush back to once I sign my discharge papers.

"Let's sell it and get whatever we can," I suggest.

Sean shakes his head. "No. This is all we get, and there's no way the four of us should unload it for the sake of unloading it. Not when one of us has time and is more than capable of getting it to the point where we can make double. We're not talking chump change, Connor. We're talking about millions."

I groan and rub the back of my neck. "I'm not agreeing to this."

Declan shrugs as though he has not a care in the world. "I'm not worried. He'll see that we're right."

"Or a bunch of assholes."

Sean grins. "We already know that."

"We meet with the lawyer tomorrow." Declan's voice is firm and authoritative, which makes me want to punch him in the throat. "After that, we'll decide what we're doing. For now, let's let Connor stew while we all drink."

I flip them off, hating that my brothers think they know me so well. Jokes on them because my mind isn't completely on the farm, a small part of it is on the woman and her little girl next door.

"What the fuck do you mean there's a stipulation?" Declan's voice rises even louder as he stares at the lawyer.

The short, pudgy lawyer dabs his bald head with a handkerchief. I love it when my brothers and I make people sweat. "It is very clear. Basically, the will states that in order for his children, Declan, Sean, Jacob, and Connor to inherit the Arrowood farm, they must each live there for a period of six months. Once that time has been fulfilled by each of his children, whether it's all at once or successional, then they will become the full owners with the authority to sell."

Sean laughs without any humor. "Motherfucking asshole is controlling us from the grave!"

"This is bullshit. There has to be a loophole." Declan says as he gets to his feet, his anger is palpable.

The lawyer shakes his head. "I'm afraid not. He was very . . . specific. If you all fail to agree, the farm will be sold and the proceeds will be donated to the foundation to help prevent child abuse."

"You're fucking kidding me," I say before I can stop myself. "The man who beat all four of his children regularly wants to donate a possible ten million dollars to prevent what he inflicted on his own kids?"

Jacob puts his hand on my arm. "He will not win."

"He wins no matter what!" I scream. "If we live on that godforsaken farm, we're doing his bidding. If we all walk away, then all the money that we're owed—and don't tell me we're not owed anything after the hell that man put us through—goes to charity!"

I can't think straight. Anger and revulsion pulses through

me with each beat of my heart. Of all the things I expected when we walked into this office, being dealt a fucked-up ultimatum wasn't one of them. I didn't think I'd be forced to live in the one place I never wanted to return to for six months.

"He thinks we won't stay." One of my brothers pipes up.

"I'm not staying. Not now. Not this way. I refuse to do this. Hell, give it to charity because those kids might actually have a chance that we didn't."

Sean stands and starts to pace. "What happens if one brother refuses?"

The lawyer clears his throat. "Then you all lose it."

I throw my hands up, wanting to punch something, and then hate myself for even the thought of it. I have never raised my fists in anger. I've fought, sure, but it was in self-defense or because I had no choice. The vow the four of us made means everything to me, and I will never hurt another person physically because I can't control myself.

"How long do we have to decide?" Declan asks, the ever responsible one who has no doubt formed a plan on how to handle this.

"Three days to decide, and someone has to be in the house within thirty," he states matter-of-factly.

Declan stands, and the rest of us follow. "We'll see you in three days with a decision."

five

"I'm hungry," Kevin slurs from the couch. "Make me something."

I close my eyes, willing myself not to mouth back at him. It only makes it worse. I have to bide my time, be smart, and keep him as even-tempered as I can.

"Sure, is there anything you'd like in particular?"

He glares at me, his anger already starting to grow. "Food, Ellie. I want food."

My throat goes dry, and I stand, forcing a smile that I hope will appease him. Once I get into the kitchen, I see Hadley at the table, working on her homework.

"Hi, sweetheart."

"Hi, Mommy."

I crouch next to her, pushing her brown hair, which is the same color as mine, back. "I want you to go play outside or stay in your room, okay?"

Her green eyes assess me, weighing what no seven-year-old should ever have to think about. "Is Daddy angry again?"

I nod. "He is, so I want you to stay out of his sight, okay?"

Disappointment flashes across her face, and I feel it in my soul. I'm letting her down. I'm failing my daughter in every way. If my mother and father were alive to see me, they'd weep. I'm not the girl they raised me to be, but I'm trying.

"Okay, Mommy. I won't bother him."

When did I become this woman?

When did I decide that it was okay for a man to treat me so? Was it when I married him, hoping I could love him enough to change him? Was it because my parents were killed the week before the wedding, and I was desperate for security? Was it when I found out I was pregnant a month after our marriage? Is this my punishment for lying for years about Hadley, suspecting that she isn't Kevin's daughter?

The wave of guilt is so intense that I worry I'll drown in it.

Before Connor reappeared a week ago, it was an easy decision. I was married to Kevin. I wanted Hadley to be *our* child because, in some part of my heart, I loved him and believed it was God's way of forgiving me for that. I thought that, if we had a baby, it would be okay. He would change because of this beautiful life that was growing inside me.

And, for a while, he did. It was as though the guy I started dating in college was back.

He was kinder, more attentive, and I had so much hope brimming inside me I couldn't breathe.

But a leopard doesn't change its spots. The man, who I saw only glimpses of in the beginning, stopped hiding years ago, and I am going to be strong enough to get away.

Hadley packs up her things and then heads to the back door. "Can I see if Connor is home?"

I can't take much more. "No, honey. Connor is a grown-up

and he'll probably be busy."

"He said I could go to the tree house anytime."

I'm not sure what tree house she's talking about, but she seems very excited by this. "Hadley, you hurt your arm a week ago . . . you can't be running around like that."

"It doesn't hurt and I won't climb it."

I don't believe her, but at the same time, I can't keep arguing with her or Kevin will get mad.

Damn it.

"Okay, where is this tree house?"

She smiles. "On his land."

I guess I asked for that. She's too smart for her own good.

I look at my little girl just a little closer. Her eyes are the same color as his. I've always thought that she had Kevin's face and that her eyes must've been like someone in my family or his. But when I saw him, saw his eyes, it was as if the universe were reminding me that I never really knew. Hadley could be Connors.

Hadley presses her hands to my cheeks. "I like Connor. He was strong and carried me. Plus, he didn't yell when he found me like I thought he would."

No, he didn't yell like her father would've. "Hadley, how did you hurt your arm? The whole story, sweetheart. You won't be in any trouble as long as you tell the truth."

She looks away, a deep breath escaping her lips. "I fell. I wasn't supposed to be out by the barn. I told Daddy I wouldn't climb up into the loft, but I wanted to see what the cows were doing. I went up there, and when I heard Daddy, I knew I would be in big trouble, and I didn't want to make him mad again. So, I jumped out, but fell on my arm and then ran. I knew he'd be upset. He's always mad."

I fight back the tears and give her a small smile. "I'm sorry."

"It's okay. I know he's tired."

And an asshole. And selfish. And mean. And angry at the world. And taking it all out on me.

Instead of telling what feels like my only friend, who absolutely should never hear it, I bob my head. "Why don't you run out back?"

She gets up from the table and slips out back to the tree outside.

Sitting under the branches of the oak tree, in the shade while little rays of light fall around her, is one of her favorite places. She looks so peaceful there, as though the ugly parts of the world haven't yet tarnished her youth. I've tried, Lord knows I have, to give her normalcy and love, but when it comes to Kevin, it's given only when he deems we've earned it.

I wonder what it would've been like had I not been drowning in grief. Would I have found someone else? Would I have not married Kevin? Would Hadley and I be on another farm, with another man who carried her when she was scared?

No, I can't do this. I can't go down a road that isn't open to me.

I shake my head and focus on getting Kevin food so my reality doesn't become a nightmare again.

I carefully make sure that I'm adding the right things and ensure I don't put too much mayonnaise on it. That set him off once.

"Ellie!" Kevin bellows.

I close my eyes, pray I did it right, and then grab the sandwich, chips, and a pickle sliced in quarters before heading back to the living room.

"Here, honey," I say with soft lightness to my voice. I've learned that the sweeter I approach him, the less venom he spits back. "If you'd like something else . . ."

"This is fine."

I release a heavy sigh internally and then sit beside him. Maybe today won't be bad and we'll pass the time like most days. Kevin isn't always mean, which is what kept me completely complacent for a while. It started gradually, leaving me wondering if I was imagining things.

Then it was like a snowball, finding strength and growing in size the longer it rolled, until it got so large that it crushed anyone in its path. Most of all—me.

It's days like this that are the scariest. When I'm unsure if I'm going to have the husband I once wanted or the man who haunts my dreams.

Do I talk? Do I wait? I walk on eggshells, afraid of choosing either one.

Kevin takes a bite, and I steel myself, hoping I step the right way. "I saw the barn door is repaired."

He grunts.

"It looks great."

"It took me hours to get it to hang correctly. My uncle was an idiot who didn't know his ass from his elbow. He didn't use the right hinges, so I'm surprised it didn't fall sooner."

His uncle and aunt were wonderful people who he inherited the farm from after they passed. Without them, we would have even less than we have now. Not that this is what I ever wanted. I had dreams. Ones that included me living back in upstate New York, working on a vineyard. That's why I was attending Penn State for business.

But then everything changed.

My parents were killed right around the time Kevin inherited the farm and . . . here I am.

I'm grateful for the farm, though, it gives us income and stability. Not to mention it's fully paid off, so we didn't inherit any debt with it. Of course, I don't see a penny of what we make because Kevin has disallowed me access to anything.

I have no idea how wealthy or poor we are. It's another way for him to control me.

But I have my own income now.

Kevin has no idea that I'm being paid as a full-time teacher. He believes I'm volunteering, and I need to keep it that way. About six months ago, I opened a bank account in Hadley's name.

"I'm glad you fixed it, though. I'm sure it'll help with keeping the equipment safe."

Kevin nods. "Especially now that old man Arrowood is dead. I heard his asshole sons are back. It's all the farmhands could talk about. Like I pay them to gossip all day."

"I'm sure that was frustrating. You deal with the workers so much better than I ever could." I go for empathy and flattery. The more I let him think I'm on his side, the more likely it is that his temper will hold.

He drops his sandwich and drains the glass sitting beside him. Then he turns to me, his eyes boring into mine, and I see that it didn't work.

"Are you mocking me?"

"Kevin, stop. You're looking for something that isn't there."

His jaw clenches. "I'm tired of feeling judged by everyone."

"I'm not judging you, I'm complimenting you. There's a difference. I don't want to fight today, so please don't turn this into one."

I've never been more grateful that Hadley was outside. If this escalates, at least she won't see it.

The thing is, Kevin is always careful of where he strikes, careful not to leave marks where people will see them. And there are always marks, even if they're not visible on the outside.

He only makes mistakes when he's too drunk to care, and that isn't this time.

Kevin's eyes close, and I start to speak again. "I was being kind, and I know you don't believe me, but it's true. You're my husband, and I'm allowed to say nice things to you. You work hard, you provide for this family."

"I'm not good enough for you, Ellie."

We both know that's true.

"Don't say that. It's me who isn't good enough," I lie. I have to.

His lids lift, and I see a sad, scared man beneath it all.

This is what used to get to me. The way he would be so apologetic, so humbled, that I forgave him. I didn't understand, but I smiled and allowed him to keep treating me awfully. Kevin is my husband, he was supposed to be my protector, my world, and I'd wanted that more than anything.

I was so naïve and hopeful and in need of love that I accepted whatever form it came in.

"Don't leave me, baby."

I choke down all the words I want to say, the anger that lives inside me, and I act. Not for my own safety but for the little girl outside who will hear through the too-thin walls if his voice rises.

My hands lift so I'm cupping his cheeks, and I stare into the eyes of a man I've come to fear and resent. "Never."

"Good, because I would die, Ells. I would die if you were gone and you took my baby girl with you. I would be nothing without you. I am nothing without you. I know I'm fucked up, but it's because I love you so damn much. If you weren't so perfect, I wouldn't be trying so hard. God, you're my world."

As his forehead drops to mine, the smell of vodka fills my nose as he breathes out and I thank God that, tonight, I get sad and sorry Kevin. Not hateful and raging.

I love my classroom. It's my happy place. I've decorated the room this month in all Shakespearean things. There are quotes, photos, a fake dagger, a vial of water, and other items that I tried to get that would interest the boys. Then there are the kids who are wonderful, mostly because the teacher I replaced was a horrible woman. I don't think she liked her job, the kids, the school, herself . . . it was bad. And so, I get to reap the benefits.

I'm at my desk going over the play we're about to study when I hear a knock.

"Hello, Ellie, you look lovely today," Mrs. Symonds, the principal, says as she stands at the door.

"Thank you. I'm excited about the new material we're starting today."

I also wanted to feel good. The last week has been calm, and I've needed calm. Kevin has been working extra hard because there's been some kind of spike in something and he's pleased with it, so home has been quiet.

Hadley hasn't had any more falls, and her arm is doing well, and every bruise on my body has faded without any new ones appearing.

Not to mention my bank account grew a little more with my direct deposit today, which means I'm that much closer to being free.

There's a reason to smile and feel lovely.

"What is it that you're teaching today?"

"*Romeo and Juliet*," I say with a smile. It's one of my favorite pieces of literature. In some way, I think that all love is star-crossed. There's a barrier that each human has to overcome in order to share their heart or at least their life with another person. As much as I love a good happily ever after, in life, that's not always possible.

"Ahh, the great Shakespeare. I've always been more of a Bronte or Austen girl myself."

I grin. "Me too, but this one is definitely fun to teach."

"I agree."

Mrs. Symonds is a wonderful principal. She's fair, laughs with the kids, and has a firm hand. I also think she's part witch or magician since she seems to have eyes everywhere. Nothing gets by her, and though the kids seem to *think* they're getting away with something, it's never the case.

All of us hear and watch, share information, and intervene whenever it's necessary.

"So, how are you settling in here?"

"I love it. The kids are wonderful and seem to be excited about learning."

She nods. "That's great to hear. I know Mrs. Williams departing was a bit sudden, but she was an asset to us here. Sure, her attitude was a bit gruff, and she was a stickler when it came to grammar and demanded a lot of her students, but we are a close bunch."

Mrs. Williams was a pain in the ass according to everyone.

"She definitely made an impression."

"How have you been getting along with the other teachers?"

I'm not sure where she's going with this. Paranoia starts to build and I give a hesitant smile. "They're really nice."

She eyes me curiously. "Really? I've noticed that you don't seem to eat with them during your lunch, did anything happen?"

And apparently, her eyes are on her staff as well.

"No, no, nothing like that all. Everything is great."

Other than I've been isolating myself to keep people from seeing things and gossiping. This town is small. It's bad enough I have a hundred students I have to conceal my life from, I don't need to add adults, who are far more perceptive, to the mix.

It helps that Kevin isn't exactly a beloved member of the community. Hell, he isn't even a part of it at all. He stays on our land, never attending a meeting or fair. He doesn't go shopping, and only had one friend, Nate, but even they don't talk anymore. He prefers it that way and likes to keep me as close to that life as possible. Over the years, people have assumed that I'm as standoffish as he is and have stopped really trying to get to know me.

She steps closer, her smile is warm, and she reminds me of my mother for a moment. It comes across that it's how she feels toward her teachers and the students. A sort of second mother who wants to protect those she loves. "I know most of them get together and work on plans, I didn't know if there was a reason that you're not a part of it . . ."

"It's just my schedule. Once I'm done here, I grab Hadley, and we get back to help on the farm."

Mrs. Symonds watches me closely, taking in not only my words but also my body language. "I can understand, we have a farm as well, but you've been here for a few months now, and I want to be sure you're settling in."

"I really am settling in."

She sits on the chair beside me, her hand extends to mine in a warm gesture. "You know, I'm always here to listen. I know it can be a big adjustment working full-time again. Plus, I know you've lived in Sugarloaf for a while, but you don't seem to have a lot of friends. If you need one, I'm happy to listen."

I now understand why people tell her things. For the first time in a long time, I want to pour my heart out. I want to rush into her arms and cry, but friends aren't something I can afford. There is a time and commitment to the truth I don't have the luxury of, but I can't tell her that.

I give a soft smile. "I'm happy here, and I feel comfortable."

"Okay, good." And then the bell rings, alerting the staff that students will be filing in. "Well, that's my cue. Just know that if you need anything, Ellie, I'm here. We're a family, and there is always room for you at the table."

I want to cry, but I don't. "Thank you, Sarah."

"Anytime. Enjoy your tragedy." My heart races for a moment, unsure of what she means, and then she tacks on. "You know . . . the play."

"Oh! Duh. Yes. We definitely will."

When she leaves, I turn and release a heavy sigh, all the while wondering if anyone in this town believes my lies.

six

"So, you're going back to Sugarloaf?" Quinn, another SEAL I served with, asks.

"I'm going to hell."

Liam chuckles and lifts his beer. "I'll meet you there, buddy. Hell, we all will."

Today, I'm officially out of the navy and heading back to serve my six-month sentence in Pennsyl-fucking-vania. It's been two weeks since I signed my discharge papers, and there's a part of me that is anxious to go back.

A part of me that has found something I thought I'd never see again.

Quinn nods. "It could be worse."

"Yeah, how?" I ask.

"You could be in love with a girl who wants nothing to do with you."

Ellie's face flashes in my mind because she most definitely

doesn't want anything to do with me. I can't even be a little excited about her being there or finally knowing who she is because she's married. So, no, it couldn't be worse.

He continues. "Not that I know what that's like since I'm very happy at this time."

Liam watches me and smirks. "Oh, I think he is in love with a girl who wants nothing to do with him. What's her name, Arrow? Angel?"

"Fuck you."

Quinn's eyes light up. "Really? How come I've never heard of this angel?"

Because I only ever allowed her in my dreams.

Because I knew that if she was within reach, I would be tormented.

Because you two are idiots who like to use knowledge to make your stupid jokes and not understand what that night was for me.

"Both of you can suck my dick."

As much as these two drive me nuts, I'm going to miss this. The brotherhood, the camaraderie that only a team like ours builds. I would die for these two and any other SEAL. We live by a code, one that reminds me of how it is with my own brothers.

"That offer doesn't appeal to me. What about you, Quinn?"

"Nope. I'm very happy with my girl."

"Yeah. Now." I roll my eyes.

A year ago, Quinn was not as buoyant as he is right now. In fact, I don't think I'd ever seen a man that low. I'm still not sure how he endured the hell he went through.

I also don't know why I agreed to have drinks with them. I have no one to blame but myself for this conversation. When they're each on their own, they're bad enough, but put them together and they're a damn tsunami, wiping out everything in its path.

"And tell us," Liam's voice is conspiratorial, "are you going to find her?"

"Like I'm going to tell you two assholes anything?"

"He already did," Quinn tells Liam without looking at me. "See that face? He's haunted. He probably saw her when he went back, maybe a girlfriend from high school?"

"I'm guessing she was his first," Liam adds on.

"Could be. I mean, he looks pathetic. I've looked around, and there's not a line of girls willing to drop their panties for him."

Liam shrugs. "Maybe he has a small wanker? That could be it."

"I'm thinking it's the pathetic thing. No girl wants a man who is that broken."

"I'm right here!" I growl the words at Quinn.

They both keep talking as though I said nothing.

Liam looks over at me as his voice fills with amusement. "Could be the attitude. He is a bit hostile."

"I bet she snubbed him because, look at him, he's not all that good looking." Quinn shrugs.

"Who wants to deal with a grumpy, ugly, and unemployed former SEAL? It's the whole damn package."

I huff.

"Who wants to deal with you two?" I say under my breath.

"Well, we happen to have two gorgeous women in our lives that do," Quinn answers. "But, seriously, did you see her?"

"Yeah, and I also saw her kid and she has a husband."

Liam lets out a whistle. "Well, that definitely fucks that one up."

"No shit."

"Kid cute?" Quinn asks.

"Yeah, she is. She got hurt and hid on my farm. I found her and brought her home. Didn't know who her mom was until I walked up to the house."

The whole situation with Hadley still has me on edge. I don't know what it is, but that day, the things she said, still has my hackles up. The thing is, I can't tell if it's because I fucking hate that Ellie is married or if my instincts are right about the injury.

"My advice? Stay away. Don't be *that* guy."

"I have no plans on fucking up a marriage and a family, Liam, but thanks for the vote of confidence."

He shakes his head. "I don't think anyone ever sets out to do it. I also don't think you're a bad guy, Connor, but I think things happen. I've seen lines get crossed, and if this woman means anything to you, your heart is going to talk before your head."

"Or his dick."

I roll my eyes. They act as though I haven't had a lifetime of using restraint. I have never crossed a line like that. Doing so would make me closer to being a dirtbag like my father. He was selfish and did what was best for him, not caring about the damage left in his wake and expecting others to clean it up. I will never be like him.

"Thanks for all this unsolicited advice. I really appreciate the confidence and trust you two have shown."

"Don't take it that way," Liam says quickly.

Quinn nods. "We just get it. We've loved a woman past the point of reason."

Jesus. They're like a bunch of old ladies. "I don't love her. I don't fucking know her. All I know is that what feels like a million years ago, we had a night. One night that . . . why the fuck am I telling you this?"

Liam chuckles. "Because whether it was one night or a lifetime, it meant something and you're fucked in the head over it."

Yeah, it meant something . . . that I'm going to need to immerse myself in fixing that house and getting out with as little contact as possible. That's all it can ever mean.

I'm standing in this rundown barn, in the only spot that I can get a signal. I move one inch to the right, I lose Declan. I've been back here for two days, and I hate this place more than ever.

Sure, the house is quiet and no one is threatening to punch anyone, but it feels as though something is always lurking. My brothers and I spent five days cleaning as much as we could after the funeral, and Declan agreed, well, was forced, to buy all new shit.

I wanted every shred of my father gone. The bedroom furniture he slept in, the couches, the kitchen plates, all of it is gone.

We bought a few new appliances, since the old washing machine couldn't be fixed if it broke, new beds, and furniture. I didn't feel bad at all spending Declan's money.

There are two years that all of us need to live in this hellhole, it was worth every penny.

Now, I need to start fixing everything so we can sell it.

"Dec?" I say his name again, waiting to see if he hears me this time.

"I hear you. How much money do you need?"

"I need at least ten thousand more."

I hear the sigh of frustration leave my brother's mouth. "And that's just for the first barn?"

"Yup."

"Wouldn't it be cheaper to demolish it?"

"Dec, I can't move an inch or I'll lose you so I'm going to say this quickly. You told me to spend my six months working on fixing up the things that would make us money. A new barn—a good one that will actually help a farmer—would cost us around sixty thousand. So, wire me the money I need to fix this one and let me get to work. You'll get it all back when we sell, anyway."

My brother goes silent, and I have no idea if he heard any of my slight rant or if I lost connection, but I disconnect. When I turn around, I almost jump out of my skin.

"Hi, Connor!"

"Jesus!" I yell and grip my chest where my heart is now racing. "Hadley, I didn't know you were there."

"I'm very quiet when I want to be." Her smile is wide as she shifts her body from side to side.

"I see that," I say with a quiet laugh. "You remind me of how my brother Sean used to sneak around to scare me."

"How many brothers do you have? I always wanted a brother. Brother or a sister, I wouldn't be picky, but Mommy says I am enough to love all on my own. She was an only child too."

I used to dream about being an only child some days. Having three older brothers was hell most of the time. When we had Mom, life was easy and fun—mostly for them because I was the dumb one who would listen to anything they told me.

Being accepted by my brothers was all I wanted. They were cool and had all the information I wanted. I was the annoying one when I was her age.

Who was the one who jumped out of a tree to see if it hurt when they landed? Me.

Who ate the cow pie because it would make a person stronger than Popeye? Me.

Who took the blame for breaking Mom's figurine because no one would punish the baby of the brothers? Me.

And did I get punished? Yup.

"I have three older brothers. Declan, Jacob, and Sean."

"Whoa. Are they here now? Are they as big as you? Can I meet them?"

I laugh at the awe in her voice. "Nope, they all went back to their homes while I stay here to work on the farm."

Her head tilts to the side. "That's sad. You're going to be all alone."

"I like being alone. Speaking of . . . what are you doing here? Do your parents know where you are?"

"Mommy told me to go outside and play, so I came here."

Makes zero sense, but who am I to argue with a kid. "To play?"

"I wanted to climb the tree, but I promised no more climbing until my arm is better."

"Did you see the doctor?"

Hadley nods excitedly. "I did. It's just bruised and I'm supposed to wear this thing on my shoulder, but I don't like it so I take it off when Mommy isn't looking."

I snort. "Sounds like something I would do. But you really should do what your mom says."

"Promise not to tell?"

I lift my hand with my two fingers up in a peace sign. "Scouts honor."

Not that I was a scout or anything close. Hell, I'm pretty

sure that isn't even the way it should look.

Hadley moves over to where I'm standing, looking at the pile of wood that is off to the side. "Are you tearing the barn down?"

"No, I'm fixing it. I'm going to take down the damaged pieces before putting all new boards up."

"Can I watch?"

Uh. I'm not really sure what the protocol is on this. She's a seven-year-old kid who I only ever met because she was injured in my tree. "I'm not sure your parents would like that."

She shrugs. "Daddy doesn't care as long as I'm out of his way."

"What about your mom?"

Hadley purses her lips and kicks the dirt. "Maybe *you* can ask her."

Yeah, not a shot in hell. That would not help with my whole plan to avoid Ellie.

"I don't think that's a good idea."

"But we're friends," she retorts.

"We are . . ." I really don't know how to extract myself from this one. "But I have to work a lot and don't have time to go over right now."

"Please, Connor. I have no friends other than you, and I *promise* I won't be a pain. Plus, what happens if you get hurt? Who will call for help if *you* fall?"

Hadley crosses her arms over her chest, giving me the cutest lip pout ever. Jesus, I know why grown men are unable to say no to their daughters.

They know exactly how to get their way. I used to see it with Aarabelle and Liam. She led him—and every other SEAL she came in contact with—around by her pinky.

"I'm pretty sure I'll be okay."

"But how do you *know*?" she challenges.

How do I get myself into these messes?

"I guess I don't."

"See!" She perks up. "I can help. I'm a great helper. So, will you please ask Mommy if I'm allowed? She'll say yes to you. Whenever a grown-up asks, other grown-ups can't say no, it's the rule. Did you know that one time I helped fix a fence? I did it all by myself. I'll help you fix your barn too!"

This is such a bad idea. I know it, and yet, there's this pull that's telling me that I can see Ellie. Maybe I can find the flaw. Something that makes her less alluring. Something that will tell me that night wasn't what I'd built it up to be in my mind.

If I can get that version of the story to change, then I might be able to stop playing it over and over again.

I'm lying to myself. My wanting to see her has nothing to do with needing to find a flaw in her. It's just her. The woman who saved me that night when I felt at my lowest. I want to see her blue eyes staring back at me. I want to remember the way her long brown hair felt in my fingers. Does she still smell like vanilla?

I'm a fucking fool for this, but I can't stop myself.

"Okay, but if she says no, you have to promise you'll listen."

Hadley squeals and wraps her arms around my middle. "Thank you, Connor. You're the best friend anyone ever had."

Oh, God, this kid is going to break my heart.

seven

"**M**ommy!" I hear Hadley yell from outside and leap to my feet.

Kevin is asleep, and if she wakes him, there is no telling what his mood will be. He came in about thirty minutes ago, exhausted and already angry. Somehow, I was able to get him to pass out, and there's a reason people talk about letting sleeping dogs lie.

I rush out the door with my hands raised to stop her, and that's when I see him. Connor Arrowood is wearing a pair of tight jeans and a gray shirt that clings to his skin. His hair is pushed over to the side like his hands just ran through it. And then there's the scruff. It lines his jaw, making him look like sin and sex and everything I shouldn't want.

He gives me a lazy smile as he moves toward me, holding Hadley's hand.

"I found this cute kid at the barn and thought she belonged to you."

My heart is racing, but I attempt to smile. "She sure does."

"Mommy, Connor wants to ask you something." She looks up at him with joy shining in her eyes.

Once again, I'm struck at the similarities between them, and my chest aches. Could Hadley biologically be his? If she is, would that change everything?

It would. We would have nothing tying us to Kevin, and maybe he wouldn't search for us.

Or maybe it would make things worse.

He could fly off the handle and do God only knows what. If Hadley being his daughter is what is keeping her safe, I can't allow myself to see things that may be figments of my imagination.

"You wanted to ask me something?" I say to Connor.

"Well, Hadley stopped by and wanted to know if it was okay if she hung out . . . I'm not really sure of the rules or if you're comfortable with it. I'm fixing up the barn and then the house and then every other inch of the property for the next six months. Hadley was kind enough to offer to help make sure I don't fall or break my arm without the ability to call for help."

I know he says things, but my mind can't process anything after the time he's going to be here. "Six months?"

"That's my sentence here on the farm," Connor says with a huff. "In order to sell the place, each of my brothers and I have to live here."

My stomach drops. Six months of him living next door. That's a long time of trying to keep my mind from wandering, and six months of Hadley trying to become friends with him.

Six months of attempting to keep Kevin from seeing him.

I want to throw my hands in the air and scream in frustration.

If I have any hope of the last happening, I need to keep Hadley away from Connor. Not because of Kevin but because, if she forms an attachment to him, it will only hurt her when we have to run.

"Wow, that seems like a lot of work to do in six months and"—I look to my daughter—"you have a lot of homework and chores to do."

"But . . ." Her lip quivers. "I like helping, and I promise I won't be any trouble."

"What the hell is going on out here?" Kevin's deep voice booms as the front door flies open.

Dread fills me so fast I don't have time to temper it. I turn quickly. "Baby, you're awake?"

He looks at me, Hadley, and then to the man standing beside her. "Who are you?"

Hadley rushes forward. "This is Connor, Daddy. He lives next door."

I close my eyes for a second and try to think. I need to get Connor to go before Kevin's anger grows and I really pay for it. It's too late to avoid his ire entirely, so minimizing it is my only chance.

Kevin's eyes lift from Hadley back to Connor. "You're one of the Arrowood brothers."

"I am." Connor's voice is deeper than Kevin's, and I swear the testosterone in the air is enough to make me choke. "I take it you're Hadley's father? It's nice to meet you."

"How do you know my daughter?"

I step toward him, my hand on his chest and a soft smile on my lips. "Hadley wandered a bit too far, and Connor was nice enough to make sure she found her way home."

Kevin takes another step down so he's off the steps. His hand snakes around my back and grips my shoulder. "Well, that was very nice of him. Hadley, go on out back for a minute. And then you can check on the horses."

She looks to me, and I give her the smile I've perfected.

"Okay, Daddy."

"Thanks, my sweet girl. And don't wander off this time."

Hadley turns, the fear in her eyes is there, but she smiles up at him. "I won't."

"That's my good girl."

My husband is great at illusions. To anyone watching, he's being loving and attentive. He's always been this way. He would never give anyone room to gossip. When we do go out in public, he dotes on me. He touches my face with tenderness. His hand holds mine, and he smiles as he watches me.

It's so easy to believe the lies.

I can even get swept up in them. And I know better.

Still, I wish he would love me that way all the time. I want to remember how his hands touched me in love and not anger. My heart aches for the kind man who offered to help me and didn't cut me down.

It's stupid, and I know it. He won't ever be that man, and that's why I'm leaving.

His hand moves down my back, gripping my hip. There's a fresh bruise on that side, and I pray he doesn't remember or he'll find a way to use it. "It seems welcome home is in order. I'm Kevin and this is my *wife*, Ellie."

Connor's eyes narrow slightly, but he steps forward, hand extended. Kevin has no choice but to release me. They shake hands, and I can hear the thunder echo in the background.

"It's great to meet you both." Connor's hand moves to me.

I take it, shaking as briefly as I can, and retreat back to my husband. I move toward him, trying to force myself into his embrace. Kevin wraps his arm back around me, and I smile up at him.

Please let this be enough.

"Hadley didn't cause you any trouble, did she?"

"Not at all. I meant to stop over here when I moved back in the other day, but I got sidetracked. It's been a while since I've been in town, and I didn't know who took the Walcott farm since they didn't have kids."

Kevin nods slowly. "Yeah, my uncle left it to me. For the first time in over fifteen years, we're profitable. I know your father had a big dip a few years back."

"Doesn't surprise me," Connor says without emotion. "I'm shocked there is a building still standing."

"Hopefully, you do better than he did. It's doubtful you can turn it around but, who knows, right?"

I want to gasp at the insult, but I hold it back. Kevin isn't usually this rude in front of other people. He likes for everyone to think he's wonderful. Or at least he did for a while.

Connor chuckles as though it doesn't bother him. "I'm sure I will, Kevin. Anyway, I should get back to work. I'll see you around."

"Thanks for bringing Hadley home," I say as he turns.

Kevin's hand clutches my side, and I wince, the sound of sucking in air through my teeth seems a hundred times louder than it is.

Connor's brow furrows as his attention moves to where Kevin's fingers are on the bruise he left the other day that's hidden under my dress.

"No problem," he says in an easy voice. His eyes, however, are tinted with a calculated knowing that makes me uneasy. "I'll be around if you need anything."

"We're fine, but thanks."

And with that, Kevin turns us, and I let him lead me back into the house. As we ascend the steps, I fight the urge to run away from my husband. He's angry, and there won't be any of the kindness I hoped for.

The door slams, and he starts to pace. I watch the clock

tick as my mind goes through a million scenarios, all of them center around ways to cope with his inevitable loss of control.

He stops moving after almost five minutes, his eyes on me. "Did you sleep with him?"

My heart sputters, and my mouth gapes open. Of all the things that I thought, this was not one of them. "What?"

"You heard me, Ellie! Don't fucking play games with me."

I have no idea how to answer this. Does he know? Did he see Hadley has Connor's eyes? Or am I making it up because she has Kevin's nose? All of this is crazy. I have no idea if he's asking if I slept with Connor eight years ago or if I slept with him yesterday.

"No! I didn't sleep with him!" I scream and turn as though he's wounded me. Really, I do it so he won't see any lies in my face. "How could you ask me that?"

"I saw that way he looked at you! Like he knows you. Like he's had what's mine."

I shake my head and spin back to face Kevin. "You're accusing me of cheating on you because of how a stranger looked at me?"

He shakes his head. "I saw it."

"You want to see it, Kevin. How could I have slept with him when I've never met him before? How could I do that to us when he told you himself that he just got here! How?"

I hold on to the idea that he's not smart enough to go back to before we were married.

"I don't know, but . . . I swear to God!" Kevin steps forward, his hands squeezing my arms in the same spot the old bruises faded a few days ago. "If you even look at him again, Ellie. I won't be able to stop myself. If you hurt me . . ."

Tears I fought back fall. Not just from the emotional pain I've endured but also because he's breaking me. "You're hurting me, Kevin. You hurt me each time you do this."

His grip is so hard that I know I'll bruise even worse. "You will never leave me. Do you understand? I'll not be responsible. I'll . . . I'll . . ."

"You'll what?"

His fingers tighten first and then release. "I'm trying to hold on to you!"

"By hitting me? Kicking me? Telling me I'm worthless? Threatening me?" I ask with an unamused laugh. "You think that doing this is going to make us better?"

I watch the agony flash across his face. Sometimes, my tears, pain, and guilt work. There are times when he sees the man he's become and we go through a period of bliss. But that is always short-lived, and then the next time he's angry, it's almost as if I pay tenfold.

I don't want the bliss this time.

The false life is almost worse because I know it's going to end.

He steps forward, his eyes fill with rage and he slaps me across the face. "You think talking back to me makes it better?"

My fingers touch the spot he hit, eyes filling with tears. "Why do you do this?"

His face is close, teeth clenched. "Because you're mine. You and Hadley are all I have, and I won't fucking lose you."

A tear falls down my face. "You're killing me, Kevin. You're killing me each time you hit me or grab me or tell me what a horrible wife I am. I'm breaking, and it's by your hands."

"My hands? What about your hands? You're the one with another man."

I can't take this. "I've been with you since I was seventeen! When do you think I had time or any desire for someone else? I loved you so much! I married you, raised our daughter together, and taken hit after hit from you."

Kevin looks as though I've slapped him. His eyes are filled with pain, and I take a step toward him. I don't know why there is an urge to comfort him. Maybe it's because I've trained myself to do it. Maybe it's because, somewhere deep inside me, I love him when I know I shouldn't.

"You make me crazy, Ellie. You have no idea how much I love you. I would do anything for you. It's just . . . when I see you like that, I see my life without you, and I can't do it."

"I don't want to be like this," I say as the words take on double meaning.

I don't want to fight with him any more than I want to look in the mirror and see a sad, pathetic woman who allows him to beat on her. Hadley needs me to be more.

I need a little more time, and then I will get us out of here. If I work a bit more, I'll have enough to find a house in a small town far enough away from here that he won't look for us. Kevin would expect me to go back to New York, which is where my parents are from. He wouldn't look for me south or west.

If I can save enough, I'll make it work and give Hadley the life she deserves. I wanted more time, but I don't think I can last that long.

Kevin steps closer, and I force my feet not to move. His hands gently cup my cheeks. "I love you, Ells. I love you, and I won't ever hurt you again. I promise."

I close my eyes and lean in as his lips touch my forehead.

Promises break. Bruises heal. But nothing erases the scars that abuse leaves.

Then his eyes meet mine and gone is the tender man with sweet promises. "But if you try to leave, Ellie. I'll kill you both. And I'll kill her first and make you watch what you've finally forced me to do."

eight

I lie here, staring at the ceiling, waiting for his breathing to even out.

"If you try to leave, Ellie. I'll kill you both."

In all the years, Kevin has never threatened to kill me or ever hurt Hadley.

"If you try to leave, Ellie. I'll kill you both."

He will kill us. I have to go now. For Hadley. For me. For any chance of a life. I can't wait any longer.

"If you try to leave, Ellie. I'll kill you both."

It doesn't matter that I don't have enough money hidden away or a plan. I have enough to get us out of here and on a bus to somewhere else. There's no way I am keeping my daughter here another night. He's crazy, jealous, and if that's the threat I got after him meeting Connor once, I can't imagine what would happen if he found out the truth.

My body is tingling with anxiety. I feel as though my

nerves are being pulled so tight they'll snap.

Kevin is a light sleeper. If he hears the car start, he'll wake up, and my daughter and I will be dead. I'll have to go completely on foot.

Hadley is going to slow me down a bit, but we'll avoid walking on any main roads.

Please, God, if you were ever listening, I need you right now.

A snore tears through the silence, and it's now or never.

I creep out of the bed, grab the dress I hid between the bed and the nightstand, and tug it over my head. When we were getting ready for bed, I stashed a bag in the tub and cracked the window in the bathroom so I could at least take a few things.

Once I'm inside the bathroom, I toss the bag outside and pray I can get out of the room without being heard. That'll be half the battle.

Ever so slowly, I creep out of the room. He shifts, and I freeze, praying he won't open his eyes.

Another second passes, and he doesn't, so I keep going.

That's all that keeps going through my mind. I have to keep moving.

Hadley's door is ajar, which was my doing because it makes the most noise.

I softly shake her, and my voice is barely audible as I urge, "Hadley, baby, wake up for Momma."

Her little eyes open, and she darts up. "Momma?"

"*Shh*," I say quickly, needing her to be as quiet as possible. "We have to go, sweetheart. I need you to make no noise, can you do that?"

She nods, and I smile softly. "Okay, get dressed and grab your blanket and bear."

Hadley moves slowly, and I rush to get a few things of

hers for us to take. My heart is racing, only the sounds of our breathing filling the air. After a few seconds, I take her hand in mine.

"What about Daddy?" Her voice is low, but I can hear the ache.

"We have to go, baby. No matter what, we have to get out of here, and we can't wake Daddy. Do you trust me?"

Hadley's eyes fill with tears, but she bobs her head.

Here is, once again, where I feel like the worst mother in the world. No child should have to sneak out of their home in the middle of the night like this. A house should be a safe place that makes everything bad in the world disappear when you enter the door. Instead, it's been a place of yelling and bruises. But no more.

Never again will he hurt me, and he'll have to kill me to get to Hadley.

"Okay, we need to be *super* quiet," I whisper. "No matter what, we have to keep going once we're out of the door, all right?"

Hadley wipes a tear and nods.

"That's my big girl. If Daddy wakes up, I want you to run back to your room and close the door. Lock it if you can or put things in front of it. Just do not let anyone in but me, okay?"

I know I'm scaring her, but I don't have time to debate and I don't want her to hesitate. "I'm scared."

"I'm sorry, but we have to go."

"Will we come back?"

I shake my head and then place my fingers to her lips. It's now or never.

I still don't know if going out the back is the best way, but it's really the only option. The front door is too close to where he sleeps, and I'm not going to have Hadley climb out the window alone. If we can get around the house undetected, we have a much better chance.

I pull her with me, watching each creak and noise that seems to be amplified in the total silence. We get to the door, and I pull slowly, there is no noise other than the sound of our breathing. We get outside, and I pull Hadley's sweatshirt around her, zipping it up as I look in her face.

"Okay, we have to go."

"Mommy?" Her big eyes are filled with so much fear.

"It's okay. We have to go. I'm so sorry, Hadley. I know you love your daddy and this is hard, but we . . . we have to go."

I wish I could tell her everything, but I can't. It's too much for this sweet girl with a huge heart to comprehend. One day, she'll look back and see that I was doing what I felt was best—or maybe she'll hate me forever. Either way, she'll be alive to do it.

That's all that matters.

I grab her hand and lead her to where I dropped my own bag out of the window. Once I have it securely next to hers over my shoulder, we walk quickly around the corner of the house. I can't slow down, at least not until we're away from the house.

Hadley practically runs beside me as we make our way past the car and farther down the drive.

And that's when I hear it.

The sound of the wooden screen door slam against the side of the house.

He's awake.

He's here.

He's going to kill me.

I feel it in my body, the awareness of everything around me. The way the air tastes of dew and moonlight. How the scent of cows and fresh-cut wood fill my nose. If he catches me, it'll be the last time I ever breathe and smell.

I look down at my beautiful girl, fighting back any tears over the fact that I might never see her again. My sweet, bright light in my life. The only thing I've fought to live for.

"Run, Hadley," I say breathlessly. "Run as far and as fast as you can. Run to someone who will protect you. Run and don't look back at me. Don't stop. Don't listen to anything else, just run."

"Mommy?"

I can feel Kevin bearing down on us. Hear his rapid foot-falls getting closer. The only chance I have is to let him take me so she can run. He can't go after both of us.

"*Run!*"

My heart feels as though it's leaving my body as she does what I say.

"Hadley!" Kevin bellows.

"Run, Hadley! Run and don't come back!" I scream as loudly as I can, needing my girl to get away from here.

Kevin grips the back of my head, pulling my hair so hard I yelp. "Going somewhere?"

I could lie, but it won't matter. He knows why we were sneaking out in the middle of the night. There's no getting out of this, and for once, I refuse to back down and be afraid. The worst will come, but Hadley will be nowhere near when it does.

There is a small . . . so very, very small comfort in knowing that when he kills me, he'll go to jail and she'll be free of him.

"You won't get her."

"Oh, you think you're noble? You think she won't come home to her daddy?"

I laugh because the funny part is, she might not be his. Still, there's some self-preservation left inside me that keeps my mouth shut. I might feel brave, but I'm not fool enough to make this worse.

"Something funny, Ellie?"

"This," I say through gritted teeth as the pain from him practically ripping my hair out throbs. "That you say you love me and Hadley, and yet, you'd stoop to this."

"I need you."

"You need to stop hurting us."

Kevin's lips graze my neck, and the grip of his hands loosen. "I've loved you from the first moment I saw you. I knew you'd leave me someday. I fought to keep you. Then we had Hadley, and I believed that we would be fine. I should've known you could never be loyal to me."

I close my eyes, forcing any emotion back down. I can't show any weakness. "Let me go, Kevin. Let me go and be happy."

He shoves me away so hard I fall, my hands and knees hitting the dirt so hard they burn with fresh scrapes. "You want to be happy and leave me to handle it all? No. I told you what would happen. I warned you not to try to walk away from me."

"Why? Why do you want me? You don't love me, and I don't want this!"

A fresh anger fills his gaze, and I don't have enough time to move before his foot connects with my ribs.

I feel the agony before I can draw a breath. The side where I was already bruised now feels crushed.

I struggle to stand, to get air in my lungs, but the pain is too great.

"You don't want this?" Kevin yells as he pushes me back to the ground.

"Kevin!"

"You don't want what? Me? You want someone else?"

His hand grabs my arm, hoisting me to my knees.

"I want you to stop!" I somehow get out.

"You could've stopped it all."

Yeah, by never marrying him. By leaving a million years ago. I could've done so many things differently, but I didn't. I chose to live with a man who has torn me down. While I felt I had no way out, I ultimately gave him the ability to hurt me. Now, he plans to do that, and I'm already broken and unsure of how to stop it.

"Kevin, please," I beg, knowing it might be my only chance.

"Please what? Please don't hurt you? Did you think I wouldn't be the one who was hurt when I found my wife and daughter gone? Did you not think of me when you were sneaking out of this house, trying to steal my child? No, you were only thinking about yourself!"

My tears fall now, unable to stop them. The pain in my chest is so bad it has spots flaring to life in my vision. Every ounce of strength I have, I use to keep him talking. The longer I hold his attention, the more time that Hadley has to run.

"I begged you," I say, my eyes meeting his, giving in to the emotions that are eating me alive. "I believed your promises that you wouldn't hit me. I fed into each lie, allowed you to control me. I let you do all of this because, at some point, I loved you. I wanted Hadley to have a father, but you broke each promise. You say I'm selfish, but what about this, Kevin? What about the bruises and injuries?"

He gets down on his knees beside me. "Don't you see how much I fucking love you? If you didn't make me so angry all the time!" Then he gets to his feet and starts to pace. "You defy me and think I'm stupid. Well, I'm not stupid am I, Ellie? Look who is on the ground at my feet now. All because you couldn't keep your legs closed."

The blame falling to me again makes me want to choke

him. I've tried so hard to make him happy. I've done everything he asked and kept our home the way he said he wanted it. I have cooked meals the way he wanted and acted exactly how he expected me to act. I did it all, and nothing was ever good enough.

I rise, not willing to be on the ground anymore. He watches me, and I step away from him, my back hitting the car.

I'm trapped.

"If you loved me, you would stop this. You wouldn't have hit me in the first place, and I wouldn't be leaving." My hands are against the cold metal as he advances quickly.

I tremble, fear hitting me as I know what's going to come. He's out of his mind with rage. "No! You just don't see. You don't fucking see!" He rears back, hitting me so hard that my vision blurs. The world around me tilts, and my hand cups my cheek, the sting so deep I know I'll feel it for days. "You're mine! You're my wife, and you'll obey me. You promised to stay!"

"And you promised to cherish me!"

Hadley.

All I keep in my mind is that sweet little girl and the hope she's still running, finding someone to give her shelter.

I stay upright, staring into his vengeful eyes. "You can hit me, break me, cut me down, but I am not staying!"

Kevin grips my hair again, pulling me up to my feet. The pain is so bad I scream, unable to hold it back. Everything feels heavy and even breathing feels like work.

He hauls me back toward the house as I try to keep up, stumbling along the way.

"You don't have to stay, Ellie, but you're not going anywhere."

nine

"Just tonight. No names. No anything. Just . . . I need to feel." Her voice is pleading.

"Feel me."

Her deep blue eyes stare into mine, and I swear she sees all my demons and chases them away.

Tonight, I'm not some kid who has dealt with his drunk dad, who thanked him with his fists and vitriol. I'm not the child of the man who threatened to ruin my life with the lies my brothers and I have told—to protect him.

I'm not Connor Arrowood, the youngest brother, the troublemaker who barely made it out of high school.

Right now, to her, my Angel, I'm a god. She looks at me with so much hope and honesty that it humbles me.

"Tomorrow . . ." I say as I gently brush my thumb across her cheek.

"No tomorrows."

I want to tell her that tomorrow I leave for boot camp. She should know that, even though we are agreeing to only one night, I'll come back for her. She just has to wait.

"There's more," I start, but her hand covers my lips.

"There's nothing but tonight. I want us to get lost in each other, can you give me that?"

I'll give her everything.

Her hand lowers, and she replaces it with her mouth. I kiss her, giving her the answer through touch.

We barely say a word as we slowly undress each other in a hotel room three towns over from Sugarloaf. I'm here to remember. I'm here to forget. I'm not even sure why I came, but maybe it was for her.

I'm eighteen years old but feel as if I've lived a thirty-year-old's life. Dealing with the loss of my mother, my drunk father, the beatings, the lies, and having to make decisions I never should've had to make—because of him.

Right now, I don't feel any of that. I'm a guy who is going to love a woman who is far better than he is.

"Connor!"

I look around, not knowing where the sound is coming from. No one else is here. It's only my Angel and me.

"Connor! Connor! Help!"

I shoot up out of bed, my dream fading away as I search for the noise.

"Please! Be home! *Please*! Connor, I need you!"

Hadley.

I jump out of bed, throwing my shorts on as I rush to the door. "Hadley?"

When I open the door, she's standing there, hair plastered to her face and eyes red rimmed. She grabs my hand, pulling me. "You have to come! You have to help!"

"Come where?"

"Hurry!" she screams.

Hadley is trembling, gripping my hand so tight that I can almost feel the fear inside her. She stares at me, broken, sad, and terrified. Images of what can be wrong flash in my mind because I remember that look. I remember running with my face a mess, praying I could find some help.

Before I go there, I need her to tell me what happened so I can prepare. I use my years of training to slow down my rapid heart rate and the urge to rush over.

I squat down to her level, gripping both her small hands in mine. "I need you to tell me what's wrong?"

Her head moves to where her house would be and then back to me. "She told me to run."

"Your mother?"

She nods. "He . . . he was . . . we tried."

I scoop her up quickly, gathering her in my arms and rushing into the house. Once I know she's safely in the house, I sit her down and try to get more from her. "Is it your dad?" Hadley cries harder, and there's a painful tightness in my throat. I want to hold her, comfort this kid who is falling apart, but I urge her gaze back to mine. "I need you to tell me so I can help her."

"He had her, but she made me run and told me not to stop."

Fuck.

For just a second, I'm Hadley. I'm running, remembering how Declan screamed until I couldn't hear him as I fled. I can feel the fear inside my body as I wouldn't stop, finding that tree, praying he wouldn't follow me.

Declan protected me and I will do anything to do the same for Ellie now.

"Okay, I want you to stay here, lock the door behind me, and call 9-1-1 right away. Tell them what happened."

"I'm scared."

I shake my head, pulling on my bravest face. "I know you are, but you got to me and now I need you to call the police so that we can make sure everyone is safe. I will come back here as soon as I can."

"With Mommy?"

I really fucking hope so. I know better than to make promises I can't keep.

"I'm going to try. Just don't answer the door unless it's me or Sheriff Mendoza . . . is he still the sheriff?" She nods. "Good, only us, okay?"

I hate that I'm leaving her alone in this broken house, but Ellie needs help. If she had Hadley run . . . it was to protect her, like my brothers did for me.

"Please help her, Connor," Hadley pleads, and I want nothing more than to give her what she asks.

This kid has somehow felt safe enough to come to me for help. I can't let her down, no matter what.

"I'm going now. Remember to call and don't let *anyone* but me, your mom, or Sheriff Mendoza in." I remind her again. I want to specifically tell her not to let her father in, but she's terrified enough.

"I promise."

With that, I pull her in for a quick hug, grab my gun out of the entry table, and run.

My legs don't stop. I don't think about anything other than getting to her . . . fast. I can't stop, slow, or falter. I know that taking the road might be the easiest, but cutting across the field is faster, so that's what I do.

I leap over the fence, moving at a pace I haven't set in a long time. During my last deployment, I was restricted from running, but right now, nothing hurts. I'm running on pure adrenaline and the need to get to Ellie.

In my gut, I knew something wasn't right. If that son of a bitch hurt Hadley that day, I'll kill him. I have to stop myself from going down that line of thinking because I'm already trying to rein my anger in that he's hurt Ellie.

As I move across the wet grass, I think about that night. I remember how she felt so secure in my arms. I've held that memory for so long that the idea of that being all we'd ever have is killing me. Ellie means something to me, whether it's reciprocated or not, she's been my talisman.

I've dreamed of her so many times and then replayed the memory of that night just to have her close again.

I've created hundreds of different scenarios for what would have happened if I'd only woken up earlier, of how the last eight years of my life would have played out.

My heart is racing as the light from the house in front of me cuts through the night. I move even quicker, knowing that each second that passes could mean anything.

I pull my gun out, keeping it down by my side as I move. The ranch-style house should make it easier for me to gain access through a window if I have to. There is a small porch on the front, and the bay window is bright with light from inside. That's most likely where they are. I do a fast assessment of the house, trying to determine the best way in. It's eerily quiet, the moon overhead is bright, giving me enough light to see but not be seen.

I step closer and see the curtain move in the front.

I'm hoping the sheriff is close, but it's Sugarloaf, so I'm not overly hopeful, and there's not a chance in hell I'm waiting for them to show up before I go in.

"Kevin." I hear a mumble coming through the window. "Don't do this."

Ellie's voice sounds broken and raspy. Not at all like the beautiful, sweet and almost song-like quality that it was earlier.

"Do you think I want my wife to leave me? I'm the man who has supported you, loved you, provided a life for you, and then I wake up to find you stealing my daughter?"

I look through the window and see her lying on the floor in front of the fireplace as he walks around the room. I survey the area, deciding the front door is the best entry to get to her quickly.

"I was bringing her somewhere safe," she tries to yell, but her arm is supporting her chest, and it looks as if she can barely draw a full breath. "You hit me for the last time."

The motherfucker hurt her.

Red fills my vision, and all my thoughtful planning goes out the window.

I move to the front of the house, tuck my gun in my waistband, and kick the door open so hard that the wood splinters. I walk forward, no longer giving a shit about anything other than the bastard who raised his hand to a woman.

"What the fuck?" He stumbles back and then comes forward. "Came to save your whore?"

"I heard some noise, wanted to see what's going on over here."

He shakes his head. We both know I couldn't hear a damn thing almost a mile down the road, but I really don't give a shit about what he thinks. I care about the woman on the floor and the little girl at my house who is scared out of her mind.

Because of this scumbag.

"Get out of my house."

"I'd really like to, but I have a strict rule about men who hit people smaller than them." I step closer, making a fist and releasing it. "You see, I think a real man would pick on someone his own size, you know?"

"Fuck off."

"How about you man up to me? I bet that would make you

feel more like a man than hitting a woman would."

I circle him, stalking my prey, ready to pounce the second I see that Ellie is out of the way.

However, the blue and red headlights fill the room, and I see the panic in his eyes.

Kevin moves to the left as if to bolt down the hallway and probably out a back door, but I lunge for him. My arms wrap around his body, and I let momentum and gravity pull us both to the floor. He lands a punch to the side of my face, and I swing back, a loud *thwack* echoing around me.

That's all there is time for before hands are yanking me back. "Let him go, son. I'll take it from here," Sheriff Mendoza says.

He grabs Kevin, and I rush over to Ellie, who is sitting huddled on the floor. "Are you okay?"

She shakes her head.

"We need to get you to the hospital."

"Hadley?"

"She's safe," I tell her quickly. "She's at my house."

"I need to get to her." Ellie tries to get up but cries out.

"Ellie?"

"My ribs. My stomach . . ."

I clench my teeth to stop myself from doing something I'll end up in jail for. She's hurt and survived God only knows what. For her, I need not to be anything like the man she just saw.

"Can you walk?" Her lip trembles, and she tries to turn away, to hide the bruise forming on her cheek. I lift my hand, but she jerks away. "I'm sorry."

"No." She tries to stop me. "I need Hadley, and I need to get out of here."

"I won't hurt you."

"Is she somewhere safe?"

"She's at my place," I answer.

Her eyes meet mine and tears fall. "Thank you for coming for me."

If she only knew that she's what kept me coming back time after time. It was the night we shared, the smile, the laughter, and everything she gave me that once. I felt alive, worthy. As though I could be someone's hero. I would come back for her every day of my life even if I knew she could never be mine.

"I'm glad I got here in time."

She wraps her arm around her stomach and gasps. "Ellie?"

"It just hurts."

I want to rip his arms off. How dare he do this to his family? His wife and daughter should be all that matters, and he broke them both tonight.

I glance back over to where he's standing, arms behind his back, and I hope those metal cuffs are so tight they are digging into his skin. He watches me, and I move to obscure her from his view. He doesn't deserve to look at her.

She makes another sound, and I don't know how to help her. Never have I felt so inept before. "What do I do?"

The tears that have been brimming fall along with my heart. "Just get me to Hadley."

I nod, and then Sheriff Mendoza calls our attention. "Ellie, I have a few questions I need to ask."

"Okay. But I have to get to Hadley."

The quiver in her voice tells me she's on the brink of losing it. She needs to see her daughter. "Would it be possible to have her give you her statement there, where they're both safe?" I ask.

Mendoza looks to her and then nods. "Of course. I'll have Deputy McCabe bring Kevin down to the station, and I'll drive you both over."

Ellie looks as though she's ready to break. Her hands are shaking, and she keeps sucking in air when she moves. "Can you stand?" I ask her quietly.

"Help me?" I put my hands out, not knowing where to touch, but she can barely move to take the offered help.

Fuck this. I lean down, and as carefully as I can, take her into my arms. "I'm sorry," I say as I hear her squeak.

"Don't apologize, thank you. I don't think I could walk."

I lift her, cradling her as gently as possible to my chest. "I won't let you fall."

And God help me, I won't let him hurt her again.

ten

The sun is coming up as I sit on Connor's porch swing, a blanket draped around my shoulders and a cup of tea in my hands. I'm numb, that's all I can process. Nothing feels real. It's almost as if I've settled into a dream-like state and have been watching everything that has happened, not living it.

Even though, I know that isn't true. The pain I feel burring through my chest every time I take a breath is proof.

The other thing I feel is safe, or at least the safest I can be. Connor has been at my side or within view each moment, making sure I know I am protected and my daughter is as well. He was there when I refused the ambulance, knowing I couldn't leave Hadley and that I wouldn't allow her to see me in a hospital.

He sat in the back of the police car with me as silent tears drifted down my face. I was in pain, yes, but more so . . . broken. When we reached the entry to the driveway, he squeezed my hand gently in reassurance. I wiped my eyes and shoved down my sadness because I needed to be strong again. Hadley needed that.

Nothing could've stopped me from getting to her, so he ensured I was out of the car and standing before he went and opened the door. She rushed out, terror etched on her face, and then relief.

All I could do was touch her face, and give her assurance I was okay. Whether she knows it or not, she's the bravest person I've ever known. My daughter saved my life, and I will never be able to forgive myself for it.

I comforted Hadley as much as I could before giving my statement and allowing the police to take photos of my injuries. As Connor bandaged my ribs, he had explained that they would need them for the court case. While he worked, I learned that he was a medic in the navy, which is why he wouldn't let the EMT, Sydney, touch me.

It was a whole other level of humiliation, but I was grateful for my ability to shut myself down and be numb to it all. I let Connor do what he could and pretended I was on the beach, away from it all. I simply held my daughter, forgetting the pain, as she drifted off.

The door creeks open, and I startle, but Connor raises his hands immediately. "It's just me. I'm coming to check on you."

I do my best to relax back into the swing. "I'm . . . here."

"How are you holding up?"

I shrug. "I'm not really sure. I'm still processing it all."

"You did great with Sheriff Mendoza."

I laugh internally. I didn't do great with anything. My entire life has been a series of errors, trying to get away last night being the biggest. Last night, I sat there, telling him and the sheriff the story, hating myself, berating myself, as tears fell down my face.

There was nothing great about any of it.

"I'm not so sure of that. I was a mess."

"You didn't lie, and you told him everything when you didn't have to. I've seen . . . there are people who cover up abuse because it's easier. You were brave. You may not feel that way, and I'm sure you have your reasons for not leaving sooner, but you were, and I'm sure Hadley will see it that way."

I look out at the sunrise, wishing I could find some solace in knowing that I lived to see it again, but I can't. Regrets are what fill me, and there isn't a slice of bravery there. "If I were brave, I never would've let it get this far. I would've left after the first time he made me feel weak and small. If so many things didn't happen . . . if only I had run when he raised his hand to me that first time, my daughter never would've seen a bruise on her mother or a tear fall because he'd hurt me."

"It's easy to look at it that way, taking on the blame or playing the what-if game, but we make the choices we think are best at the time. We all have regrets."

He can't possibly mean that. People who aren't in the situation look at it differently. I've heard people talk about those in bad relationships and how they wouldn't do this and they wouldn't do that. If someone isn't living in those shoes, they can't say what they'd do.

I never thought I'd be in an abusive relationship, but here I am.

When I was growing up, I was this smart girl who thought she would find a man who treated her well, and if they didn't, they'd be gone. Then I met Kevin and was in this whirlwind relationship where he became my entire world and I became an outsider in my own story.

I am the one to blame.

"While I appreciate that, I disagree. I knew I needed to get out, but I made the choice to stay and hope he would change.

That will forever be on me because I was too scared to see that he never would."

Connor takes a sip of his coffee and offers me a sad smile. "I disagree with your disagree." I let out a soft laugh and wince. "Are you okay? I really wish you'd have seen a doctor."

I was checked out by the EMT named Sydney, and I only allowed that to convince her I wasn't in grave danger. But my side is in so much pain that I wouldn't be surprised if I had a cracked rib. "I'll go tomorrow when she's in school."

"I need to at least clean the cut under your eye."

"I appreciate that you want to help," I say softly. "But I'm sure I can manage."

Connor moves to rest against the rail, big arms crossed over his chest as though he could fight off the world if it came for him. "I understand if you'd rather that, but at least allow me to check your ribs. I'm sure they're broken, and I want to make sure there are no signs of something more serious, especially if you're putting off going to the doctor."

"Okay," I agree, knowing I won't be able to look at it or touch anything there. Hell, I can barely breathe without wanting to cry. "I still can't believe this is how last night went. I'm so . . . tired but don't think I can sleep. All I keep seeing is his face and feeling the pain when he kicked me."

We both fall silent. I don't know why I'm admitting any of this to him.

After a few minutes of comfortable silence, Connor clears his throat. "Ellie, did your husband ever hit Hadley?" he asks with no traces of judgment, just curiosity.

"Not that I know of. He threatened . . . well, it's why I finally left last night. He said if I tried to leave, he'd kill us both, and I believed him. I knew I had to leave. I knew that one more night was too many and didn't care that my plan wasn't in place or that we had no money or nowhere to go. I couldn't stay another minute. I think he really would've killed me if you hadn't shown up."

"You did right. Abuse never ends, hell, even if the abuser dies, you can still feel the effects."

My eyes lift, and I study him as though there might be something else beneath the surface. "I'm sure I'll feel this way for a long time."

"You'll heal, and I swear, he will never hurt you again."

"I don't know how you can promise that."

Connor pushes away from the rail. "Because he sure as fuck won't hurt you if you're in my house. If you choose to go back home, then we'll come up with a lot of ways for you to protect yourself if he's released from jail. Either way, tonight, tomorrow, or until you're ready to leave, you're safe with me."

Safe. It's a word I've taken for granted so many times. When I was young, I remember my father always giving me hugs and telling me he would keep me safe. He locked doors, took precautions, and then one day, when I was at college, another car veered into their lane and killed them both. They never found the driver of the other vehicle.

Nothing kept them safe.

When I met Kevin, he fooled us all. My parents loved him, thought he was sweet, wonderful, and told me how lucky I was to have met a man like him in my freshman year of college. He inherited the farm a month before the end of the year, so he and I invited them up to see it.

They were so happy that night. They loved the land, the town, and hoped that I'd maybe live here someday. Then they were killed, and I was hollow. I thought he would fill the void of losing my parents. I was so alone. So sad, wanting for someone to make things a little better. Kevin was there, promises to take care of me, give me love, and a life. I fell for it, hook, line, and sinker until I was on his reel.

Now I feel gutted, just like a fish.

"I appreciate that, but I'm not safe anywhere. Can we not talk about this right now? My mind is . . . well, I can't handle thinking now."

"Of course, can I sit with you?" I move over, giving him room, and he settles in beside me on the swing. "I'm sorry. I shouldn't have pushed you to talk."

"No, you didn't. I'm raw and a mess, but you did nothing wrong."

"You're not a mess," Connor says and then starts speaking quickly. "Tell me about Hadley as a baby."

I look through the window for the hundredth time. I keep checking to make sure she's really there and that this isn't some alternate reality I've created in my head. Right now, I trust nothing because I'm not really sure I'm alive and this isn't limbo.

Except for the pain. Surely, there's no pain in death and there wouldn't be Hadley.

"Hadley was always, has always been, the best kid. She never fussed as an infant and slept through the night way before I probably deserved her to. It was as if she was following the baby book I read because she hit each milestone when she was supposed to."

He smiles. "She seems like a good kid."

"Yeah, she really is. I've been so lucky with her. I never really did get to thank you for how you took care of her when she hurt her arm. It means a lot that you cared. I truly appreciate you finding her and getting her home."

Connor rocks the swing gently. "I would never have let her go like that. She's been the one thing about coming back to this place that hasn't been bad. This town isn't exactly my favorite place."

"Why is that?"

He shrugs. "A lot of memories here. Lots that I tried to

forget and won't stay gone. You know, my mother used to do this each morning." I look at him, wondering what he means. "She would sit out on this swing every morning and watch the sunrise. I remember trying to wake up early to come out here with her. She said it was her slice of time where nothing could bother her."

I smile despite the hell I went through. I picture him as a young boy, coming out here just to sit with her.

"I think it's important for kids to have time like that with their parents. Hadley and I have our bedtime routine that I cherish and pray she always remembers."

"Mom did something special with each of us. She made it her goal to make us happy. She died when I was about Hadley's age."

I touch his hand. "I'm so sorry you lost her. I met your father a few times, but I didn't know him that well. I wish I had gotten to meet her, she sounds wonderful."

"My mother was a saint. I don't remember much, but what memories I do have . . . are everything. I wish I could see her face clearer in my head."

"I know what you mean. I lost my mother as well, so I know it's hard. She would be very proud of the man you became. I know we don't know each other really, but everything I've seen so far says you're a good man."

I don't know how to explain it, but since Connor came back into my life, everything has shifted. Maybe it's nothing or maybe it's the universe telling me I fucked up the night I left him sleeping in a hotel room and I should listen to it. Maybe it's my parents giving me a sign from above. Whatever it is, Connor has helped me more in the last week than anyone else has since I moved to this town.

He rescued my daughter and now me. He's been kind and hasn't made me feel small. Even now, instead of grilling me or making me talk, he's giving me something else to think of and talk about.

I've wondered about him for so long, and he's here. Right when I need someone the most.

When Connor glances over to me, his eyes look haunted. "I really hope she would be. My brothers and I have tried to live in a way that would make her proud."

"Tell me something about her," I urge. I'd rather talk about her than my own parents or what has happened.

"She made the best pie. For our birthday, she would make us our favorite one instead of making us cake. We didn't care about presents or anything as long as she made pie."

"Which was your favorite?"

"Apple."

"The same as Hadley," I say and then look toward the window again. "That girl can eat an apple pie all on her own. I'm sure mine doesn't taste near as good as what your mom made, but . . ."

"I'm sure it's perfect, Ellie."

I bite my lip to keep it from wobbling, but it's too much. I can't stop it. "God, Connor, I could've died, and then who would've made her pie? What would have happened to her if . . . if you didn't get there? How would I ever forgive myself for making her world fall apart?"

"You didn't die, you're right here."

Am I, though? Guilt and pain assault me, leaving me breathless. I've been trying so hard to keep everything at bay, but I'm a mess. Everything is a mess. "I should've never tried to leave last night. If I had been smarter and waited . . ."

"What? What do you think would've happened, Ellie? Men who use their fists don't care when it is. Men who use their power to make people submit to them don't care about the situation or the person, it's all about them. You did the right thing."

I shake my head and wipe at the tears on my face. "I did nothing right."

His eyes look inside and then back at me. "You did right for her. You didn't allow him to hurt her. You put Hadley first so that she would have pie when she wanted."

My chest aches, and not just from my injured ribs. I feel helpless, drifting away like the morning mist, becoming nothing. I was so scared that he would make good on his word that I gave him the opportunity to do just that. "I promised myself that, if he ever touched Hadley, I would leave. I vowed never to let anyone hurt her, and look . . ." My tear-filled eyes watch the little girl sleeping on the couch. She's tucked in tight as a ray of sunlight illuminates her face. "I broke my word and failed her."

But I will do anything I can to never break another promise again.

eleven

"We promise each other right now," Declan says as we all link hand to wrist so we're standing in a circle. "We vow that we will never be like him. We will protect what we love, and never get married or have kids, agreed?"

Sean bobs his head quickly. "Yes, we will never love because we might be like him."

Jacob grips my wrist tighter. "We don't raise our fists in anger, only to defend ourselves."

I tighten my fingers around Declan and Jacob as I make my pledge. "And we never have kids or come back here."

In unison, we all shake as one unit, the Arrowood brothers never break promises to each other.

I've held on to that vow that the four of us made that night like a vice. I've never allowed myself to love anyone or have a kid. Not because I think I'm anything like my father but because my word to my brothers means everything. We broke the cycle that day. We promised to protect each other by ensuring we don't have anything worth losing that would make us turn to drinking.

A man is only as strong as his word, and mine is ironclad.

Sitting here with her, I know that all my promises don't mean shit. I'd break each one for her, and that scares the fuck out of me.

I can't convince her that she did nothing wrong. Her heart and head are filled with the truths she is going to hold on to. I know it all too well.

However, I'm overcome with the need to comfort her.

She shivers, and I want to pull her into my arms, shielding her from the cold as well as everything that's haunting her. I don't want to overstep, but the need to protect her is so strong I can't stop myself. "Can I hold you?" I ask, prepared for whatever answer will come.

Her eyes lift slowly, reminding me of a wounded animal. I hate that anyone did this to her. I want to slice that man apart for ever making her fear anything. She should've been loved, protected, and cherished.

"Will you?"

I'll fucking do anything for her.

I lift my arm, inviting her to come to me.

She moves very slowly, making small noises when it hurts, but I stay completely still. She tucks herself into my side, head resting on my shoulder, and then I wrap the blankets around the both of us.

Neither of us say anything, I don't think words are necessary. Right now, I couldn't speak if I had to.

She's with me. In my arms and allowing me to give her comfort. The amount of trust she's giving me isn't unnoticed. The last six hours have been hell for her, and once again, she shows her bravery.

We rock together as the sun continues to come up, lighting the sky in warmth. Her tears soak my shirt, but I don't remark on it. If she needs to soak through a hundred shirts, I'll let her. If she wants me to hold her for days, I'll stay just like this. She may have gotten away from me that night, and our lives may be complicated, but one thing is for sure, Ellie will never feel small or broken again. I will do everything to make sure that, from this day forward, she feels protected.

"You really don't have to drive me," she says for the tenth time as we head to the preliminary hearing for her husband. "You've done so much for us already. I could've walked."

Right, like I was going to let her walk twelve miles to the courthouse. She needed a ride since she can't drive because of the medication she's taking, and I couldn't seem to let her leave my sight for more than an hour. So, my driving her is as much for her as it is for me.

"You don't have to keep saying it. If I didn't want to be here with you, I wouldn't be. I know you can't understand this, Ellie, but I need to be here with you right now."

"You do?"

"Yes. I am not making you go in that courthouse alone. If you want me to come in, I will. If you want me to stay out of it, I will. I'll do whatever you need me to. Okay?"

"Okay."

She and Hadley stayed at my house last night, mainly because I was able to convince her that she needed someone to help her move around because she can barely walk upright. The doctor verified that she has three broken ribs and there is extensive bruising. His handprint is on her arm, and there is a purple mark on her cheek from when he slapped her, but she didn't need stitches. I don't have any intention of leaving her side.

Not because I want to control her but because I want to protect her, which is where I'm struggling to keep myself in check. Ellie had no choices and no way to leave, and it made her feel helpless. My stepping in and protecting her by trying to tell her how to handle things isn't something I can do.

I don't want Ellie to have another man take from her. So, I'm choking down every response I would normally give that would leave zero room for negotiation and trying to get her to come to the decision I want. If she doesn't, which is something that hasn't happened yet, I'll have to pivot.

Sheriff Mendoza explained that today would determine if they keep Kevin in jail until the trial or if he makes bail and is released on his own.

If he's released, I don't know how I'm going to respond, and I don't know if Ellie has a plan for if that happens.

I park the car, and Ellie reaches for the handle, but she doesn't move to open the door. "I can't do this."

"Yes you can."

"No," she says with a hitch in her breath. "I can't. I can't see him."

I get out of the car, go around to the passenger side, and open her door before squatting so we're eye to eye. "He can't hurt you. He'll have to get through me to even come close to you."

Her hand lifts, and she touches my cheek for a brief moment. "You owe me nothing, Connor."

I'm not sure what she means by that. "I'm not here because I feel indebted to you. Why would you think that?"

"I don't know, but I also don't know why you're doing this."

"Because I care."

"You care?"

How does she not see? "I care about you and Hadley. You have no idea how many nights I dreamed of you, Ellie. I didn't know your name or anything but your face and how you saved me that night. Your smile, your eyes, the way you gave me trust and hope when I had none is what kept me alive. Night after night, I would replay it in my head, dreaming of my angel who came down from heaven, making me want to keep fighting. So, I may not owe you, but I do care about you. I'm doing this because I can't imagine doing anything else but being here for you. I'm doing this because you are fucking brave and strong and no one ever deserves what was done to you. You got Hadley and left. You knew that your daughter needed you to choose her, and you did. So, you have to do it again now. You have to fight and walk in there with your head held high. I'll be right beside you."

She releases a heavy breath, turmoil clear on her face. "You say these things to me." Her voice catches, and she has to clear her throat. "I'm not brave, but I want to be. I have so many things I want to say to you, but my head is such a mess."

"I'm not asking for anything. I just want you to know that you're not alone."

"I want to be the woman you see."

I know how that feels. I stand and extend my hand to her. "Then show me."

twelve

I place my hand in his and exit the car, garnering courage from him with each step I take. He thinks I'm brave. He doesn't look at me like I'm a stupid girl who was too weak to leave. Connor sees me as a woman who put her child first and left when that child's safety was threatened.

Now, I need to feel that strength again. I need to be strong, even though I want to hide in the car and never see him.

When we get to the courthouse doors, the district attorney, who was once good friends with Kevin, is standing there.

"Ellie," Nathan Hicks says with his hand raised.

My hand moves to Connor's forearm, and I hold on as we move forward. "Hi, Nate."

He looks at me, taking in the bruises and cuts that I can't hide, and his jaw clenches. When his attention moves to the man beside me, his eyes widen. "Connor? Connor Arrowood?"

"Nate, been a long time." Connor reaches out to shake his

hand.

"It's been years. You left town and none of us ever heard anything again. It's good to see you. God, I can't believe it's really you."

Connor doesn't appear to look happy to see him, but Nate is known for being an asshole. "I take it you're the prosecutor?" he asks.

I start to tremble a bit, but then Connor's other hand covers mine and squeezes.

"Yes, I am. I didn't know you knew Ellie . . ."

"He lives next door, and . . . well, I'm sure you read that Connor is who helped on the scene."

"Yes, of course. I didn't even put two and two together," Nate admits. "Well, I'm glad you both are here. This is the preliminary where we see if the judge will detain Kevin—"

My fingers tighten against Connor's arm because Nate might make this go the other way. What if he isn't on my side.

Connor's eyes meet mine, and then he steps in. "You mean Mr. Walcott. The man who beat his wife, broke three of her ribs, and put that bruise on her cheekbone, right?"

Nate bristles and then clears his throat. "Yes, I apologize, Ellie, this is all a bit strange. I knew you and Kevin argued, but I didn't know it was physical. We're going to ask that the court keep him until the trial for your and Hadley's safety. The verdict will likely depend on the report that Sheriff Mendoza submitted and the statements you make today."

"What kind of statements?"

"I don't understand all of this . . ." I confess. "I know Sheriff Mendoza explained it, but honestly, it's just too overwhelming. I'm . . . sorry . . . I shouldn't be this confused."

"Don't be sorry. You've been through a lot, so I'm happy to explain it. Today is to show the judge we have enough of a case to go to trial. If he doesn't think I have enough evidence, which we one hundred percent do, then he could dismiss it. It's why it was imperative you come."

All of this is so paralyzing. Not only am I still reeling from the entire thing but also I now have to go before the judge and look at the man who hurt me. I have to relive it in front of people, and this is the preliminary. I'll have to do it again if this goes to trial.

Connor nods and clenches his jaw. "What are you asking for, Nate?"

Nate puffs his chest out a bit and then turns to me. "What do you want, Ells? I can push for him to be detained or is there going to be someone who will post bail?"

"I don't want him released if that's what you're asking."

They can't let him go free. If they do—he'll kill me and Hadley.

There's no way he's going to let us go.

My heartbeat accelerates, and I shake so hard I worry I'll knock my teeth out. I assumed that beating his wife would mean he wouldn't be let go. Where will I go? Where will Hadley and I hide from him?

"Ellie?" Connor steps in front of me, moving me back a few steps. "Ellie, calm down."

My chest hurts, but I can't get a grip. I see his eyes as he moved toward me and feel the way my body couldn't recover from Kevin's kick. I live it right here, as though it's all happening again.

I push Connor off me, my hands raised as I move to run.

I need to get Hadley and get the hell out of here. I was so stupid. I should've run before this.

"Ellie, listen to me . . ." Connor says with his hands in the air, moving slowly. "Right now, we have to go in there and tell the judge why he can't be released, okay? If you don't do that, then we have a whole other plan. He will *not* get near you or

Hadley. Do you hear me? He won't even be able to take a step in your direction. I will be right beside you."

He doesn't understand that I can't do this. "I have to leave."

"If you leave, he walks," Nate says with an intensity in his voice I've never heard. "I know you're freaking out right now, but I'm going to ask for an outrageously high cash bail, which means he can't be released unless he has the money in hand or someone willing to pay it for him."

I laugh and shake my head. "You don't get it. I don't know what funds he has, Nate. I have no access to our accounts. I have no idea if there's some bank account, ready to send it over if they allow it. I was given a stipend to buy groceries and that's all of the money I ever saw. He could have millions and I wouldn't know it. He's mentioned the farm making profits the last few years. He got an inheritance on top of the farmlands. I have no *idea*! I don't even know what he has!"

The admission of my life makes me feel sick, but there it is, a truth that I can't pretend isn't there. Kevin could have money flowing out of his ass, and I wouldn't have a clue. He could write them a check today and be back at the house, and then what?

Nate makes a noise through his teeth. "Ellie, he would have to have that cash on him."

"He can't wire it or get his hands on it?" Connor steps in.

"No, but that's not to say he can't have someone post bail."

I can't stay in this town if he knows I'm leaving him. He'll hunt me down and that'll be the end.

It doesn't matter what kind of protection that Connor thinks he can provide by being around us.

"You can't control the outcome." Connor gently cups my cheeks, forcing me to look at him. His green eyes are filled with understanding and promise. "You can only do this one step at a time. Hadley is safe. She's in school, and the deputy there is watching over her. Right now, you have to go on the stand and explain why he can't be released. If you don't and you run instead, you'll be running forever, Ellie. Trust me, it will never end until you face it. You can do this for yourself and for Hadley."

I try to steady my breath and focus on him. He's right. I have to do it. I need to stand up for myself and for Hadley. She's what matters and I need to show why doing what I did was necessary.

"Okay," I say with a shaky voice.

Nate steps closer. "I'll do everything I can to get us the outcome we want."

"Thank you." I shake my head, willing away the tears, and walk into the courthouse with Connor and Nate on each side, praying I can do this.

I sit in revulsion as I listen to Sheriff Mendoza and then Connor take the stand, each recounting the events of that night in their own words. It sounds like a horror movie, only it's all real. It's my life. I'm the girl they describe as battered, lying on the floor when they got there.

Nate takes his time to show the judge how bad it was, and they repeat the statements they heard. He then lays out a brief account of what I said outside about Kevin's control and then explains that we don't know how much money he has available.

Connor sits beside me, not touching me, but . . . there.

"Please call the plaintiff to the stand."

"He can't hurt you, Ellie, just be strong and tell the truth," Connor's deep voice is at my ear.

I swallow the dread and focus my eyes forward. Nate is standing there, so I look to him. He's been intense and unyielding today. The worry I had about him being Kevin's friend is gone. Today, he's championing me, and the defense was unable to poke holes in Sheriff Mendoza or Connor's accounts.

I'm the last one.

I pray to God I don't get sick or lose it.

When I get to the stand, I recite what the bailiff asks me to and then sit.

Nate goes first. "Mrs. Walcott, could you please recount what happened two nights ago."

I intertwine my fingers, close my eyes, and speak. I tell them everything. I go over each word, each threat, every time he gripped my hair and kicked me. How I was pulled up and tossed around as though I were a doll. Tears fall as I keep talking, but I don't stop, not even when I begin to shake. I just speak. "I thought I was going to die. I thought that was the last time I would ever see my daughter when I told her to run and never come back. The pain was so bad as he hit and kicked me."

I feel as though I have nothing left in me. I'm drained of all the strength I had reserved, but I eventually force myself to look to Nate. His lips quiver before he controls them and hands me a tissue. "Thank you, Mrs. Walcott." He then turns to the judge. "Your Honor, based on the testimony here and the evidence I've provided, we ask that Mr. Walcott be held without bail as he has made life threatening promises against Mrs. Walcott and their daughter."

The judge nods. "The defense has its turn, then I'll render my decision."

The attorney stands, buttons his suit jacket, and heads toward me. "Mrs. Walcott, you've been through quite a trauma."

"Yes."

"One that seems to have never happened before, am I

right?"

I shake my head. "No, it's happened before."

"Really? When?"

I lick my lips, feeling sick to my stomach because I know where this is going. "I never reported it, which is what you're asking. My husband has hit me on numerous other occasions."

"Has he? Or is this some elaborate scheme that you've concocted with your lover so you could run away together?"

My lips part, and I suck in a breath. "Excuse me?"

"You and Mr. Arrowood are in a relationship are you not?"

"No, we're not. He moved here recently."

Connor's gaze meets mine, and his jaw clenches. This is the crazy talk that Kevin was saying that night.

Kevin's lawyer nods. "I see, and in that time, suddenly your husband of eight years just . . . loses it? Never having done something like this before, contrary to your words, Mrs. Walcott, there is no proof of prior incidences. You can see how some may find the timing strange. In the middle of the night, you just happen to be outside and the man who you say your husband accused you of having an affair with is who"—he lifts his fingers and does the air quote sign—"saves you?"

I will not allow this man to take this away from me. I have to stand my ground, not because it's the truth but because Hadley and I will have to run again if they let him out. We will be gone before Kevin is released from jail and no one will be able to stop me. I don't care if that means he walks free after it because I will be free from him. I'll find a way.

So, instead of cowering, which is exactly what they want, I sit a little taller and blow out a deep breath that causes pain to my side.

"My husband has hit me before. He's punched me, he's grabbed me, he's pulled my hair and thrown me to the ground. My husband has controlled me and isolated me from other people. He's trapped me in every aspect of my life and then threatened to kill our daughter and me. I can't speak on what he thinks or the excuses he's made over the years, but *everything* I have said today is true. My neighbor saved my life when our daughter ran to him for help and called 9-1-1. I'm not in any kind of romantic relationship with him. Mr. Arrowood acted as a friend when I was in danger, nothing more."

"Well, I guess we'll see about that." The attorney walks away and sits beside Kevin.

"You may step down, Mrs. Walcott."

My legs feel like jelly as I make my way back to my seat.

"Does the defense wish to make a statement?" The judge asks.

I sit here, my body trembling and my nerves shot. I was able to get through it, but this is really the worst part. None of us can control anything else. Sheriff Mendoza reenters the courtroom and sits beside me so I'm flanked by two men who are showing their sign of support and protection.

"At this time, we plead the fifth and wish to await the trial."

The judge doesn't look surprised, but I am.

Mendoza leans over, his voice a soft whisper. "They know there's enough evidence to keep the case from being thrown out and it's best to wait for the trial instead of having to recant anything he says now."

Right, God forbid he dig himself a hole. The same rights should be afforded the people who witnessed it and me—the victim.

How unfair is this all?

The judge leans forward, his arms resting on the desk in front of him, and he looks to the defense and then to the prosecutor.

"I find myself sitting in these proceedings more than I'd like to be. A family being torn apart, and there's always some flighty reason that the defense presents. As though the woman or child were asking for what happened. I'm not sure when we as judges felt that this was allowable. But it's not. Mr. Walcott, I've looked over your wife's medical records, heard her testimony, and have made note of your lack thereof. I've heard the account of the night, seen the images that the prosecution put forth, and heard how your seven-year-old daughter is who went for help, believing that her mother was going to die. Now, this isn't the trial, but it is to decide whether you're released until that trial, and if so, at what cost. Usually, the courts say one hundred thousand dollars and calls it a day, but I'm reminded of a case that is similar to this. One where the outcome of this case, I fear if I were not to follow my gut, will be much like that one. Therefore, I'm denying the request for bail."

thirteen

Relief so sweet fills me that I can barely contain myself. We're on our way back to Connor's so I can grab Hadley and my things to go back to my house. Connor's place is . . . strange. It's clean, but very sterile with its single couch and outdated television. Each bedroom has a queen size bed and a dresser, but that's it.

It's a house, but not a home.

Even though my home isn't great, it's at least comfortable.

I lean my head back in the seat and release a breath through my nose. "I can't believe they held him."

"Honestly, I can't either."

I look over at him. "You thought they'd release him?"

Connor tilts his head to the side. "I did. Usually, they go with bail, I hoped Nate could push back enough. I was prepared though if it didn't . . ."

"If it didn't, what?"

He glances over and then goes back to the road. "I wasn't sure what I'd do."

"I'm sure you had some plan."

Connor laughs. "I had some crazy ideas, that's for sure."

I'm sure he did. We get to the beginning of his driveway and Connor stops the car.

"Is everything okay?" I ask as we sit here.

He looks up at the sign that says his last name and then over to me. "My mother . . . she was sentimental in every way. She wanted us to have traditions we would pass on to our children. When we came to the driveway, she would stop the car and make us answer a question. Each of us had a different answer based on what she thought fit our needs."

"That's sweet."

My mother was the same. She was always trying to make holidays special and doing things that have stayed with me. Every year for my birthday, my mother would come into my room with a cake in her hands, and we would eat if for breakfast. It's a tradition I've carried on with my daughter, who thinks it's the best thing in the world.

"It didn't matter that, after she died, no one asked the question aloud. My brothers and I still stop the car and stare at this sign, wondering what life would've been like if she lived."

It's clear that her impact on her sons was far greater than she could ever know. "What was the question?"

"What is one truth about an arrow?"

I touch his arm, and it drops from the wheel, which he was gripping. My hand drifts down to his, taking his fingers in mine. "Tell me what your truth is?" I say softly, not wanting to break the spell of the moment.

"You can't take a shot until you break your bow."

"What does it mean?"

Connor moves his hand, covering mine completely. "It means you have to pull back on the bow, use all your might to fight against the strain in your arm as you're going for what you want. It means that if you don't break the bow, you can't ever go forward and hit the target."

My heart begins to pound hard in my chest, both of our breathing is quiet as we watch each other. The words are so poignant to my life right now. I've been unwilling to make any ripples for fear of what would come, but until I stand and change the form of my life, I'll never go anywhere.

"I can see how much your mother influenced you. Also, you did break the bow, Connor. You left this place that morning and became a SEAL and a hero. When you came back, you became a hero to Hadley and me as well. Thank you for sharing that with me."

He opens his mouth to say something but then stops. "You're welcome."

I look down at our hands, and we both pull back. "I'm sorry. I should . . . I'm clearly a mess and you're being so nice. It's been a rough couple of days, and I'm . . ."

"Ellie, stop. You don't have to explain anything to me. You didn't do anything wrong. And stop saying you're a mess, okay?"

"But I am!"

"We all are. Believe me, I may seem like a hero to you, but I'm not. I've made mistakes and lived with the consequences. I think about you, and how, if things had gone differently, that night . . ."

"I think about it too."

He leans back in the driver's seat, head back and then he turns. "I was a mess the first time I saw you after I found Hadley. I had to tell myself a million times that you were married and that whatever I felt was ridiculous. My friends were even warning me that I had to fight this urge to be around you because it wasn't right."

I'm fighting the same thing. The want to be near him.

It's hard to describe why Connor makes me feel this way, but he does. There was this undeniable chemistry the two of us shared, and then there was the actual night.

Being around him again has made it confusing and hard to decipher what I'm feeling.

I smile, knowing I have to answer him but not being able to speak that truth yet. "Okay. I'm just so tired and over-whelmed."

"I understand, but you're not a mess. Sure, the situation is, but that doesn't mean you can't find a way through it."

My eyes start to flutter closed, and I fight to keep them open. "I think the medicine is kicking in."

He nods and puts the car into drive. "Let's get you back to the house so you can rest."

I yawn. "Rest would be good."

As we ride up the long driveway, my thoughts drift in and out of various things. There's so much that has happened that it's as if my life is a series of movie clips I can't see in one sitting. There are too many.

When we stop, Connor's hand touches my face and I see him staring at me. "We're here."

"I wasn't sleeping."

"No?"

Maybe I did for, what, two seconds? I inhale deeply and open the door before he can get out. I move slowly, careful not to jostle my side too much. Between the drive, the hearing, and not sleeping for two nights, I'm dead on my feet.

I exit the car using all my strength and determination, but when I shuffle forward, I start to sink to the ground. Strong arms wrap around me, and the most gorgeous green eyes are locked on mine.

"Ellie?"

He cradles me, and my head rests on his shoulder as he walks toward his house. "Tired. I'm so, so tired. I'm fine. I can walk."

"You're in pain and on medication. You need to rest."

I need to go back to my house and put my life together. "Home."

"Take a nap and then we can talk about that. I'll be here when Hadley gets back."

I want to open my mouth and tell him everything I've been wondering since he came back into my life, but exhaustion overtakes me, and I drift off to sleep.

"That's not how you play Go Fish." Hadley's voice echoes through the small farmhouse, and I smile.

"Yes it is! You have to have two cards of the same color."

"*Noooo*," she chides. "You have to have two of the same *number.*"

"I think you're making this up," Connor says with a laugh. "I know Go Fish, and those are the rules."

"You're cheating."

"Me? Cheating?" He sounds shocked, but I can tell he's kidding.

"Yes, because I beat you three times in a row."

I lie here, still trying to wake up as I listen to them.

"I think it's you who's cheating, Hadley."

I hear her soft little sigh. "You're just a bad fisher. But you're my favorite hero."

He laughs, and my smile is automatic. "I'm glad I'm your favorite. You're my favorite seven-year-old who cheats at Go Fish."

"I'm going to miss you," she says with wistfulness in her voice.

"Miss me? Why? Are you going somewhere?"

I slowly lift myself to the edge of the bed, not knowing where this conversation is going and needing to listen.

"Mommy and I were going to run away that night, and I don't know if I'll ever see you again when we go." Her voice breaks at the end, shattering my heart with it.

This is her home. It's the only place she's ever known, and while her protection is paramount, so is her security. I need to repair any damage done.

First, is going back to that house and doing what I can to set it to rights.

I need her to see that we're okay, and I'm strong. I'm still scared to go there. Even with Kevin in jail, that house is filled with things I want to forget. Still, I want to give Hadley the courage to face things that scare her and prove she can endure.

"Well, if that does happen, we're going to have to find a way to stay in touch."

"But I don't have a phone."

"True, but you know where I live."

Hadley pauses, and I carefully make my way to the door, watching the two of them. Connor and Hadley are sitting on the floor at opposite corners of the coffee table with the cards between them. My world shines a bit brighter just watching them.

I don't know that I have any memories of Kevin ever doing something as simple as this. While I was sleeping, the two of them have been spending time together, bonding in a way that brings tears to my eyes.

"What if you move?"

"Well, I'm only staying here for six months, but I'll make sure your mom knows how to get in touch with me."

"You promise?"

He lifts his hand in some sort of salute. "I sure do."

Hadley lunges forward, wrapping her arms around his neck, and he catches himself before he's tossed backward. "You're my best friend, Connor."

He smiles over her head, hugging her back. "I'm a lucky man then."

He might be more. So much more. I owe it to him and to Hadley to find out.

I step out into the room, and our gazes touch.

"You're awake."

"I am. How long has it been?"

"Mommy!" Hadley rushes toward me. I put my hand out quickly so she doesn't barrel into me, which causes her to slow. "Sorry."

"No, no, I want a hug, just not a fast one."

I want a million hugs from her. Ones that last forever so I can hold her close.

"Were you good for Connor?"

She nods. "We went out to the barn so I could see all the cows. He has a lot of cows, but," her voice drops to a whisper, "he doesn't know what to do with them."

I laugh softly. "Did you tell him to milk them?"

"I tried, but he doesn't listen. Then we walked out to my favorite tree."

Connor walks over and ruffles her hair. "I figured you

needed to rest, so we did some outside stuff and then came back to warm up when we got cold. Did we wake you?"

"No." I smile at him, feeling so much gratitude it overwhelms me. "Not at all. Thank you for taking good care of her."

"It was nothing. Hadley and I are friends. It was fun to get to hang out for a bit."

She looks at him with a wide grin.

"Well, I think Hadley and I need to get back home."

"No!" she screams. "No! I don't want to. Please! Please, Mommy! Please don't make me go back there!"

I fall to my knees and gather her hands in mine. "Hadley, it's okay."

"I don't want to go home!" Her eyes fill with tears as her head shakes back and forth quickly. "I want to stay here—with Connor!"

"Honey, we can't. We need to go back. No one is going to hurt us there."

Her tears fall like rain, and her sniffling breaks me apart. I can see it's true fear that has her. I can't tell her that I feel the same way. The idea of going back to that house makes me want to crawl out of my skin.

"I'm scared, Mommy."

Connor kneels with us, saying, "You don't have to be scared. I can go there to make sure that there's no one else inside and that you'll be safe."

She shakes her head. "I don't want to go! You can't make me!"

Hadley rips her hands from mine, scrambles to her feet, and rushes out the door.

"Hadley!" I yell after her as I try to get up, but wince when my side screams in protest.

"Easy, I'll go get her," Connor says as he helps me stand.

"She's my daughter, I'll go. I just need a second."

"Why don't we give her a minute? She probably needs to cool off, and I know where she went."

How does he do this? How can he know what Hadley needs with such ease? It's as though he's gotten to the core of both of us without any effort at all. Connor and I had this when we met, but now he has that intuition with Hadley as well. He could see that she needed time when I couldn't.

It has to mean something, right?

"You're right. I'm so sorry. I thought she'd want to go home, and we needed to."

"Why do you need to?"

I sigh, hating that I said anything. "Because that's her home and we can't stay here forever. I'm sure you don't need the two of us driving you crazy."

"You're not driving me crazy, and you don't have to go back there if you don't want to."

"We can't stay here."

"Why?"

"Why?" I repeat. "Because . . . you're a bachelor and you have this farm to fix up and I don't think you need another broken thing to repair."

Plus, being around him makes it hard not to see the similarities between him and Hadley. Keeping the possibility of him being her biological father to myself is wrong. He deserves to know. What keeps me from saying it is how I feel when I'm around him. I want to be close, rely on him, and these are dangerous thoughts for me. It's impractical, and I worry that I'll form an attachment to a man who I know is going to leave.

If it hasn't already happened with him and Hadley.

But what if she's his?

What if all the signs that point to it are real?

I have to tell him.

He shakes his head slowly. "I'm more than able to fix up this place with you both here, and I think you and Hadley feeling safe is more important than my being a bachelor. Do you feel safe with me?"

And that's the craziest thing. I have never felt safer than when I'm around him. He's strong, steadfast, and has stepped in when I needed him most. I trust him, and I barely know him.

It's now or never.

I gather any courage I have and prepare to confess something that could forever change both their lives. "I do feel safe with you, and that's the only reason that I have the ability to speak. Connor, I have to tell you something. Or . . . tell you that there's something that is eating away at me."

She's the world, and he deserves to orbit around her as well—if it turns out that he's her father.

"You can tell me anything."

I sure hope that's true because this might not go as I imagine.

"I found out I was pregnant with Hadley about a month after my wedding. I've always wondered . . . if maybe . . . she was . . ." I trail off, afraid to say it aloud. "There's a chance that Hadley isn't Kevin's daughter."

His gaze snaps up before moving to the door she ran out off and then back to me. "You think she could be mine?"

"I don't know, but she has your eyes." The admission falls from my lips as a tear drops from my lashes.

fourteen

There's a chance Hadley could be my daughter?

It isn't . . . it can't be . . . possible. Could it?

We made love so many times that night it's hard to remember if we were careful each time. No, we were. I know I was.

"It was one night," I say. "I wore a condom."

"It was. But the timing of it all leaves the possibility. Maybe it's just wishful thinking because she's so wonderful and that night was . . ."

I don't know what to say or think. If she is my daughter, I need to know. "How long have you wondered?"

"Since the day I found out I was pregnant."

Jesus Christ. I could be a dad. I've been around Hadley all this time and hadn't known I could be her father. I sit back, trying to wrap my head around it all.

What would've happened if I had come back? Would I

have known then? Why didn't I piece any of this as a possibility when we met? I'm a fool, and yet, there's this hope inside me that she is mine.

"Why didn't you try to find me?"

Ellie's lip trembles. "How could I? I didn't know your name or where you were from. I never saw you again until a little over a month ago. I married Kevin the day after we slept together, so it wasn't as if I could say for sure."

Right. Married and . . . yeah, it was one night with no names or expectations.

"Wait, the day after?"

She nods, looking nervous and almost ashamed.

But the reality is, I could've had a child for the last seven years and missed out on it all. "Does she have any idea?"

"No, no, *God* no. I'm sorry, Connor. I should've told you when you got back here, but I couldn't risk Kevin suspecting anything."

Ellie wipes a tear away, and everything inside me springs into action. I made her cry on a night when she should feel nothing but security. I shift closer to her. "Ellie, don't cry."

"It's that . . . I didn't know. I really don't know, and she might not be yours, but there's this part of me that has always hoped she is. Because . . . you were kind to me, and that night is something . . ."

"That night is everything."

She looks at me, her eyes still brimming with vulnerability. "You told me that you dreamed of me?"

I nod. "I did. All the time. I relived that night in my head, wondering who you were, where you might be, and if you were happy."

"I wasn't."

"I know that now."

The two of us watch each other as I reel with the confessions just made. I don't know if I scare her or if she feels the connection that I do.

The sound of thunder rolling in the air snaps me out of it. The two of us blink, coming to the realization that Hadley is outside, probably hiding in a tree while a storm is rolling in.

"I'll go find her," I say before Ellie can speak.

"Connor . . ."

"We'll talk more when I get back, but I'd like you to stay here at least tonight, for Hadley." And for me, but I leave that part off.

"We'll talk when you get back."

I nod and when the thunder rolls in the distance, I feel it in my soul.

I approach the tree where I have a feeling I'll find her, and sure enough, there's a scuffling sound on the wood.

It's hard, this time, not to think about Hadley coming here as some sort of sign or fates way of stepping in. But what are the odds of Ellie's daughter finding her way to my farm and the tree that means the world to me on her own?

And does she have my eyes?

I try to picture it, but I can't.

Is she my kid? If she is, what does it mean? Can I have time with her? Does she want that? Does it even matter when I care about her and already view the two of them as a part of my life, one that I don't want to let go of?

I chastise myself because, right now, I can't get caught up in a bunch of what-ifs and maybes because there's a little girl who has been dropped into hell and is struggling to find a way through it.

I've been there.

Too many times.

I climb the wooden slats and pop my head up and smile at her. "You should probably pick another spot if you don't want me to find you, but then I know how hard it is to avoid this tree when you know it has magical powers to keep you safe."

Her lip quivers. "I don't want to go back there. I don't want to go to the house again. I want to stay here—with you."

"Well, running away isn't going to change whatever choice your mom makes."

Hadley's frown falls deeper. "I'm scared."

I don't blame her. "You know that your mother would never make you go back home if it weren't safe. She's probably a little scared too."

"Mommies and daddies aren't afraid of anything."

"Oh, sure they are. Grown-ups get scared of things all the time."

Hadley crosses her arms over her chest and stares at me. "No, they don't."

I let out a low chuckle. "I get scared."

"No way! You're the strongest boy in the world. You're just saying that."

I love that she thinks that highly of me. I want to be the hero she sees me as, but heroes always fall the farthest when they fail their charge. She's had enough of that.

"If you come down from the tree, I'll tell you all about mine."

Hadley seems to mull it over and then sighs. "You're going to take me back and make me go home."

I know how she feels. When Declan or Sean would come

get me from here, I would drag my feet. Going back to where you feel as though you're only going to run away from again is horrible. If I could've lived in this tree, I would've. My father had no idea I was there, and I could finally breathe.

However, the one thing I always respected was that my brothers never lied when it mattered. They told me what we had to do, and we protected each other, like I'll do for her.

"I am going to take you back, but I promise that no matter what, you are going to be okay."

It's hard being a kid and even harder when you feel like the world around you is crumbling. Everything I know about her has shown that she isn't going to openly defy anyone. She loves her mother, but I imagine she feels lost.

"Why can't we stay with you?" she asks as she starts to move toward me.

"Because you have to do what your mother says."

"I'd rather stay up here."

I chuckle to myself as the thunder rumbles again, and I give her a pointed look. "You know, once the lightning comes, I'm going to need to rush back to the house."

Her head whips to me quickly. "You'll leave me here . . . all by myself in the storm?"

No, but I need to get her down because the tree isn't a safe place to hide out in a lightning storm. I can already see flashes in the distance.

I give her a dramatic sigh. "I'm afraid of lightning . . . I won't be able to stay. So, either you come down and I tell you all about my fears while we go back to the house or you stay here in the storm—you pick."

Hadley moves to the edge. "Fine. I'll go with you. But *only* because you're scared."

I smile and duck my head before she can see it. "I'll meet you at the bottom."

Once she's safely on the ground, I find myself staring at her a little closer. Her eyes are the same color as mine and my brothers' eyes, which are green with small flecks of gold. We used to be beaten for it because they reminded Dad of our mother. We had her eyes.

Now, looking at Hadley, I see it.

Or maybe I'm fucking wishing it were true because then she would be mine. I would never let that fucking asshole touch her or her mother again, not that I would let that happen if Hadley weren't mine.

Still, I have never wanted something to be so true in my entire life.

I don't care about any vows I made in the past because I would die before I'd let anything happen to Hadley or Ellie. I've known it from the minute I saw Ellie eight years ago, and that need for her is still as strong, but now, it's the same with Hadley.

This little girl will own my heart, regardless of whose blood runs in her veins.

She and I start walking and her posture rips at my soul. Her shoulders are slumped in defeat and the normal chatter I've come to know as her is gone. It's as though we're walking toward some horrible fate. I wish I could take it away from her, keep them both with me where I know they're both safe. I refuse to take even an ounce of control away from her mother, though.

"Connor?" Hadley asks as we move through the field.

"Yeah?"

"What are you scared of?"

So many things come to mind, all of which revolve around people I love. "When I was little, I was terrified of storms. I was stuck up in that tree for a big one where the bolts were hitting the ground. It was so bad that even the cows were scared. I was so afraid that it took my older brothers coming to find me before I would leave."

"What about now?" she asks.

Now, I'm afraid that she's my daughter and I'm never going to deserve her. I'm scared she won't be my daughter and the part of me that has this bit of hope will never recover from the loss of what was never mine to begin with. Mostly, I'm afraid I won't be able to protect her or Ellie.

"Well, I don't know. Mostly, I worry about the people I care about."

"Like me?"

I nod with a grin. "You bet. We're friends."

"I'm scared of my dad."

Bile churns in my stomach and guilt fills me. If I had known there was a possibility of her, I could've saved her from it all. We both slow down, and I put my hand on her shoulder. "Your dad can't hurt you now," I reassure her.

She looks away and then back to me. "He hurt my mom and was always yelling at us."

This kid should've known a life with fairy tales, sunshine, and tea parties. Her father should've given her hope and been a man she looked up to. He robbed her of that, and I'd like to kill him for it.

I'll do what I can to ease her worries. "I was up in the tree during that storm because my dad was angry a lot. He would yell and sometimes he'd hit my brothers and me."

"But you're so strong."

"Now I am, but I wasn't then. I remember being scared a lot when I was younger. It wasn't until I grew up and went into the military that I finally realized I didn't have to be scared anymore."

I don't want her to wait that long, but there is hope.

"I want to be a grown-up."

I laugh. "It's not all it's cracked up to be, Squirt."

The house comes into view, and Hadley sighs. "When I'm a grown-up, I'll get to do what I want and won't have to go anywhere I don't want to."

The ignorance of youth. I sure as fuck don't want to be in Sugarloaf or have to fix up the farm I never wanted to see again. Nor did I want to get out of the navy, but I had no choice. However, coming back here has given me something I never thought I'd get . . . a second chance.

fifteen

"She's all tucked in and fast asleep," I say as I make my way into the living room where Connor is sitting making a list of something.

He looks up and smiles. "Good. She's probably exhausted."

We all are. At both Hadley and Connor's insistence, I decided to stay another night here. Ultimately, I made the decision to stay because Connor and I have a lot we need to talk about. My want for Hadley to feel comfortable, even if it means this conversation will be anything but for me, was another reason.

"Yeah . . . do you think that we could talk?"

He puts the paper down and nods. "I think that's probably a good idea."

"How about we go on the porch, that way she doesn't overhear if she wakes up."

"Sounds good."

I release a deep breath through my nose and follow him out. We sit on the porch swing, and I shiver from the drop in air temperature, but I have so much to say, I don't give myself a second to think about it.

"I want to tell you that I really have no idea if it's possible. I'd like to explain, if that's okay?"

"Of course."

I plan to bare my soul and hope I make it out of this without crumbling.

"I met you the night before I married Kevin. In some part of my brain, I knew I didn't love him and shouldn't marry him, but I felt like . . . I had to. I truly believed he loved me and was just protective—maybe a bit jealous and insecure. It was the way he talked to or about me, you know? I convinced myself that once our relationship was secure, he'd be too. I was wrong. In my heart, I knew it wouldn't matter and I shouldn't do it. I went to the bar that night because I was lost and that was the last place my parents were. They meant everything to me. They were . . . they were killed in a hit and run close to the bar a week prior, and I'd been a mess since their death. My entire world was gone just like that and I thought, well, I thought that if I could feel them then I'd know what to do. But then you said hello, and I was so lost. It took one word for my entire life to feel as though it had been righted. You were so wonderful, and you looked at me like I was special and beautiful. We danced in that bar, and I wanted one night that every girl dreams of. Even if it could only be that solitary night? Even if it was so wrong?"

"But it didn't have to be that once."

He's right. If I hadn't left before he woke, I might have never married Kevin. Even if Connor had still left, maybe I would've found the courage to walk away, seeing what I could've had. I was so naïve and didn't want the morning sun to wipe away the night we shared in darkness. Instead of facing the possibilities, I settled for what I thought was my only option.

I hadn't really thought Connor could have been more because he was just as happy spending that night wrapped in anonymity as I was.

"I think we'd be lying if we said that was true. You were running from something too, if I remember correctly."

We used each other to escape the reality of our lives. As much as I would like to believe there could be more, it wasn't true. And I've done enough pretending to know the difference.

He looks out at the horizon and grips the bottom of the swing. "I was."

"You're not married, so it couldn't be that." I attempt a little levity.

Clearly, it didn't work because he now looks as if he's haunted by something.

"The night we met . . ." He trails off.

I reach out, placing my hand on his, and his other hand covers mine. The shiver I experience this time has nothing to do with the cold. "The night we met?" I struggle to keep my voice even.

Connor's face shows no emotion, but the air around us feels heavy. It's strange, and yet, I remember this same exact feeling the night we met. It was as though I felt his touch so deeply that I would never be the same. Our hearts became tangled as we bared ourselves in ways that I didn't know were possible.

"It was so much more . . ."

"I know what you mean."

He shakes his head, breaking us both from the odd connection. "My father was an abusive drunk who beat the shit out of me and my brothers."

A piece of me shatters from that one sentence. "Connor . . ."

"No, I don't talk about this well, so let me try to get it out."

I press my lips together tightly, giving him the silence he asks for.

"When my mother died, he became a completely different person. He drank constantly, and when the alcohol stopped numbing the pain, he decided to spread it around. My brothers took what they could to protect me since I was the youngest and by far the smallest."

My chest aches, but I hold in any sound as he keeps talking.

"When they left, it became a lot harder to avoid him. I learned that running made it worse. When I came back, I paid for it."

I wrap my fingers around his, giving him whatever support I can lend. I can't fathom the betrayal he must've felt when the one person he needed the most was the person breaking him. He's been so steadfast in his support for me, giving me what I needed without asking, and I have no idea if it's hurt him at all.

Did he relive what he endured?

Does he look at me and see a weak woman, even though he's the one telling me how strong I am?

"I'm so sorry. You never deserved that from anyone, least of all your father."

"No one deserves to be hit, Ellie. No one. It doesn't matter whose hand it comes from—it's wrong and unforgivable. I vowed that I would never be like him, and I want you to understand how much I mean it. I would never hit someone in anger unless I'm trying to protect what's important to me."

I lift my other hand and gently touch his cheek. "You don't have to try very hard to convince me. I see who you are. There isn't a trace of that man inside you."

His fingers wrap around my wrist, pulling my hand down. "I've worked really fucking hard to make sure of that. My brothers as well. The night we met was probably the lowest I've ever felt. My father was in a state for months before my graduation. He was drinking more, finding ways to catch me off guard. I knew I had to get out of here, and I wasn't smart like Declan or Jacob so there wouldn't be any scholarships. I didn't play baseball like Sean, so sports were out. I knew it was jail or the military, so I enlisted while I was a senior and never told him. That night, I let him know that I was leaving, and he lost it. He came at me hard, yelling and saying things I will never forget. He punched me, and I swung back. We fought, man to man, and it was the first time and only time I had let my emotions get the better of me."

"You can't for one minute think that any of it was your fault. You were defending yourself."

He runs his hand over his face. "I fought my father when he was out of his skull. I don't fault myself, but make no mistake that it wasn't because I was pissed. I had ten years of rage from the beatings he inflicted and the hell he put us through built up inside me."

It's different. I know he probably won't see it that way, but this isn't the same at all. He didn't go looking for a fight, he responded to what was in front of him.

"And if I had gotten a bat and took it to Kevin's head, what would you say to me?"

"Good."

"But you fighting off your own attacker is different how?"

Connor's hands clench and then he rubs his leg, seeming uncomfortable. I understand him in a way that maybe no one else can. I've lived it, fought with the guilt, and spent years thinking that maybe in some way I did deserve it because that was what I'd been told. I've fought every day with the decision to stay one minute past the first time.

Being a victim doesn't just happen in the moment, it follows me every second. I recognize it, and I hate that it's a bond we share. I'm also grateful I'm not alone.

"Regardless," Connor begins again, "a few hours after I woke up without you there, I was on a bus to basic training and haven't come back until he died a few weeks ago."

So many questions float around in my mind. If Connor had come back, even once, would it have been different? If I'd run into him, I would've felt something or maybe he would have fought for me. There are a million what-ifs but only one truth, and it's this moment in time.

"I've often wondered if I was being punished for that night . . ."

He gets to his feet so fast that I gasp, but then his hands are on the back of the swing, steadying the movement. "Don't ever say that. What we shared isn't something that anyone would punish someone for. How could it be?"

"Because it was wrong of me! I was getting married the next day. I didn't regret what we did, I still don't regret it, but I should have never ever gone back to that room with you."

"I don't understand."

"I married him. I went through with it, and all the while, I . . ." I can't say it. If I do, it'll be a mistake. But then I look up and see the look in his eyes, see the way he's silently begging me to give him my truth, and God, I want to. "I wished it could've been you. The man who smiled at me with the softest and most loving expression. You looked at me as though you needed me, and I know it was wrong, but I needed you."

When he sits back down, his head falls in his hands before turning to look at me. "I did need you."

"But we weren't each other's to have."

"No, I guess we weren't."

I lean back, turning just enough to still be able to look at him and wondering if the moment we're sharing now could've been our daily life. Would we be sitting on the porch, talking at night, enjoying an honesty I'd never known existed until this moment?

"If things had gone differently that night, if I were braver and stayed, do you think we could've been something more?"

Connor lifts his body back up, his arm going across the back of the swing. I can see how easily I would fit into his side, as though I were made to go there, but I stay where I am because we've yet to talk about Hadley.

"I don't know. Sometimes, when I envisioned what we may have been, it was so much more, but I think that the fantasy of that time was just that. I was fucked up when we met, dealing with emotions I wasn't mature enough to handle. That night was peace, but in the morning, it was gone . . . like you."

"I was never gone, I was lost."

"And what about now?"

I look away, letting the question settle over me. "I'd like to say that I'm finding my way. I'm not lost, but I'm not found. I'm . . . hopeful that I'll be able to get where I should be."

Connor takes my hand in his. "That's all any of us are doing, Ellie."

"Some better than others."

He laughs once, the sound echoing around us. "I'm the eternal bachelor, sworn never to have a family or a real relationship. I push everyone away. I'm not doing a damn thing better than anyone."

That leaves me sitting here wondering if he's upset with my possible revelation. "And what if Hadley is yours?"

"Then I'll be the father I never had, and that girl will never have to fear for you or herself again."

sixteen

"Connor, Connor, Connor!" Hadley yells as she runs out to the barn.

I've been working non-stop since she left for school. I finished my surprise about an hour ago and came to get some of the work I actually should've been doing for the farm done.

"Hey! How was school?"

"Good. I got to talk to the whole class about how a Navy SEAL rescued me when I hurt my arm."

Ellie is walking slowly behind her with a huge grin on her face that makes my heart stutter. God, she's beautiful.

The sun is off to the side of her, and the skirt of her dress is blowing just slightly around her legs. She has a wrap around her shoulders, and her long brown hair is down. She looks breathtaking.

"Hey," I say with a hitch in my throat.

"Hey." Ellie's eyes brighten as she gets nearer.

"How was school for you?"

Ellie shrugs. "It was good, but I can't wait for Hadley to tell you all about her day."

I look down at her as she smiles so hard I worry her cheeks could break. "So, you talked about me, huh?"

"I did! I did! And now you're going to come to school with me!"

"Uh—" I stammer. "I'm what?"

Her eyes go wide, and she starts speaking at her normal speed, which is Mach ten or twenty and still too fast for a normal man to keep up with. "I was telling them how you found me in the tree but that I didn't really want to be found but you're so smart and saved me. I told them about how you carried me with one arm because you're like Hercules. Then I changed my mind because you're even better because you know how to use a gun since you were in the military. Then I was saying how, again, you came and helped me when I was in trouble and how you're a hero *and* fought in the war *and* how you're not afraid of anything except storms when you were little." She draws a huge breath and keeps going. "Then I said I was going to bring you for show and tell because everyone wants to meet you because you're my best friend. Plus, no one has an adult for a best friend like I do. They didn't believe it, but you are, and Mom says I can't tell people you'll come to school and that I have to ask. Connor, will you come to school with me?"

When she finally stops, she smiles and looks pleased with herself. I'm just in shock. "I don't know about that."

"You have to. You don't want me to fail, do you? Show and tell is for a grade."

I don't, right? I mean, that's the right answer, but it's also the absolute last thing I want to do. What the hell am I going to show and tell?

"No, I don't want you to fail, but I'm sure we can find something else that's even better."

"It has to be you. I even wrote a paper about you so that it was approved by Mrs. Flannigan, and she's mean. She doesn't like kids, but they let her be a teacher anyway."

Oh, Jesus. "Right, but I'm not really sure people want to meet me."

"You're the coolest. My friends will love you!" Hadley's little voice sounds very sure of herself there.

I need to get out of this—quick. "I am sure there are a million other things that are much cooler and better options."

Her lip juts out into a pout.

"But you're what I want to bring."

I look over to Ellie for help, but she leans against the door opening with a knowing grin. There's no way to say no to this kid. Especially not with the lip thing and the big eyes staring at me all innocently. Damn it.

"Ten minutes."

Hadley leaps up and squeals. "You're the best!"

No, she is, and I'm completely wrapped around her finger. If this kid is mine, I'm in even more trouble than I thought. There's no way I'll want to let her go. For each day I spend with her there are hundreds more I want to make up for. There are seven years I missed, and if she's my daughter, I'm going to want to make sure there isn't a single one added to it.

"I think you're overestimating how much people will want to meet me."

Hadley shrugs. "My best friend is the coolest. Everyone is going to be so jealous. Can you wear your uniform?"

Ellie laughs and then covers it with a cough. "That's enough, Hadley. Connor is working hard, and we need to get your homework done."

"First," I say with a little too much enthusiasm, "I have something to show you."

"You do?"

I nod at Hadley. "Yup. Let's take a walk."

"Can Mom come?"

"Of course, we can all go . . . if she wants."

We both look back to Ellie, who shrugs and pushes toward us. "I think a little fresh air would be good for all of us."

The three of us head out of the barn and start to head toward the tree, Hadley between us. I think about how we probably look right now. A family with a mother and father who adore the child between them. In many ways, that would be the picture's story because I do adore Hadley and I care very much about Ellie. In some ways, I love her, which is crazy, but it's there.

Ellie has been the woman I've felt passion, love, and longing for almost my entire adult life.

I know she isn't ready for anything. Hell, she's still married and about to deal with her husband's trial, but . . . it's as though time didn't pass for me. She's been mine this whole time, and now I have to wait until she's ready for me—again.

"Meet you there!" Hadley runs off, leaving the two of us behind.

"So, how did fixing up the barn go?" Ellie asks after a few seconds, her hands clasped in front of her.

"I didn't get much done, actually. I was working on something else . . ."

"Yeah?"

"Something for Hadley."

Ellie's eyes find mine and there is a sea's worth of questions floating in them. "You didn't have to . . ."

"I know. Look, I know we talked last night, but I want

to know if she's biologically mine. If she's not, I will do my damnedest to respect that she is his, but I hope you understand that, regardless of the test results, it doesn't change how much I like her. She's a good kid, and she's . . . well, she . . ."

"You care about her."

I look up with a grin. "I do. And I care about her mother too."

"We both kind of like you as well," Ellie says with a smirk. "Just a little."

"Also, you guys can stay with me until you feel safe to return."

Ellie releases a breath through her nose as her fingers graze the top of the hay that's growing in the field. "Hadley would stay here forever with you. I don't know that she'll ever feel safe at that house, and I can't blame her, but . . . you don't need two troublesome females around you."

I don't want to tell her that it's exactly what I need, that them staying here has made being in this house easier. The memories aren't so loud when they are around, and I much prefer seeing their faces than the ghost of my father when I enter the room.

Instead, I try to give her a part of that truth. "You're not bothering me at all. And if Hadley . . ."

"Is yours," she finishes.

"If it is the case, then I really am grateful for the time I have right now."

Ellie's fingers move to the side, brushing against mine. I don't know if she did it on purpose, but I'm not one to let a moment pass me by. My hand slides into hers, and I hold on. She looks to me, and I watch her, waiting for a clue as to what she wants.

"And if she's not?"

"Then I have a pretty cool best friend."

Her smile makes my heart flip over in my chest. I want her to look at me like this each day. I want to be the man who makes my angel look like she could fly. Her wings may have been broken years ago, but I'm really good at restoring things.

Neither of us says a word as we near the tree, but Ellie pulls her hand back when we hear Hadley yell. "Whoa! This is the best thing in the world!"

I look at the fully decked out tree house that I spent hours building and then to both of them. Ellie's eyes glaze over with moisture as she watches Hadley, who is already climbing the steps.

"You did this?"

"Every kid should have a safe place."

Ellie turns to me, her lips parted, the sun casting a soft glow over her face as it dips closer to the horizon. Her voice is soft. "You spent your whole day doing this for her? Connor . . ."

I shove my hands into my pockets to avoid touching her face. She's so damn beautiful. "This tree was where I would run if I could get away from my father. It's where I found Hadley, and it doesn't have to hold the same memories for her as it did for me. I did it for both of us, and for you."

"For me?"

Yes, for her. As I was building, I kept thinking of my mother. It was as though she was there with me, telling me how proud she was as she smiled. "I can't take a shot if I don't break the bow, Ellie. I'm strong enough to hold off on releasing the arrow, until you're ready."

Her eyes widen, and her breath hitches.

It was worth it.

The sweat, frustration, and deviation of plans just to see that look. We may have lost our chance years ago, but I'm not a kid anymore, and I have my target set. I'm waiting for the sights to align.

seventeen

"I appreciate you meeting me like this," I say to Nate's friend Sydney as we sit in the teacher lounge.

"Not a problem at all, honestly."

Sydney was the volunteer EMT on scene, but she is also a lawyer I hired to help me draw up divorce papers.

"I know this is weird . . ."

"Why?"

"Just that you were there, and then you and Connor were arguing."

She laughs through her nose. "Connor and I have argued like that since . . . well, forever. He's lucky I didn't deck him for the way he tried to push me away. It is as though that man thinks he can come back here and suddenly be king of the castle. I don't think so. He made his choices, and while he may think he's a new man, he can kiss my ass if he's going to order me around."

A pang of jealousy hits me in the gut, and I do my best to ignore it. It's clear they've had some kind of relationship. I wonder if he loves her or if she still loves him.

Sydney is what I would call an old-world beauty. She's the type of regal-looking woman you would expect to find in New York or London, not Sugarloaf. Her golden hair is pulled back into a low knot with wisps of hair falling out. She's wearing a black pants suit with the most beautiful red heels I've ever seen. Everything about her says confidence where I feel small and insignificant.

"I didn't know . . ."

"Didn't know what?"

I feel awkward, but there's obviously history between them. "That you two were together."

Sydney rears back, her lips are parted, but there is a smile of amusement tugging at them. "Oh, no, it's nothing like that. Connor is like a little brother to me. I dated his older idiot brother, Declan, from the time I was thirteen until the asshole left town and never returned. All of them are the same, though. Domineering, protective, and attractive. Oh, and stupidity runs in their veins."

My body breathes a sigh of relief. I don't know why since Connor and I are just friends who possibly have a child together, but it's there.

"I'm sorry to assume."

"Don't be sorry." She smiles, giving me a feeling of reassurance. "Are you okay to talk about this with me? I want to be sure you're comfortable. If you worry I'll betray you because I know Connor, I can promise you that not only is it illegal and I'd lose my license but also that I would never tell anyone what we spoke about, even if there weren't that threat. Not to mention, it will bug him to no end and I would get far too much joy out of that."

I'm not comfortable talking to anyone, but Sydney seems

kind, and she was there that night. She isn't looking at me with judgment, and that's about the most I can ask for. "No, it's not that, and I don't think you would. I'm sure you can imagine that this is humiliating, and I . . ."

"You don't have to feel that way with me."

I wish it were that simple. I'd like for all of this to be a bad dream I'm about to wake up from. "I'm okay. I want this over with."

"I can understand that. I know you've been through a lot and this will be no different. Right now we have the temporary order of protection for both you and Hadley, which then allows us to move forward with the divorce once the ninety-day waiting period is up. I don't think we'll have any problems proving fault since we have photos and a police officer's testimony of your husband's abuse. If it's okay with you."

My hands start to tremble and I feel sick to my stomach. This is the reason that so many women stay quiet. The fear of speaking out and it falling on deaf ears. If I go before the judge and tell him everything, what if he deems it's not enough and lets him out? Sure, the judge refused bail, which makes me want to believe the courts will rule in my favor, but even Nate said that was the luck of us drawing a judge who was on a mission. What if I have one who doesn't feel that way for the divorce? Without the conviction, Kevin could contest the divorce and use this as another way of controlling me.

"Do you mean they still might not believe me? They might think I'm lying about the abuse and not convict him? Even when there are witnesses and everything?"

Sydney puts her pen down and places her hand on mine. "Ellie, it doesn't matter if the case doesn't go as planned. We know what happened, and I believe you. You're not alone. You didn't do anything wrong, and no matter what, I'll help you get out of this as quickly as possible."

"I don't want him to hurt us again."

"I know, and I'm going to do everything I can to prevent it."

I push out a deep breath and drop my chin to my chest, saying, "I should've done this years ago."

"You're strong to do it at all. I want to say I'm sorry." She squeezes my hand. "You've lived here a long time, and none of us ever reached out. I always assumed you didn't want to be a part of the community."

I shake my head as the feelings of loneliness resurface with a vengeance. "I wasn't allowed to really be a part of things."

"I see that now."

"Plus, it's hard to have friends when you're covering bruises."

Sydney pulls her hand back, and her shoulders slump. "I hope you know that you don't have to cover anything anymore, Ellie. I'd really like to be your friend, if you'd like to be mine."

A friend. It's such a simple word and yet it's something I haven't had in so long, I don't even know what it means. Still, Sydney is kind and offering me an olive branch that I never would've taken before. "I'd really like that."

She smiles. "Good. Now, let's go over the details and get our information ready so we can file the second we're allowed to, okay?"

"Okay."

I'm going to do everything I can to put this behind me, and this is step one.

"Mommy?" Hadley asks as we walk through the field to get

to our home to get some clothes and things we need. It's been a week of making it work, but that isn't really possible anymore. We need more clothes and supplies if we're going to keep staying with Connor.

"Yes?"

"Why did Daddy hit you?"

My hand tightens just a bit as the question catches me off guard. I'm not sure how to answer her. Hadley may be only seven, but she's smart and sees things. She isn't young and gullible.

This is a chance for me to help guide her into not making the same mistakes that I did. I want her to know that it's not okay. No one should ever lay their hands on her, especially not in anger. I stayed too long, made too many excuses, but not anymore.

I straighten up a bit and work to make my voice sound confident. "He hit me because he was angry and couldn't control himself. It's never okay to do that, you know that, right? It was wrong of him to do it."

"Is he sorry?"

No, I doubt he was.

"I sure hope so."

"Does he love us?"

Oh, my heart is breaking apart. "I think he loves you very much."

Hadley is, of course, too smart to miss that I left myself out. "Does he love you, Mommy?"

"I believe he tries really hard, but . . ." Now I'm going to break her world. "But when you love someone, you never want to hurt them. What he did is never okay to do, and it is never the way you show someone you care about them. Do you understand?"

She looks up at me, and I pray she hears what I'm saying.

"I think so."

I squat down in the field of straw and pray that this little girl will never allow someone to hurt her. "It doesn't matter if it's a daddy, a husband, a friend, or someone you don't know. No one should ever be allowed to hurt you. You should tell someone right away if it happens. Don't ever be afraid that it's your fault because it's not ever your fault."

Hadley bobs her head but her gaze never leaves mine. "I love you, Mommy."

"I love you, sweet girl. I want you to know that what happened will never happen again. You and I won't live with Daddy anymore."

"Why not?"

Protecting her from the truth has been all I've ever done. I don't want her to hate him, but I want her to see strength from me. She should always understand that the choice I'm making right now may not be easy, but that it's the right one. I can't be married to him. I won't let him be around Hadley and let her think that it's the way a marriage should be.

"Because I'm not going to stay married to him anymore. We're going to move out of that house, and we're going to be okay."

A tear falls down her face, and I wish I could take it away from her. "Did I do something wrong?"

"No, baby. You did nothing, and neither did I. I'm doing this because I have to protect us. I know it's scary and a lot to worry about, but I want you to know that I love you very much and I'm going to do whatever I have to so that we're safe."

"But doesn't he love me?"

"Who could resist loving you?" I ask her.

"If he loved me, he wouldn't want us to leave."

Telling her was what I feared. I never want Hadley to think this is her fault. "Do you like when Daddy yells at us?"

She shakes her head.

"Me either. I don't want either one of us to be afraid anymore. You and I, we're strong girls and no one is going to yell at us anymore. You are the best little girl any mother could ask for and part of my job is to protect you."

"Will he come back for us?"

"No, he won't be around us anymore." No matter what I have to do, I'll keep that promise. "We'll find somewhere to live that we both love."

"Can we stay with Connor?"

I smile softly. Comfort fills my soul that he's come to mean so much to her. "No, honey. Connor isn't staying in Sugarloaf for long, and while he's been very good to us, he has his farm he needs to deal with."

And I'm not even close to ready at this point for that.

"I think he likes you."

"I think he likes *you*!" I say with a giggle. "You got a tree house on his farm and he's going for show and tell."

And he might be your dad.

"I'm going to be sad when he leaves."

I will too. I will miss the way he looks at me as well as his unwavering strength and understanding and support.

"Well, we have to make the next few months super special then. Come on, let's keep walking."

We make our way through the field as she tells me about her day. She's a little quieter than normal, less animated, and I hate that this conversation dulled her. I know that if I don't stand up now, I'll never get up off the ground.

When the house comes into view, a wave of nausea hits me like a brick. All of it rushes back to me, and I can hear the sounds in my ears, the rush of breath coming from my lungs when he kicked me the loudest of all.

All of it took place right here—in my home.

Hadley's breathing accelerates, and I squeeze her hand tight. "It's okay, we're going to get our things and then go back, but no one can hurt us, okay?"

I'm not sure if I'm trying to reassure her or myself at this point. Maybe we both needed to hear it.

"He's not here?"

"No, baby, he's not here."

I hate that my child is so afraid, so I tell myself to be the strength she needs to see and take a step forward. Using my determination to thrust me closer to the house that was a horror just a week ago, I hold on to the need I have to protect Hadley. I recall each time that Kevin took something from me, and I refuse to give him anything else.

I hold her little hand tighter, showing her that even if we hit rock bottom, the only way to go after that is up.

As we get to the front door, another sense of dread hits me. I don't know what the house looks like. All Hadley has ever known is the perfect home. I was meticulous at making sure everything was clean and in its place so that Kevin couldn't use it as a reason to hit me.

When I left that night, there were definitely things knocked over.

Shit.

I open the door, which someone had clearly had replaced, and hope it's not as bad as I fear it will be.

Then I stop, stunned.

Everything is in its place.

The photo that was thrown across the room is sitting back on the sofa table as though it had never been touched. The lamp that Kevin threatened to bash over my head isn't on the floor where he dropped it. It's sitting on the end table.

I don't understand. How? Who came in and cleaned?

Hadley releases my hand when she spots her beloved doll over in the corner. "Phoebe!" She runs at full speed, lifting it into her arms and hugging it tightly. "Can I bring her back to Connor's?"

"I'm sure he won't mind." I smile softly, relieved that she got past her fears and thankful that someone had come in and cleaned up so Hadley didn't have to see the destruction.

eighteen

When we get back to Connor's house with a bag of clothes each, there's a very expensive SUV parked next to his.

"Who is that, Mommy?" Hadley asks.

"I don't know."

We walk toward the car and the driver door opens, a pair of red heels hit the dirt, and I smile.

"Hi, Sydney," I say as I make my way over.

"I was hoping I'd find you here."

"Hadley, this is Miss Sydney."

Sydney extends her hand. "It's nice to meet you."

They shake, and Hadley looks up to the house. "It's nice to meet you too. You have really pretty shoes."

"Thank you." Sydney's voice is laced with a smile. "You have very pretty eyes."

My heart lurches to a stop as I wonder if she sees it. If Sydney knows the brothers as well as she says she does, will she be observant enough to figure it out?

"Thank you, Miss Sydney. Mommy, can I go find Connor?"

"I don't think . . ."

"Please! I have to help with the barn. I'm sure he's there. He said once I was done with school I could help him because he needs help. Yesterday, he let the chickens out the wrong door, and I had to chase them so they'd go back in. You can't let the chickens run around when the cows are there." Hadley huffs as though it's common knowledge. "I told him, but he said he was trying to get things done so he could go back to repairing the house. Then we found another problem in the fence, so he was upset."

"Well, then, don't you think he has a lot to do and you'll be in the way?" I ask, hoping she'll leave him be.

Sydney laughs. "I think you should go find him and let him know all the other things that are broken."

"You know Connor?" The suspicion in her voice rings clear.

"I do. I knew him when he was a little boy who would follow me around, asking to ride my horses."

"Really?"

"Yup."

Hadley's brow furrows as she looks Sydney up and down. "Did you know he's my best friend and he thinks I'm the best."

"He is? Well, he's a lucky guy," Sydney's voice is light and playful. "I wish I had a best friend like you, but . . . he got you first."

She nods once. "He did. And he calls me Squirt."

Sydney's smile grows. "You have a nickname from him?"

"I do."

"Wow, do know that Connor loves nicknames. When we were little, I gave him the best one and since you're his best friend, I think you should have it."

Hadley claps her hands together and squeals. "Really?"

"Absolutely! You should call him Duckie. He loved it so much, and he would laugh so hard hearing it again!" Sydney's smile tells me that he will not do that.

"Okay! Can I go, Mom?"

"I guess so, but if you don't find him in the barn, please come right back."

"I will!" Hadley yells over her shoulder since she's already running away from us.

Sydney gives a soft laugh. "She's adorable."

I watch her run at full speed, hair swaying side to side, and my chest feels lighter. She looks so carefree, like she should be. I try to remember any other time I'd seen her like this, and I come up short.

Sure, she's been happy in the last seven years, but it's different. Right now, I don't see the hesitancy to just be a kid. It's as if she's really found a sense of safety that allows her to . . . be free.

"She's all that matters to me."

"And it seems she's smitten with Connor."

I nod. "The two of them have formed an instant bond."

Sydney's shoulders go back, and she fidgets a bit. I know she's thinking it, based on her comment about her eyes. If Sydney dated his oldest brother, surely, she saw the resemblance. "Connor is a good man."

"He is."

"He's been through a lot. They all have been, and . . . did you and Connor know each other before?"

I stop her right there. "Connor and I slept together eight years ago, and yes, I know that Hadley has his eyes . . . and his smile."

She exhales. "I didn't want to pry, but it was . . . impossible not to see. At least for me because, well, I fell in love with those eyes when I was a little girl."

If it was so easy for Sydney to see, I can't help but wonder if Connor's father ever noticed. He used to look at Hadley with a wash of confusion, but he never said anything or even so much as hinted at it. Maybe he knew? Maybe that was why he was always so nice to us. I figured it was because he was lonely, but what if he saw the similarity?

"Would you like to sit?" I offer. "It's a long story."

Sydney and I walk up to the porch, and I can see the unease in her. "This house, it has a lot of memories for me. I haven't been here since the night Declan left." She lets out a half-laugh. "I thought if I could avoid it for long enough, it wouldn't hurt, but . . ."

"Houses have truths that don't ever die."

She looks up at me and shrugs. "I guess so, but love sure as hell does."

Isn't that the truth?

We sit, and I relay the story of how Connor and I met and all that happened after. It feels easier this time, telling Sydney. I'm able to go through it, and she just listens.

"Wow," she says once I'm done.

"Yeah."

"And he knows that you have doubts?"

"He does," I reply with a bit of hesitancy.

He hasn't really brought it up. I keep waiting for him to ask for a paternity test, but it has yet to come. I would think that would've been the first thing he wanted. Unless, he doesn't want to know.

Which doesn't make sense given his personality.

Connor is fiercely protective of his family. He's made that clear when he speaks of his brothers or his mother. I would think that Hadley would be no different, especially since he already seems to care for her.

"Well, this is a bit of a revelation."

"Will it change things for the divorce?"

Sydney shakes her head. "Nope. If anything, it'll make it easier for you since we won't have to fight about any kind of child support or visitation. Did you guys get a test yet?"

"No, we sort of . . . it hasn't really . . . I've been waiting for him to . . . ask for one. I don't want to push him. It's a lot to take in, especially when that night was supposed to just be that. I didn't even know his name until a few weeks ago."

She laughs and her eyes are filled with disbelief. "You're kidding me."

"Nope."

"I don't know whether to be in awe or be in shock. It's like those stories that you hear about when people find their way back together after fifty years, but this is so much more amazing."

I don't know if it's anything other than happening. Connor has saved me, and not only from the situation that happened with Kevin. If I had never had that one night with him, if I hadn't known that there was more than what I had, I would have given up a long time ago.

"Well, that's all of it."

Sydney leans back in her seat. "That's so insane, and yet, so Connor."

"What's so Connor?" His deep voice causes me to jump.

"Hey. Hi. We were just talking about you."

He and Hadley share a look and then start to climb the

stairs. "I figured that much. Nice to see you, Syd. Anything I can do for you?"

She gets up, hand on her hip and head tilted. "You can start by telling me how much you've missed me."

"I would, Goose, but it seems that my friend Hadley here is calling me Duckie. Any idea how that came about?"

Her smile is wide as she bursts out laughing. "God, that night was the best thing ever." She turns back to me. "You see, the Arrowood brothers are inherently evil, at least to each other. There is nothing off-limits, and if they know your weakness, they use it. Connor here was afraid of this pond on my farm. It could've been because Declan, Jacob, and Sean told him that if you put your toes in, they'd fall off, but only if your name started with a C."

Connor moves up the steps. "Don't let her fool you, she is far from innocent here. Syd was the sister I never wanted."

"Please, I was always nice to you," she defends.

"The hell you were!"

"Anyway," Sydney starts in after giving him an eye roll. "We told Connor we wanted to play Duck, Duck, Goose, but the only way to play was to act like a duck."

I see this going very badly. Connor glares at her with a sort of brotherly affection under all that gruff. "In the water."

"Of the pond at my house," Sydney tacks on. "Then his brothers tossed him in and forced him to be the duck. Oh, you should've seen him, terrified that his toes were going to fall off but making duck sounds at the same time. It was priceless."

Sydney's arms are wrapped around her stomach as she laughs. I can't help but join in because his expression right now is priceless. It's as though he still hasn't gotten over it and he hates that she's telling stories he clearly would rather I not know.

"Did he catch any of you?" I ask.

"Nope, he was quacking and running away."

He moves closer to me. "Yeah, you should all be so proud of torturing a six-year-old. And you can laugh now, but when my mother showed up, none of you assholes were at that time."

Sydney rolls her eyes again. "You got all of us grounded for a month."

"Deservingly."

"Please, it was two feet of water, you big baby."

Connor turns to me. "Do you see why I left this town? It's filled with horribly mean people who have no remorse."

I shrug. "I think you survived okay."

He shakes his head and then turns to Sydney. "What are you doing here anyway? No one invited you, that's for sure."

"Well . . ." Sydney moves to me, placing her hand on my shoulder. "Ellie and I are now best friends, Duckie. You're going to have to accept this as a fact and realize that, if you're hanging around her, it will include some time with me."

He grins as though it doesn't bother him in the least. "It's all good, Syd. I know exactly how to handle you."

Oh, Lord. That sounds ominous. However, this volley back and forth is the most fun I've had in years. These two clearly adore one another but have no problem giving the other shit. It's what I always imagined having a sibling would be like.

"And how exactly is that?" she asks.

His grin spreads, and there's a look of mischief in his eyes. "I'll call Declan."

And with that, I see that Sydney and I may both be captivated by an Arrowood.

"Hey," Connor says with an easy smile as he makes his way into the living room where I'm grading papers. It's been a crazy night, and I'm still trying to get caught back up from being out of work after the beating.

"He—" Complete words die on my tongue as I look up and get a look at him. He must've just gotten out of the shower because he's in a pair of gym shorts and no shirt with damp hair. There are a few drops of water rolling down his chest.

My throat goes dry as I drink him in. I can see each muscle with perfect clarity as though he's in high definition. His hair is slicked back, and my fingers itch to touch it. He rubs his hand against the smooth skin of his chest, and then up to his neck. I've seen him with his shirt off, hell, I've seen him naked, but this . . . this body is a whole new world of wow.

I turn to keep myself from swooning off the chair.

"Working?" he asks as he moves behind me, reading over my shoulder.

Oh my God. Get a grip, Ellie.

But I can't because I can feel the heat coming off his chest and smell the musky soap that he used.

His arm comes down to the right of me, resting his hand on the table, using it to hold his body up.

"Uh-huh," I stay, completely frozen, afraid that if I move, I might accidentally touch him, which then might lead to me saying or doing something incredibly dumb. That seems to be something I've been fighting a bit harder with each day I'm here.

Kissing him is all I think about.

Wondering if we fit together the way we did all those years ago fills my fantasies.

It's dangerous ground, but the injuries might be worth it.

"Need help?"

I shake my head and try to focus on the very non-sexy

English papers about punctuating dialogue I should be grading.

"Ellie?"

I move my head to the side to look up at his face, hoping that maybe that will be better than the muscles in his arm that are so close. "Yeah?"

He grins, eyes crinkling, and I realize I made a grave mistake. His face is really what's beautiful, and when he smiles, well, it's damn near impossible not to get lost.

But I don't need to be lost.

I need to keep my head on straight, get a divorce, and get the hell out of here.

"You going to stay up much later?"

No, in fact, I'm going to my room right now so I don't do anything I regret. "I'm done, actually."

"I was asking because I have to get up early tomorrow. I want to work on the main house instead of the barn. I'd like to check the house and lock up, but I usually wait until you're in bed."

"Yeah, all done. Not a big deal. Main house is good. Locks and all that," I stammer like a fool.

"You all right?"

"I'm great," I say way too quickly, gathering the papers into stacks that make no sense but needing to do something with my hands. "I'm just tired, you know, working and all the other stuff. Plus, Sydney has the divorce papers all drawn up, and it's been a lot to sort through."

"So, you're going through with it?"

I look up, pulling the papers to my chest as though they're some kind of barrier of protection. "Of course."

"I hadn't heard anything."

I wasn't sure what to tell him. It's one of those things I

don't really want to talk about, but at the same time, Connor and I have spent the last two weeks practically living together, which is strange.

"I'm sorry, I sort of . . . have been waiting since we can't serve him for a bit."

He shakes his head. "Don't apologize, you don't owe me any explanations."

No, maybe I don't owe it to him, but I guess I could've mentioned it. But then I think about the last few times we've talked and how those conversations have been about what he's working on here or my job. We've been almost avoiding talking about things that are personal.

I don't know why that is, but there's something that's been bothering me for a few days now.

"Connor, can I ask you something?" I say before I have time to stop myself.

"Of course."

I swallow the nerves since it's too late to go back now. "Do you want to find out if Hadley is yours?"

His eyes meet mine, and my heart races as I wait for him to say something—anything.

"More than anything."

"Then why haven't you said anything?"

He moves closer, pulling the papers from my hands and placing them down on the table. "Because you've been through hell and so has she. While I want to know if she is my daughter more than I've wanted anything in my entire life, I also won't be selfish and demand it happen now. I can wait, Ellie. I can wait until you're ready."

"Ready for what?"

He lifts his hand, pushing the hair off my face. His voice is soft, careful, and yet, there's a confidence underlying it all. "Me."

nineteen

"How are things going?" Sean asks after avoiding my phone calls the last two weeks.

"Like you give a fuck."

I get that my brother is some big-time baseball player, but he's fucking annoying when he thinks no one else's time is as valuable as his. Declan is helping figure out the land values thanks to one of his clients who deals in real estate, Jacob is doing . . . God knows what, but Sean was going to reach out to some guy named Zach Hennington who he played baseball with to figure out the damn cows since he has a cattle ranch.

I'm failing at this part. I have no clue what to do with the animals other than what a very adorable seven-year-old who instructs me to do. Which I have no clue if that's even right, but it's better than what I've been doing so far. Ellie's farm-hands have been helping me a bit when I have questions, but they're busy running her farm.

Even though I grew up around the animals, I never really

cared much about learning how to run it. I did my chores, which were usually mending fences or the carpentry type things, and my brothers dealt with the animals.

"Look, I'm busy," he explains. "I did my best, but I have shit going on."

"And I don't?" I throw back at him. "I know absolutely nothing about cows, Sean. You're supposed to handle that part."

"I gave Dec his number."

I huff and curse under my breath. Declan is just as bad lately at calling me back. In fact, the three of them can kiss my fucking ass. I've been here a month, busting my ass, with absolutely no help other than Declan getting funds to me, which was something I had to call ten times about, while they live their lives, oblivious to the shit I'm dealing with.

"A lot of good that does me, asshole. I need some help. All of you guys were supposed to do something, and instead, I'm doing it all on my own—like always."

"What crawled up your ass? You're even more of an asshole than usual."

I sit on the bale of hay, rubbing my fingers across my forehead. I could tell him everything. A part of me wants to, and Sean is the only brother who knows about my angel, but even telling him a sliver of what's going on will force me to answer too many questions.

Still, my brothers are all I've ever had.

They're family.

They have never turned their backs on me and to be honest, I feel like I'm drowning right now.

"Connor?"

"I found her," I say before I have a chance to think better of it.

"Found who?"

"*Her.*"

Sean goes silent for a second and then lets out a breathy laugh. "No shit?"

"She's here . . . in fucking Sugarloaf, and that's not even all of it . . ."

I tell him everything. I talk and talk, probably saying more in this one conversation than I've said to my brother in the last ten years. He doesn't say a word as I unload the last few weeks and all the revelations. I even go over details that I don't want to remember but can't seem to forget.

I tell him about Ellie, Hadley, the tree, the house, the beating, and how they're living here.

Once I'm done, I feel like I've completed a workout and can't catch my breath. My heart aches, head pounds, and I'm winded.

"So, it seems you've been rather busy, baby brother."

"That's all you have to say?"

"No, but . . . I'm not really sure I can gather anything more than that."

A lot of help he is. "Thanks, Sean."

"Look, you just told me that the girl you spent the last eight years dreaming about, who is apparently some ethereal being who walks on water, is staying with you because she just left an abusive husband. On top of that, you might have a kid with said woman? Give me a fucking second to digest all this."

I release a heavy breath through my nose and then look up at the ceiling. What a damn mess. "I'm not sure what to do."

"Do?"

"About Ellie. I can't get my head straight. I look at her, and my heart races. I think about her, and I fight the urge to find her. It's ridiculous. Then there's the fact that all I want is more."

I've tried to deny my growing feelings. Ellie isn't ready to even think about anything with me. I've waited for her for so long that the last thing I want is for it to fall apart because I pushed her too hard. I want her to want me. I don't want it to be because of her ex.

"Tell me that you haven't . . . ."

"What?"

He hesitates, which is very unlike him. "You didn't do anything . . . with her . . . like after her attack?"

If he were in front of me, I'd lay his ass out. "If you're asking if I've slept with Ellie again, the answer is no. No, I am not a selfish asshole who would take advantage of a woman who is in the middle of hell."

"I didn't mean it like that. Simmer the fuck down. I'm saying that this situation is pretty nuts, and I also know what it's like to feel something, even when it's wrong."

Sean has been in love with his best friend for the last twelve years. The problem is, she's in love with someone else. His only saving grace is that she lives here and he doesn't have to see her anymore.

"I didn't say there aren't feelings."

"I figured. And then there's the kid."

Yeah, then there's Hadley. "If she's mine . . ."

"You need to find out."

I blow out a deep breath and get to my feet. "The chances are that she's not."

"Okay, and there's a chance she is. You said she has the Arrowood eyes, right?"

"Even Syd noticed it," I tell him.

Sean bursts out laughing. "Sydney . . . like Declan's Sydney?"

"The same one."

"How the fuck are you handling all this on your own, Connor? You're back in Sugarloaf, which is bad enough, but now you've got this girl, a possible daughter, and Sydney. Hell, next you're going to tell me that Devney and her boyfriend are coming for dinner."

I smirk. "That's your mess, brother."

"Yeah, well, I guess we all have shit to deal with, huh?"

"Some more than others."

I'm not sure how I feel at this point. More than anything, I want to know if Hadley is mine, but there's a lot of things that could happen once that knowledge is revealed. Right now, I'm not her father. I don't have to parent her. I get to enjoy spending time with her. Then there are feelings for Ellie that are unexplainable.

I love her.

I know it. I know that it's also the absolute last thing she needs to hear from me.

She doesn't need to hear that she is the only woman I want, and I will wait an eternity if that's what it takes to earn her.

The hell she's endured might take her that long to get over as well. But if I know Hadley is mine, I'm not sure I'll be able to hold back.

I'll want them both to be mine.

"I feel like the bastard knew all this . . . ." I admit something that's been on my mind.

"Dad?"

My father was a bastard, but him putting bullshit stipulations in his will wasn't like him. Why did he care about us being here? What the hell did any of it matter if we kept it for two years or not? Unless he suspected as well. There's a reason that he wanted us all to return here, and not just for some sort of nostalgic bullshit.

"Why else did he want us here?"

Sean goes quiet for a second and then snorts. "You know, I wouldn't doubt it."

"Declan has unresolved issues with Syd. You love Devney and never grew a pair to tell her. I might have a daughter, and well, who knows what the fuck we're going to uncover with Jacob."

"I don't love Devney." He tries to sound convincing.

"Sure you don't."

"She's getting married."

"And she wouldn't marry that idiot if she thought there was even a chance of having you. We both know it."

Sean's voice is low and full of frustration. "We also made a vow."

We did, but we were kids then. Clearly, shit has changed. "Well, I might have a kid, and if that's the case, the vow is no longer valid."

Which is another thing I'm struggling with. My word to my brothers is everything, but I'm willing to endure their wrath if it means I can have her.

twenty

It's late and I can't sleep. I toss and turn in a large and empty bed, my mind going in a million directions. I'm in one of his brother's old rooms while Connor is on the other side of the wall. The three of us have fallen into a strange routine over the last three weeks.

Each day, I take Hadley back to our house, do something menial, and try to spend a bit more time there than we spent the day before.

Today, she struggled more than usual. She was antsy and kept looking around. A book fell out of my bag, making a loud *thwack* noise and causing her to run out of the house. I don't know how we'll return to living here if she's this fearful.

Then my thoughts move to how I don't really seem to be in a rush to move back home either. Connor has been nothing but sweet and thoughtful. He's always doing little things with Hadley or making sure I'm okay. Then there's the way he looks at me, heat and want in his eyes that sends currents through my body. Just like the night we met, there's chemistry that hasn't ebbed.

I think about how, on the other side of the wall, he's sleeping. What would it be like to go through his door instead of mine at the end of the day?

It's a thought I shouldn't be entertaining at all.

I huff and rise out of bed, tug on an off-the-shoulder sweatshirt and head out to the kitchen. Maybe moving around for a few minutes will help me settle and get some sleep.

I go to the fridge, grab the milk, and pour a glass. I stand there, hands on the counter, wondering how this is my life.

When I turn around, I nearly drop the milk when I see a profile of someone in the darkness standing in the doorway. Fear grips me so tightly I can't draw breath. I open my mouth to scream, but the voice stops me.

"It's just me," Connor says quickly, hands up in the air. "You're okay."

"Jesus Christ, I almost had a heart attack."

I thought it was Kevin waiting for me, watching me, ready to drag me back to my house and finish what he started.

Maybe Hadley isn't the only one who is still not okay.

"Sorry, I heard something and came to check." He steps into the room.

My heart is racing so fast that I clutch the milk jug, trying to catch my breath. "I was thirsty, and I thought I was quiet."

He moves slowly until he's standing in front of me and then gently pulls the milk from my clutches. "I hear everything, I blame it on years of being in the military and sleeping in half measures. I didn't mean to scare you."

I wish I could say he doesn't scare me, but in so many ways he does. He's the man I find myself thinking of during the day. The guy my daughter wants to be around. And if I'm truly honest with myself, who I want to be with too.

I have never felt as connected to someone as I do with him. It's as though the time we spent apart only had us growing closer together.

Which is crazy.

Can two people belong to one another without ever actually being together? Can you love someone without knowing them? I've always believed in soul mates, and standing here in front of him, I can't deny that we're something . . . more.

"I couldn't sleep," I say instead of responding to his declaration.

"Why not?"

Because I was lying in bed, wondering about you and why I can't seem to leave.

"Just a lot on my mind."

Mostly him but a lot about Kevin also. I got the court date today, and I've been struggling with it. I'm not ready to talk about what happened again. I feel like I finally got to the point where I'm not living it each day, so dragging up all those emotions in front of the court is daunting. Not because I don't want to see Kevin go to jail for what he did but because I don't want to have to go back to feeling like I did in the days following his arrest.

"Because we have a date?"

A date? We have a date? My chest tightens and I rack my brain to see when I agreed to that. "We do?"

"For the trial."

I mentally slap my hand against my head. Of course he meant the damn trial and not us. We're not dating, we're . . . avoiding the fact that we have feelings.

I'm a poster child for mental health right now.

"Yeah, I knew what you meant. It's just late, and I'm tired, but the trial date is good. I mean—that we have one and it's five months out. I'm ready for there to be a resolution and . . ."

And your lips are so close.

I can feel the heat of your body as you stand so close to me.

Connor's cologne fills the air around us, and I inhale, letting it fill me up.

"Ellie?"

"Huh?" I keep looking at his lips and committing the way they move when he says my name to memory.

Slowly, my gaze lifts to his. I see the hunger swirling as he watches me. I want him so badly. I don't know if it's because we're standing in the dark, only the silver rays from the moon illuminating the space around us. Maybe it's the fact that he smells so damn good. Or maybe it's because I'm lonely when I'm not near him.

"Connor?" His name is a whisper in the wind.

"Yeah?"

My heart is racing as I grapple with what I want to do, each second feeling like years passing until I stop allowing myself to think. I've thought so much, and it's never turned out well for me.

I want to do.

I want to be.

I want to live.

I close the distance between us so fast that he doesn't have time to react, and I press my lips to his. It doesn't take but a second for him to respond. His arms wrap around my waist and he pulls me to him. Our lips move together softly, but the passion is so intense that I feel as though I could melt.

My thumb brushes against the stubble on his cheek, reveling in the tiny prickles against my skin. He makes a noise in the back of his throat, and I swallow it as I allow him to deepen the kiss.

While I may have started this kiss, Connor is leading it.

His strong arms tighten as he tilts me back slightly, delving deeper into my mouth.

The memories that I've clung to have faded so much more than I thought because kissing Connor is nothing like I remember. It's as if I've been living in black-and-white but have just steeped into full color and the vividness of life around me is blinding.

It's almost as though this isn't real and I'll awaken back in my bed in a moment. If this is a dream, I pray I sleep forever.

Slowly, I move my hands from his face down to his neck as his lips trail down my jaw. "God, Ellie," Connor's voice is deep and lusty.

"Kiss me."

He pulls back, his eyes watching me as though he realized who he is and what we're doing. "Is this a dream?"

I know how he feels. "No, I'm real. We're real."

His nose slides against mine, and I preen at the low grumble that comes from his chest. "I don't want to push you. I can wait. I *will* wait. I'll wait forever for you."

I appreciate that more than he knows. He tilts my head up to where he can watch me a little closer. "I don't want you to wait to kiss me."

His eyes close, and slowly, he kisses me. His soft lips touch mine gently, our breaths mingling as neither of us moves. I feel dizzy, breathless. It's almost as though I'm suspended and desperate for him to tether me to the world.

I start to move toward him, unable to resist, and then I hear the only thing that could stop me.

"Mommy? Are you in here?"

I step back so fast I almost stumble and turn wide eyes to the doorway to the kitchen. "Hi, sweetheart. What's wrong? Can't sleep? Need some water?"

"Connor!" She perks up as soon as she realizes he's in the

room as well. "I didn't know you were here too!"

"Hey, Squirt."

She looks to him and then to me. "Let's get you something to drink and then back to bed." Maybe if I can usher her out of here fast enough, she won't ask any questions.

"Why are you both in the dark?"

So much for that idea.

Connor laughs and scoops her up. "Because the lights are too bright. Let's all get back to bed before the sun comes up and we all melt."

Hadley giggles. "We don't melt in the sun."

"We don't?"

"No!" Her voice is high and filled with amusement. "People don't melt, Connor."

"Well, look at that. You taught me something. Now, Mommy can bring you something to drink and I'll super tuck you in."

He looks back at me and winks before heading out.

I stand in a daze, my fingers touching my lips remembering the kiss we shared and wishing it were me he was tucking in too.

I'm in so much damn trouble.

Nate's office is exactly what I pictured it to be, which is to say it's the opposite of Sydney's. Hers was white with gray furniture, modern décor, and nothing at all overbearing or lawyerly. Hers felt like an inviting and clean place where she wants her clients to be calm and open. Whereas everything about

Nate's screams "look at me!"

His desk takes up a third of the room with bookcases lining the back. He has a large, leather wingback chair that's tufted and dark. There is no art, only his diplomas and a few photos of him with the mayor and other people of the county.

"Do you have any questions?" Nate asks as he turns in his chair to face me.

Sydney taps her pen and then looks to Nate. "What are the safety measures being taken for Hadley upon the reading of the verdict."

He shakes his head, eyes narrowed at her like she's being ridiculous. "Really, Syd?"

"Don't Syd me. If he's found not guilty or if he's released until sentencing, do you think he's going to leave them alone?"

The pit that's been sitting like a rock in my stomach turns over, sending a new wave of anxiety through me. I really wish Connor were with me, but because he's also a witness, he isn't allowed to talk to the prosecution at the same time as I am.

Not like we couldn't plan some coup if we wanted to since we live in the same house, but whatever.

Nate shifts in his seat and then looks down. "I don't know. I guess we could happen to have a deputy at the school."

"I would appreciate that," I say with a soft smile. "I know this is hard on everyone. It's a small town, we all know each other."

"It doesn't matter," Sydney cuts me off. "I don't care if I knew him, you, or anything else. What I saw that night, Ellie . . . well, I want to make sure that this never happens to you again."

My body feels cold, and I move my hands up and down to try to ward off the chill. I never want to go through it again either. The safety and security I've started to become accustom to is going to fade unless he's found guilty.

On top of that, I've been told that the time he's been held can be used toward time served. Kevin doesn't have any prior arrests and he isn't considered to be dangerous. The fact that he was held at all still seems to have Nate and Sydney mystified.

"No one can control that, Syd. My biggest worry is the hearing," I admit.

Nate sits up straight. "What has you worried?"

The easier question to answer would be what am I *not* worried about. There is nothing easy about this process. I have no idea what to expect. Sure, they've gone over scenarios, but that's not etched in stone. If Kevin is released, there is no way he'll let this go. I will have ruined his life, so I'll have to pay.

He isn't going to fall at my feet and apologize. We're serving him with divorce papers, I'm not at his precious house keeping things the way he wants them. Not to mention I haven't even checked on the farm. For all I know, the workers are stealing cows, and I don't care.

What I do care about is my and Hadley's safety. So, yes, I'm worried.

"Everything. But what if they don't believe the evidence?"

Nate and Sydney share a glance, and then Nathan speaks. "I can't control the way it goes, God knows I wish I could. What I can do is present the truth in the best way I know how. I'll paint the picture and hope they see it. That's why we're going to have a lot of these talks and a lot of rehashing things. I have four months to build a case."

"That doesn't change the fact that they might not believe me."

Sydney breaks in, gripping my hand in hers. "Your story doesn't change based on the ending. There is nothing we can do but tell the truth, Ellie. You're a strong, beautiful woman who has been through hell. You did what you needed to do for Hadley. You showed her what strength and courage looks like.

The verdict doesn't change that. We have a few months to prepare for all of this, so if he is cleared of charges, we'll have a plan in place to keep you safe."

A tear falls down my face because those words from her mean everything. I don't know that I'll ever believe them, though. For so long, I thought my truth didn't matter. I saw myself as weak and stupid. No matter what others have said about me, I thought I deserved it.

I knew better than to marry him.

Hell, I slept with another man the night before I married him because a part of me wanted an out. I was too weak to take it.

I got up, got dressed, and left without taking the chance on Connor.

Now look at me.

My fingers swipe at the tears that continue to fall. "I'm so scared."

"I know you are, but you're so brave."

"It's not just that . . . for so long, he's been able to make me do whatever he wants. It's like this sick game that he plays, and it makes me feel stupid and vulnerable and what if he's let out that day?" I ask. "What then?"

Sydney's eyes are filled with concern but also determination. "Then we will all be around to make sure you're safe. Not that you'll have to worry because Connor will kill anyone who tries to hurt you or Hadley."

I look up, fear gripping me so tightly it hurts to breathe. "That's what I'm afraid of. I'll ruin someone else's life because of the mess I've made."

twenty-one

I walk through the grass, dew sticking to my legs as I move closer to my destination. I woke up early, and since Connor and Hadley were already out working on the barn, I thought it was time to come get some much-needed advice from the people I love the most.

It's been years since I've been here. Time that I've spent trying to piece my broken life together the best way I could. As the days passed, as time slipped away and my world became more complicated than I ever thought it would be, one thing has always remained steadfast. I love these people, and I know they loved me.

I hold the bundle of white daisies that I picked up on my way, my hand shaking as I get closer. The smell of clean morning air swirls around me, hints of grass and a little bit of cow is inevitable.

Still, I'm transported back to the day I buried them eight years ago.

That day, I stood here alone and sad, feeling as though nothing would ever be the same. And it hasn't been. The night they died forever altered my life.

That person stole my family and future.

Now, I'm going to get it back.

Just a few more steps and I'll be able to see the plaques where their names are etched. They're small, simple, and mark the resting places of the two people who were most dear to me.

I stop, my heart is racing as I stare down.

The grass is overgrown to the point where I can barely make out the names, but there's a bouquet of dried up flowers lying above them. "Hi, Mom," I say as I squat, tearing the blades away to reveal what should've never been forgotten. "I know it's been a while and . . . well . . . a lot has happened. I'm hoping you're watching from above and know that you're a grandma to a perfect girl. Her name is Hadley because—" I stop speaking as I trace the letters of my mother's name, Hadley Joanne Cody. "I guess you can guess why. I needed you beside me still. She reminds me of you. She's smart, funny, has the biggest smile. Dad would love her, too, she's as curious and clever as he was. You would've loved her. You both would have. I'm not sure that you'd be so proud of me, though," I confess. "You see, I ran away from all the things you taught me about family and respect. I think that's why I stayed away from here for so long. I was sure you'd think I was foolish. My own heart was breaking because of the choices I made and coming here was the last place I could go, but I was stupid, Mom. You wouldn't have judged me. You would've helped me."

My mother was the best person in this world. She loved with an intensity that rivaled anything else. I've tried so hard to be that way with Hadley. To love her like it was my last day. So many times, I feared it might really be, and I hoped that knowing the love I had for her was so strong that it would get her through.

My own mother loved me that much.

And I still didn't do right by her.

"I'm sorry, Mom. I'm sorry I wasn't strong like you." I look over at the gravesite where my father rests. "I'm sorry I didn't find a man like you, Daddy."

A tear falls down my cheek. "I'm sorry that I was afraid and wanted to believe I could change someone. I'm sorry that I let the person who took you away go free. I don't know who was driving that car, but I want you to know that I've never forgotten."

For a while, I had hope. But when the police said they had no information or any reports of damage matching the accident, the case went cold.

As did my heart.

"I have so much to tell you." My voice shakes. "A confession of sorts to the people who raised me to do better. I married Kevin, even after I told you I didn't think I would. I thought he would be like you hoped, but he wasn't. I think I knew, even in college, that there was something dark inside him. Now, I'm . . . well . . . I'm making changes. Ones that you would be proud of."

I try to think about what I would say if Hadley were in my situation. I know my mother would place her hand on mine and give it a squeeze. She would tell me that I'm smart and that I know what I need to do, just to get on and do it now.

"I filed for divorce from Kevin after he . . . ." My voice trembles as a tear forms. "He hit me. He would've killed me, and well, he didn't because of Connor. I told you about him the last time I was here, only I didn't know his name. I bet you probably thought I would marry him since I went on and on about him. Then there's the possibility that he might be Hadley's father, which is a whole other thing."

After I left Connor that night, I came here. I laid my soul bare to my parents, knowing I could never tell another soul about what I felt. I was ashamed but also filled with hope. I told them about how he held me, cared for me, and how I was going to be okay now.

"He's back, and I don't know what any of it means, but I can't stop thinking about him. I want to be near him. I find myself dreaming of him during the day and then restless at night, thinking about kissing him again. I worry that it's too soon to be feeling these feelings." My hand moves against the cool metal, and I wonder if I'm being crazy. Connor and I haven't known each other long, and yet, it's as though no one else in the world has ever known me better. He's been patient, caring, and kind. I know he wants me—I can see it in his eyes, but he fights it.

We both do.

"I care about him, Mom. I know he cares about me, but what if I'm wrong about him? What if he doesn't want us if Hadley isn't his? What if he finds out that Hadley is his and does want a family but I'm too broken? It's too much, and I'm scared. God, I'm so scared to make the same mistakes, but . . . I don't know how much longer I'll be able to resist him. And that's what scares me the most. If only you were here to tell me what to do, Mom."

"Are you avoiding me?" Connor's deep voice causes me to startle as I stand facing the moon.

Once I get my heart to stop racing, I shake my head. "Not any more than you're avoiding me."

Hadley went to bed two hours ago, and I worked on papers while Connor was out doing something on the farm. We've seen each other in passing since the kiss last night, but it's been as though we're orbiting each other, not quite able to stop the spinning. I've wanted to talk to him, but we haven't had time or Hadley has been around.

I was hoping he'd find me out here so we could figure out whatever is going on between us.

"Ahh, that's where you're wrong. I'm not doing anything like that, Angel. I'm just working and trying to get this damn barn fixed up so we can move the cows, which your foreman said I needed to do by the end of the week."

The wind blows, pushing my hair in front of my face, and I pull the blanket that's wrapped around my shoulders a little tighter. Snow will be here soon, and it makes sense to move the cattle to the closer pasture.

"How did you grow up on a dairy farm and not retain any information about running it?"

Connor shrugs with that swagger I've come to look for. "I had no intention of ever living on or running one, so it wasn't information I cared about."

I guess that makes sense. "Will you tell me about your childhood?"

"There's not much to it."

My head tilts to the side. I don't believe that for a minute. "You grew up here with three older brothers. There had to be something you can tell me about."

He moves closer, his eyes looking out at the fields in front of us. "Do you see that tree out there?"

"Yes."

"That's where my brother convinced me that I was a descendant of Superman and that flying was in my blood. He also told me that he had a vile of kryptonite, and if I didn't take my chances on the flying thing, I would die."

I laugh once and cover my mouth with the blanket. "And did you fly?"

He huffs. "No, and I broke my nose and two ribs. But"—

Connor's grin grows—"the whooping that Sean got for making me do it was almost worth it. I swear that he couldn't sit for three days."

"Boys," I say with a huff.

"You have no idea. We were the town hell raisers. My mother would walk around apologizing and swearing she raised us to do better. But four boys with a lot of time on their hands and wild imaginations were a mixture she couldn't contain."

I love hearing these kinds of stories about him. "I wished I had siblings."

"I wished I didn't."

"You would've been very lonely on this vast farm with no one to get in trouble with."

Connor tilts his head to the side. "Maybe you're right. When my brothers left, it was hard on me. I was stuck here—alone—and I hated it. Although, if Mom had been alive, maybe it wouldn't have been that way."

"How did she die?" I ask and immediately wish I could take it back.

I remember the pain in Connor's eyes when he spoke of his mother, and I know my own when I think of mine. It's hard to lose a parent. They created you, molded you into the person you are, and when they aren't there any longer, it's as though a piece of your whole existence is gone. I've grappled with losing both of mine in an instant. There was no goodbye or chance to say things we needed to. I have no closure, and I hope that Connor did get some, no matter how much it probably isn't a comfort.

"Cancer. It was fast and it was fierce. We found out, and then it feels like I blinked and she was gone. My brothers and I were . . . a fucking mess, but my father, well," his voice is soft and filled with pain, "we buried him alongside her that day only his body didn't go into the hole. He was never the same, and neither was the life we thought we had."

I reach out, taking his hand in mine. "I don't know that any of us get back to the life we thought we had after tragedy strikes. Someone or something rips it away, and we're left drifting."

His eyes watch mine with an intensity that makes my stomach clench. "Are you still drifting, Ellie?"

I shake my head. "No, I don't think I am."

"Why not?"

"Because you won't let me."

He lifts his hand, cupping my cheek as he stares down at me. "Will you let me kiss you again?"

I've both wanted and avoided this moment. Equal parts of me being torn apart by desire and fear. I want to kiss him again, to feel his lips on mine and give myself over to the moment. Then I worry that, if I were to let myself hope for more and I lose him, it will break me even more than I already have been broken.

But my resolve is not that strong.

Resisting him is futile, and I'm only lying to myself when I say I want to resist. There's nothing I want more than to be his.

So, I push my fear to the bottom and ask the only question left that matters. "Will you hurt me, Connor?"

"Never."

And I believe him.

"Then, yes, I'll let you kiss me."

twenty-two

I wait just a beat in case she changes her mind. The first kiss was everything, but fear had me holding back, the grip I had on my restraint unyielding. This time, I don't think I can hold back.

But I'll try.

She's everything I want and need, and she's here. I want to pull her into my arms, kiss her until she forgets every bad thing that's ever happened to her, and give her new memories filled with all the things she should've had.

I want it all, and I want it with her.

Slowly, I bring my other hand up and frame her face in my hands. The bruises that marred her skin a month ago are gone, leaving only her gorgeous blue eyes, which have no hint of fear in them. Each day, she heals a little more, and each day, I hope I show her the man I am.

I won't hurt her. I won't ever take what she isn't willing to give. I will only cherish her because she's a fucking angel.

Our lips move closer together, each breath given over to the moment. I feel the warmth of her body as she leans in.

"You're everything I remembered and nothing I was prepared for," I say right before I kiss her.

At first, I go slow, just letting our lips touch and not wanting to scare her with the insane desire I feel for her. I keep myself in check, using every ounce of training I've endured. Patience is what she needs, and it's the last thing I feel when I'm this close to her.

Her hands slide up my back, causing the blanket to fall from her shoulders. And then I kiss her like I've wanted to. My tongue slides against hers, and the taste of her is enough to make me want to fucking die.

This is heaven.

This is why she's an angel sent down to me.

Everything about her is perfect.

I moan, unable to stop myself as I kiss Ellie the way I've dreamed of for so long. Our tongues move together as I drink her in. She has no idea what she does to me, and in some ways, I hope she never does.

Ellie consumes my thoughts and dreams. Just a smile can set my entire world ablaze. I'm so far gone, and I don't even know how it happened. One minute I was here, in this fucking town I hate and surrounded by ghosts, and the next, I was never wanting to leave my house because she and Hadley were there.

She pulls back, resting her forehead to mine. "When you kiss me like this, I can't think."

"I don't want you to think, I want you to feel."

Her blue eyes lift to mine, and her vulnerability humbles me. "That has always been my downfall. If I used my head more, I never would have gotten into the position I'm in."

Ellie steps back, and I let her go even though I want to hold her against me. She and I both have demons, and when they're awoken, I know how hard it is to silence them again.

"I don't want to take away your choices."

She turns quickly. "I don't think you do. I can't make the same mistakes again, Connor. I jumped feet first into a relationship with a man who I knew wasn't right for me. I let him . . . hurt me. I gave him power over me in a way that I never should've. He broke things inside me, trust that I don't know can be repaired. I will never be whole or the woman who isn't a little damaged."

I move toward her, unable to stay back, but I restrain myself from touching her. "I don't care if there are pieces of you that are damaged. I don't care if every inch of you is scarred. Believe me, there are parts of me that are so fucking mangled it would take a miracle to straighten them. It's not about perfection or being whole—it's you being you."

Ellie looks away, tucking her hair behind her ear. "You say these things, and I have to stop myself from falling."

"If you fall, I'll catch you."

"What if I take you down with me?"

"I'll shelter you so you don't get injured."

"And if you're hurt in the process?" Ellie's voice is barely a whisper.

"I can handle it." I inch closer, my hand lifting and tucking the other side of her hair behind her ears. "What I can't handle is causing you or Hadley pain. I want to make you happy, Angel, not make you cry."

Her fingers wrap around my wrist as my palm moves to cradle her jaw. But she doesn't tug my touch away. "It's just that when you kiss me, I forget myself. I can't let that happen."

I rest my lips against her forehead, trying to think of what to say to assure her. I don't want her to forget herself, only the things around her. I want to give her power and freedom.

When I go to open my mouth, she lifts her head and speaks. "I want you, Connor. I think I've always wanted you, but that's not what I had. I left that night, and we can't pretend the last eight years haven't happened. I know that you're worried that, if you find out Hadley is yours, you won't be able to pull back, and I'm worried that if we don't, I won't be able to move forward."

My heart pounds against my chest. "It won't matter if she is or isn't."

"It matters to me."

Which is what I fear too. If she finds out that Kevin is Hadley's father, will she walk away from me? Will she fear that he'll want Hadley and run? Will she go off and not tell anyone to protect them both? I won't be able to handle it if she does. I want her to be ours. I want that night to have created something so perfect that it lives between us now. However, if it matters to her, then I'll give her the answers she wants, damn the consequences.

"Is this what you need?" I ask.

"I think it is."

"Then . . . I'll take the test tomorrow if that's what will make you happy and feel secure."

"It is. I want to know one way or the other."

"I'll do anything for you, Ellie."

Ellie launches herself at me, her arms wrap around my neck, and I steady us and hold her in my arms. Her lips are on mine an instant later, and all the worries I have disappear.

Maybe she's right, we can't move on if we don't face what's behind us. God, if that's true, I'm going to have a lot of baggage to unpack.

twenty-three

I'm so damn tired. Today was a crazy day at work. I have been trying to step out of my comfort zone and meet the other teachers, but I have horrible social skills. If they don't have kids, I have nothing to contribute to the conversation.

They were talking about shopping today, and I tried. I really did. I also failed and ended up faking a stomach ache and hiding in my classroom to eat.

"Connor?" I call out as I enter the house. "Hadley?"

No one answers.

Maybe they're both working on the tractor again. Connor finished with the barn last night and said he needed to get the equipment going next. There are so many repairs to be made that I don't know how his brothers expect him to get even half of it done before his six-month sentence is up.

Not even six months now.

It's been almost two months since my assault. Time is

dwindling without even knowing it. What happens when it's up? Will he stay or leave? Will I stay or leave is another question. I don't have the answers to either question.

I release a sigh because I'm not ready to face any of this right now. I grab the mail off the counter and toss the bills, my bank statement for the account I never changed the address to, and then stop cold before tossing the last envelope.

The DNA test results.

I take the envelope and rush into my room. I can't open it without him. I can't sit here and not look, though. Hadley is my daughter and this is her entire life, but what if the results aren't what I hope for?

I knew that would be a possibility, but it would still suck. Now it's here, and while I thought that I could handle whatever the results were . . . maybe I was wrong. Am I ready for Connor to be her father? Am I okay with knowing that . . . Kevin . . . could be a part of her and we'll never be rid of him? There's so much at stake here.

Instead of allowing myself to go down the rabbit hole, I force myself to get a grip. Connor is a good man and won't push, that much I'm sure of. He may want to, but he will never do anything to hurt Hadley or me. I have to trust that regardless of what this test says, I know my path.

I'm going to get my divorce and start living the life I deserve. Whether that means Connor is a part of it or not is irrelevant. I'm saving my money, working in a job I love, and somewhat living with my could-be baby daddy because my house is too scary for my daughter to be in for more than ten minutes. Yeah, I've got it all together now.

I sit on the bed, tilt my face to the ceiling, and release a heavy breath. I've got this. I need to take it step by step. First one is to find my daughter and Connor, lure him away from her, and make him open the results. Then I can freak out.

Instead of any of that, I put my hand down and don't feel

the comforter, but find satin. Huh?

When I get to my feet and look down, there's my black satin dress that was hanging in the closet at my house. It is the only nice thing I own, and I've only worn it on very special occasions. Kevin didn't want me to dress nicely since it might draw attention to me.

"What is this?" I ask as I pick up the note.

Ellie,

Meet me at 8 PM at the bar where we met. Hadley is with Syd for the night, all is well. We deserve some time . . . just us.

Connor

"What exactly are you up to Connor Arrowood?" I ask aloud as I clutch the note to my chest. Regardless of whatever it is, he did something that no one has ever done before.

Tried.

I'm all nerves as I get out of the black Town Car that happened to be parked outside the house once I emerged. It was pretty impressive and very thoughtful. I smooth the dress down and push my hair back. I was in a hurry to get ready since I didn't find the note until seven thirty and knew it would take about twenty minutes to get over there.

Still, even with rushing around, I'm about fifteen minutes late. The envelope containing the results of the DNA test is in my purse, and I worry when the moment will be right to bring it up.

I step out onto the curb and am thrown back in time. It's

exactly as I remember. The bar is old with a neon sign that is still only partially illuminated, making it read AR instead of BAR. The windows have old shutters that are in desperate need of repair, and the music is a low country sound that speaks to the sadness of those who come here.

But inside, sadness isn't waiting for me—Connor is.

I push through the door, suddenly anxious to see him, and when I take in what's in front of me, I can't breathe.

Connor is the only person inside, no other patrons or even a bartender. The dingy inside has been cleaned, and the faint scent of pine and lemon is lingering under the scents of the candles lit all around the room. There's a small table in the middle of the dance floor with a tablecloth, two place settings, and a bouquet of roses. His hand casually rests on the back of the chair as he smiles and watches me.

"You're late."

I smile back. "I didn't get adequate notice."

He starts to move toward me, not in a rush but not overly slow either. His stride is confident, as though he knew I would come even if it took me a while. "You look beautiful."

"So do you. Well, handsome. You look handsome," I correct.

All the worries that plagued me are gone. Connor pushes them all away just by being near me. "I wanted us to have a real date."

"I see that. Typically, one asks the girl, right?"

He shrugs as he comes to a stop in front of me. "I don't think there's anything typical about us, Angel."

He's right on that one.

Connor's hand slides up my arm, leaving a trail of goose bumps in its wake before his thumb brushes against my jaw. "Don't lose yourself." His voice is low and has an edge of warning. "I'm going to kiss you, and I need one of us to have some control."

My breaths are coming in quick succession, and I can't quite keep up with what he's saying. Control? Kissing?

Before I can think too much more on it, his lips are on mine. He kisses me softly at first, sweetly, slow pecks that cause my toes to curl. I hold on to his shoulders, needing the support because I would swear I'm melting.

Then the kiss becomes more intense, and I'm not even sure what planet I'm on anymore. I feel weightless, floating off into a sea of desire where he is all that exists.

The music is gone, the bar fades away, and it's just the two of us.

Our mouths move together, not rough or needy, but exploratory—as though we have no time but the present. It's magical, wonderful, and I never want it to end. The sound of my heartbeat fills my ears as I open my lips for him. His tongue melts against mine, and I moan.

God, kissing like this is criminal.

He tilts my head to the side, urging me to give him better access, and I give it freely. I would give up everything to make this kiss last forever.

My fingers dig into his shoulders as his lips move down to kiss my neck. "You were supposed to keep your wits," he says against my skin before pressing another soft kiss at the hollow of my throat.

"You know what kissing you does to me?"

He straightens, a triumphant smile on his arrogant face. "Yes, and I like the results."

I grin and take a step back, wobbling a bit, which makes him grin wider. "Watch yourself."

"Yeah, you watch yourself too. You're not as unaffected as you'd like to pretend."

Connor chuckles, a deep throaty sound that makes me

want to kiss him again.

"I never said I was. When it comes to you, Ellie, I have no restraint."

"I think you have a lot more than you'd care to admit."

He raises one brow. "How so?"

"Well, I've been in your house for two months now and you haven't done anything more than kiss me."

After the words are out of my mouth I want to slap myself.

"Did you want me to do more?"

Yes. No. I don't know. "I shouldn't and that's why I'm glad you haven't. I'm still technically married, and there's this part of me that doesn't want us to do more than what we have for that reason." Not that I think any God in heaven wouldn't understand after all I've dealt with. Still, I think it's more of starting a new thing. I want my relationship with Connor to never bear any black marks.

We had the night together years ago, and I should never have done that.

"No, that's . . ." I cover my face with my hands. "I'm not good at any of this, so please forget I said that."

"Please explain," he urges as we sit.

"The next time we're together, I want it to be right. No husband, no secrets, no things that are hanging over our heads. I want you and me to be everything."

He reaches his hand out over the table, and I place mine in it. "I told you that I'd wait forever for you, and I mean it. I feel like these eight years have been my training mission."

I try to smile, but I feel stupid. "I'm sorry."

"Sorry for what?"

"That I'm basically telling you we have to wait until my divorce is final."

"Tell me this, can I kiss you?"

"Yes."

"Can I hold you?"

I nod. "Of course."

"Can we go on dates?"

"I hope we do."

Connor smiles. "Then, until you're ready for anything more, we'll do just that. I'm not in a rush."

"And what about when your six months are up?" I ask.

"Then we figure it out."

I don't know why I hoped for something else. It's unfair of me to expect him to make promises of more, and I really am grateful he doesn't. Connor tells me the truth—always. He's honest with me, knowing that I can't handle games.

"Okay, we figure it out," I say in solidarity.

"Now, tonight, we're on our first official date, and I plan to woo you."

I lean back and extend my hand. "By all means, woo away."

The dinner is great. Connor and I laugh, tell more stories of when we were younger, and talk about good times. We both steer clear of heavy topics and enjoy each other's company. He had the bar serve us mozzarella sticks for an appetizer on plates he brought from home, cheeseburgers for the main course, and he had the fries separated to be our side dishes. It was cute, thoughtful, and absolutely perfect.

"Tell me about your parents," Connor says as we sit, waiting for the desert.

"Not sure what to say. They were amazing, really wonderful. They died tragically, and it's all still a mystery as to what happened."

"A mystery?"

I nod. "They never found the car that hit them, so the case went cold."

"I'm so sorry." His voice is filled with empathy.

For the first time, I don't feel quite so sad. It's funny how healing happens in ways you don't realize. Before, talking about them would make me depressed, but in this moment, I want to remember the good and not the bad. I'm tired of always going back to what it was like when they died.

"I've been stuck for so long and . . . I don't know. I guess I forgot just how much my parents loved each other. It was sometimes almost gross to watch. My father was always kissing her." I laugh once. "I remember one time I walked into the kitchen and he had her up against the wall. I was sixteen, so I fully knew what they were doing."

Connor smiles. "I never saw any of that, thank God. To me, my mother died a born again virgin."

He's so stupid. "From what you've told me about your father's undying love for her, I'm going to guess that isn't true. Also, she had four boys in five years. That's a lot of sex."

His face scrunches. "No, that's one time each, and they never touched again."

"Is that what you'd want if we were together?" My fingers slide against his palm.

He clears his throat. "No. Once I have you, Ellie, you're going to want more time with me as well."

"Is that so?"

Not that I doubt him in the least. I want him now. Touching him, kissing him, is a drug that I can't quit. I can't imagine how it will be when we finally make love again.

"Most definitely."

"I look forward to the challenge."

Connor rises to his feet and comes around the table. "They say that dancing is like having sex with your clothes on."

"They do?"

"Yes. Will you dance with me?"

"Now? But there's no music."

He grins as he extends his hand. "We don't need it."

I place my hand in his and we walk a little away from the table, which took up most of the dance floor. Connor stops, and I step into his arms. Together, we sway, our cheeks resting on each other's, arms holding on to one another. He was right. We don't need music.

I close my eyes and commit this moment to memory. Here we are, in the bar where we met so many years ago, dancing just like we did that night.

I feel it all, the warmth of his body, the strong muscles that make me feel safe, and the way I seem to fit perfectly against him.

Connor pulls back so our eyes meet. "I could stay like this with you forever."

"Me too."

And I want to. With him, the world is filled with possibilities and safety.

"Tell me what you're thinking," Connor urges.

I want to confess it all to him because he needs to know what I'm feeling. "That when I'm with you, I'm not the broken woman I sometimes feel like. That you look at me in a way I only dreamed was possible. It scares me, yes, but it humbles me as well. I think about how much I want something more with you even though it feels like it should be way too soon."

His thumb strokes my cheek. "I think if we were anyone else, it would be. You've been mine since the night we met in this bar. When we gave ourselves to each other, it wasn't the way either of us planned. I know you, Ellie. I see you for all that you are, and I think that maybe you're just starting to see yourself."

He's the man who wants to slay dragons and has the fortitude to do it. I don't fear telling him things. He is the calm in the storm that rages around me.

I shake my head, looking away. "I don't deserve you."

His thumb lifts my chin so our gazes lock once more. "It's me who doesn't deserve you, Angel, but I'll be damned if I'm going to give you up."

We stay like this, just moving to the sound of our heartbeats, making our own music.

After a few more beats, I look up at him, hoping what I'm about to say doesn't destroy the perfect night we've been enjoying. "I got something today."

"Is it about the court case? I got my subpoena today too."

"No, it's not about that," I chew on my lip nervously.

"Ellie." Connor's concern is laced in my name. "I promise, it'll be okay. I'll be right beside you, and with the way the judge ruled the last time, I'm sure that it'll go your way."

"No, I know. It's not that. I know you won't let him hurt us," I say. "I actually got something else—results, really." I try to ignore the sliver of fear in his eyes as I walk over to my purse. I pull the envelope out and hold it in my hand. "I didn't open it. I really wanted to, but I thought it should be something we do together—that is, if you want. Or I can open it and tell you."

Connor steps closer, his fingers grazing mine as he takes the envelope. His eyes study the plain manila envelope with the company name and the address label before he raises them back to me.

"We do it together."

I nod, unable to use my voice even if I wanted to. It feels as though something is sitting on my throat as the enormity of this moment washes over me.

We're going to find out if she's his.

My hands are shaking, and so are his as he lifts the paper

from the envelope.

Connor looks at me once more. "I mean it, Ellie, this changes nothing about how I feel. I love Hadley, and whatever is going on with us isn't going to stop because of this. If she's mine, I swear right now, that I'll protect her with my life. I'll follow your lead on how we handle it because she's what matters. If I'm not, then she will never know anything different. But regardless of whether I'm her father or not, she will never fear that man again. Neither of you will."

"But don't you see, everything will change."

He shakes his head. "No, it won't."

"If she's yours, then you will want to make up for all the time you lost. You'll have needs because, as a parent, that's how it is. You will love in a way that you don't ever fully understand. She will become your world, as she should, and that will bring big changes for all of us. So, while you think it won't . . . it will. Let's at least acknowledge that."

Connor puts the paper down on the table and pulls me into his arms, eyes searching mine. "I have thought about you since that night we met. I've wanted you, craved you, loved you in some way for eight years. The only thing that this will change is that the family I thought I would never have is now in front of me. The woman I thought I might have conjured up is still real and we still have a chance to have something. Maybe something will change, but the way I feel about us and what we're doing won't."

I touch my hand to his lips, wishing that the words he spoke could somehow absorb into me because no one has ever said anything more beautiful. "It won't for me either."

"Good."

I kiss him once, because he's close and I can't seem to help it, and then step out of his embrace and grab the letter.

With shaky hands, I lift the fold and then lower the other, and then tears fill my vision after I read the first line.

twenty-four

I have a daughter.

I have a little girl. Ellie and I have a child. That's what keeps going in my mind on repeat. It's as though I'm waiting for the ink to change in front of me, telling me it isn't real. Hadley is my daughter.

Ellie's hands drop from the paper, and I look into her blue eyes. "She's mine."

"She is."

I want to say something more than this, but nothing seems adequate enough. I wanted it so badly but wouldn't allow myself to hope it could really happen. Hadley and I bonded instantly, and over the last few months, she's become so much more than the girl I found in the tree.

"I don't know what to say," I admit as I read the words over again. Ellie wipes at her eyes and that snaps me out of it. "Are you okay?"

She nods quickly. "I wanted this to be the results. God, I practically convinced myself it had to be, but . . . I worried so much she wouldn't be. It was one night and we were careful—at least, I thought we were, but then the timing and I . . ."

"I'm so fucking happy."

Ellie laughs through her tears. "I am too. I wanted it to be you."

I pull her back to me and kiss her roughly. I'm over the fucking moon. I really wasn't sure I'd feel this way. Of course, I wanted her to be my daughter since the moment Ellie said it, but I couldn't know what it would feel like to find out she is.

For so long, I've been resigned to being single and never having children.

Now, I'm standing before a woman I love and just found out that I have a daughter.

My heart is racing, and I'm not sure whether I want to scream, laugh, or both at the same time. "It's like everything inside me is ready to burst. I can't explain it. I wish a lot of things were different, but then . . ."

Ellie looks away and her breathing accelerates. "Connor, I'm sorry. I'm so, so sorry."

"Sorry?"

I have no idea what she has to be sorry about.

"Sorry that I never found you. I'm sorry I married that horrible man and let him raise her. I'm so sorry she didn't know what life could've been like with you!" Ellie sobs, and I pull her to my chest. She cries, and I hold her. "I'm sorry I didn't do more for her! I'm sorry!"

I can't imagine how she feels because, if her emotions are anything like what I'm enduring, she's overwhelmed.

I have a little girl who I missed getting to watch grow up, but I don't blame Ellie. How the hell could she have found me? Walked around a town that I didn't live in, asking for a guy whose name she didn't know? Sure, if she knew I was an Arrowood, it would've been different, but she didn't even have that much.

"You did the best you could. You didn't know she was mine until just now. You protected her, Ellie."

She lifts her head, and I wipe away the moisture under her eyes. "She should've never needed it."

"We can't change the mistakes we've made. Lord knows I've tried to atone for mine."

If she knew the things I've done to erase the things I want to forget, she might run. The day I left this town was the day I shed who I once was. All of my brothers did the same. When we were here, we were forced into a life we didn't want. My father broke us, and I've done everything I could to rebuild. I served my country and tried to do good. I've never allowed the shit that happened to affect who I am now.

"I feel like I can never make this right for her or you. She should've known you. Look how much she loves you already."

"And I'll be there for her the rest of my life."

"You know this means . . . everything I was worried about with the divorce won't matter. Kevin will never be able to touch her. He isn't her father, and he has no rights to her," she says as her eyes fill with relief.

No, her ex will never be around Hadley or Ellie ever again.

"In order for that to happen, we're going to have to tell her."

She takes a step back and then turns. "I know."

"Do you not want to?"

Ellie spins around. "No, I do. But we can't just spring this on her. She doesn't know we met before. She's only ever known Kevin as her father. While I don't think she'll react badly, I think she'll be confused."

I nod. The last thing I want to do is make this harder on either of them. And even when you have an abusive parent, you still love them and want them to love you—maybe even more so than if you had a loving parent. I would beg God to let my father see that we were good kids. I wanted him to be proud of us and would often do things to earn his approval.

It never came, and I was only left more disappointed until I finally stopped caring.

"And we'll both be there to help her through."

Ellie gives me a soft smile. "We have a daughter."

I take the step toward her, closing the distance. "We do. And soon, I hope to have you."

twenty-five

"**M**om, watch this!" Hadley yells as she spins on the tire swing that Connor hung for her off the edge of the tree house.

He's been working on it at least an hour of each day, making it more special than she could ever imagine. This last week, she's been here until one of us comes to drag her home.

"Hadley, it's getting cold, and you have homework."

"But I like it here!"

"I know you do, but you have to get your schoolwork done. And we have to go home to get some things."

She mutters under her breath as she slogs her feet toward me. "Can't you go?"

It's been months of this, and I'm starting to think it's not real fear anymore and that she just likes being at Connor's.

"No, we both need to go."

Mainly because once the divorce happens, it won't be my

house any longer, so we need to get everything out. Kevin owns all of the land and the house on his farm. I don't know anything about it and it was his family's home, not mine, so I have no rights to it even if I wanted it.

"I hate it there."

"You know that nothing can hurt us there, don't you?"

Hadley looks up at me, her green eyes wide and trusting. "I know. Daddy's in jail."

And that is the saddest thing. She only feels safe because Kevin is in jail.

I've come close to telling her that Connor is her daddy so many times. I've wanted to blurt it out instead of agonizing over every word I want to say. It's been hard knowing the truth and keeping it from her, but Connor and I decided to wait. I want Kevin to be served with the papers, which happens this week. This is also the week I'll be filing for dissolution of paternal rights due to the fact that DNA has proven Kevin is not her father.

Sydney was able to get Kevin to agree to a DNA test, and she is holding those results for legal proceedings.

All of it is messy and ugly, but each step has been necessary to get him removed from my life.

"All right, how about you run back and get started on your homework and I'll meet you there in a bit?"

Hadley grins and takes off running.

I start back toward the house, not in a rush as I enjoy the crisp, fall air. It reminds me of my mother. She loved this time of year. Our house smelled like apples, pumpkins, and spices. Baking gave her a great sense of joy, and my father loved all things horror themed, so Halloween was his favorite holiday.

I move through the tall grass, just breathing without worry. It's a totally different life for me now. I don't worry about having dinner on the table or making sure the house is immaculate. As my way of thanking Connor, I do cook and clean up, but it's appreciated not expected.

And he demands that the cook doesn't clean. So, I get to sit there after the meal and . . . do nothing.

When I get closer to the house, I see his tall frame with the sun at his back.

God, he's gorgeous.

His ball cap is backward, hiding the hair I love to run my fingers through, and his white shirt is straining against his muscles as he lifts the bale of hay.

Apparently, farming is really freaking sexy.

I stand a few feet away, chewing on my thumb as I drink him in.

He tosses the bale with little effort, and I let out a soft sigh.

Our eyes meet, and he flashes me one of his effortless smiles. "Hi there."

"Hi, yourself."

"Like what you see?"

Do I ever. Instead of giving him the satisfaction of my response, I shrug. "It's all right, I guess . . ."

His voice dances with amusement. "You guess?"

"Well, I mean, you're okay and all."

And then he lunges for me. I squeal and run, but I don't have a chance in hell of him not catching me. Connor grabs me and pulls me up into his arms. My legs kick, and then Hadley rushes outside.

"Connor!" she yells, and he takes off with me in his arms.

"You can't catch us!"

My arms are wrapped around his neck as he circles and Hadley follows. "You got my mom!"

"I do, and if you want her back, you have to catch us!"

I laugh as he ducks and dodges her. She laughs hysterically as she chases him and, in this moment, I'm the happiest I've ever been.

There's nothing weighing me down.

In his arms, running around this field, with our daughter chasing us—I smile, and it feels like the world is smiling with us.

"The petition for divorce has officially been filed. The judge will review the case and, regardless of whether Kevin signs it or not, he'll render a decision because Kevin's in jail awaiting trial."

I don't even know what to say. It's been months of waiting for the stupid time restriction to run out, and Sydney has been vigilant as she counted down the time until she could strike.

"And the paternity?"

She pulls out the copy of it. "He was served it at the same time as he received his version of the results. Do you want to see?"

I nod. I know that Hadley isn't his, but it'll be nice to see it for myself. "Did you look?"

"No, I didn't think it was my place."

I smile. Sydney has become a trusted friend, which is something I never had before. Hadley loves her, and she loves giving Connor shit. It's been fun spending time with her. "Thank you, Syd."

"Don't mention it, but please open the damn thing so I can stop the internal suspense."

I do as she asks, grinning as I read the results.

"I take it that he's not her father?"

"No," I say with tears of joy. "No, he's not, but we knew that already, this sort of . . . confirms it all again."

"So . . . Connor?"

"Yeah, he's her father."

Sydney leans back in her chair, the look of surprise is evident on her face. "I thought so, I mean, Hadley has the Arrowood eyes, but I wasn't sure how it could be possible."

"I always hoped."

She smiles. "I once did too. Listen," Sydney says before pausing. "I want to warn you, as a friend, the Arrowood brothers have a lot of . . . baggage. I dated Declan for what feels like my whole life. He kissed me when I was eight years old, told me we were going to get married, and that was that. I loved him with my whole heart, and I really believed he was my forever, but he changed. Day by day, the boy I knew disappeared at the hands of his father. It was impossible to watch, but we had a plan. And then he took off and never came back. Loving those boys is easy, but losing them, well, it's not something we ever really get over."

My first instinct is to defend Connor, which is an urge I tamper down. Sydney isn't telling me this to hurt me, she's being a friend. I also hear the pain in her voice. It's clear that she's never gotten over the loss of Declan.

"I know they had a rough childhood."

She snorts. "Ellie, whatever he's told you . . . double it. Those boys went through hell and it was horrible to watch. Connor bore more of it than we probably know because he was the last one living at home. Declan was the first to leave, and well, while I was in college, so was he. We were fine, it was great, even. We went to schools close to each other, but then once Connor left for boot camp, Declan was done with me. I was depressed and shut myself off when he left."

"I'm sorry he hurt you."

"Me too. The sad part is that I would've run with him. I would've followed that man to the ends of the earth, but he told me to stay and that he didn't want me anymore. He wanted to start over and that meant we were through."

Sydney may be doing the best she can to mask the hurt in her voice, but I hear it in each syllable. I also hear the love she still has for him. But Connor isn't Declan, and I'm not her. We've talked about things, and I have to believe that after everything I've been through, Connor isn't keeping some deep dark thing from me that's going to make him run again.

We've already sorted that part out.

"I know that you and his brother had issues, but we're not young or going into this with eyes half open. Connor knows my demons, and he's told me about his. I appreciate that you want to help me, and I hear your words, truly I do, but there's something between us. We have a child together and . . . I don't know, Sydney, it's just so . . ."

"Easy to love him?"

I want to shake my head in denial. I don't love him, at least not like that yet. I know I could. I know my heart wants to leap, but I keep my head in check. Love is powerful and can be used against someone if its bearer doesn't have good intentions, and I refuse to leap again without first knowing what I'm leaping into.

"Easy to want to love him at least."

Syd extends her hand and covers mine. "I'm not telling you to stay away from him or anything like that, I want you to be careful. Seeing you or Hadley experience even half the pain that I have . . . well, I'd do just about anything to make sure that doesn't happen."

"I appreciate that."

She smiles. "Now, let's celebrate your upcoming divorce and get food!"

I grab my purse with the widest grin and nod. "Yes. Let's."

Today is filled with possibilities and joy, and I plan to enjoy both, but there's something niggling at the back of my head, telling me I'm not there yet.

I'm not sure why I'm here.

Every instinct and red light is flashing, warning me to turn back.

But here I am in Luzerne County Prison with a wall of glass separating me from an empty room.

My hands are tingling because my nerves are through the roof. I know he can't hurt me, touch me, or do anything at this point. Yet, just knowing I'll see Kevin makes me feel sick.

Still, I need to say these things. I need to face him and let him know that I'm not afraid.

Well, I am, but I won't show it.

On the other side of the glass divider, a row of inmates all dressed in their orange jumpsuits start to file in. I grasp my hands in my lap below the counter and wait.

He walks slowly, eyes not meeting mine until he sits down.

This man has been the cause of my fear for so damn long, he's tormented me, haunted me, and now when I look at him, he seems so small.

Kevin sits and takes the phone off the wall, and I do the same.

"Are you here to kick me when I'm down?" His deep voice rasps through the line.

"It would be no different from what you did to me." His eyes close, head falling forward, but he keeps the phone to his ear. "I'm not here for that. I'm here because . . . well, I don't really even know, but I felt that I wanted to have some closure, regardless of how the trial goes."

He laughs once. "Closure. You're my fucking wife, Ellie. You cheated on me, and you want closure. How the *fuck*," he says through gritted teeth, "could you lie to me for seven years about her being my daughter. Were you that desperate to be loved that you manipulated me all this time? I gave you everything, and this is what I learn?"

"Gave me everything? You hit me, Kevin. You hit me when you couldn't control me. You called me fat, ugly, worthless. You withheld love, affection, and used sex as a weapon. You beat me both physically and emotionally. I didn't know if Hadley was yours, and I didn't manipulate you. It was honestly more plausible than my getting pregnant the one time I was with someone else—*before* we were married."

He slams his hand on the counter, and I jump. "One time. You're a fucking liar and a cheat. You want a divorce? Fine! I'm all too happy to be done with you and her."

My chest tightens and tears threaten to form. I don't care that he says he's happy to be done with me, I really don't, but I thought maybe he'd have some slight affection toward Hadley. I don't know why since he's a bastard in every sense, but she adored him. "She meant so little to you?"

Kevin shakes his head, reminding me of how callous he really is. "Why are you here? Did you want me to have to look at you in the eyes and tell you, what? I signed your fucking papers. I don't want to be married to a gold digger who fucks other men. You want a divorce, go. Take your bastard child and leave."

"I came because a part of me felt bad for you, silly me. I thought that maybe it really hurt you and you wanted answers."

When Kevin leans forward, anger fills his eyes. "You put me in jail, divorced me, and then told me the brat I've been raising for seven years isn't even mine. Feel bad? I'm fucking relieved to be done with you, and when the judge hears what a whore you are, I'm pretty sure I won't be in here after the trial. If I were you, Ellie, I'd do what I could to avoid running into me—ever."

And with that, he hangs the phone up and stands.

I look at the man I once loved and wanted to make happy who is now a stranger to me. I came here for closure, and I guess that's exactly what I got. There was no love between us. It was possession and control. That was all we were to him, nothing but expendable property all along.

twenty-six

"What do you mean you have a kid?" Declan asks after I get done informing him of what's happened the last week.

I've been avoiding his calls, saying I have no service and texting him updates instead. I don't need a lecture or a reminder of what my brothers and I vowed to each other. None of that matters anymore. We're adults, and if any of them don't understand, they can fuck right the hell off.

"I have a daughter."

Silence fills the other end of the phone. "You've been there for what, almost four months? How the fuck did you father a kid in that little of time?"

I sigh and launch into the explanation of Ellie and Hadley. I've held that night close to the chest. There was no reason to tell anyone because it was just mine. Telling Declan everything now makes me feel like a tool. He's always been more of a father than anything and has the most guilt and disappointment over the things we've endured and done.

"Jesus Christ, Connor."

I picture my brother in his fancy high-rise office, flopping down in his chair with his hand over his face.

"Look, I know you're probably pissed at me, but I'm happy. I love this little girl, and I'm falling hard for Ellie. I can't explain it, but it's like she's this perfect other half of me. I'm not asking your permission or asking for anything else other than your understanding."

Declan releases a low, long sigh. "I get it more than anyone, brother. I've had that kind of love before."

"Speaking of Syd, she's Ellie's best friend."

"You've seen her?" There's an animation in his voice that wasn't there a moment ago. He can pretend with anyone else, but he can't with me. He loves her. He always has, and she's the reason my brother will never find happiness.

"She was here the other night."

"Fuck. I can't see her."

"You're not going to have a choice when you're back in Sugarloaf for your six-month sentence," I remind him.

My brother may be some big shot in New York City, but Sydney will bring him to his knees.

"And what are you planning to do with your new family? Are you moving? Going to get a job? Do something else?"

This is the main reason for my call. He's going to lose his shit, but my other brothers will be worse. If I have any hope of selling this idea to them, I'll need Declan on my side.

"I'd like to buy a parcel of the land."

"I'm sorry, *what*?" He nearly chokes on the words.

"Hadley has only ever known Sugarloaf as her home, and we have enough acreage to buy a part of it. There is no mortgage, so I'd like to buy some of it."

"Are you fucking insane? You want to stay in fucking Sugarloaf? Do you remember the reasons we left, Connor? Of all the damn things I thought I would listen to, this has to be the most asinine thing ever!"

Now it's my turn to yell. "Yes, I'm fucking insane because I want to be a father to my kid! I want to give her what we didn't have—stability. You may run from the things you love, Declan, but I don't. I found the woman I literally dreamed of for eight years, and I'm not letting her go. If she wants me to live here and be buried on this land, I will."

He huffs and doesn't say anything. We're both pissed off, and our tempers are known to get the better of us. We also love a good verbal sparring with each other, so I doubt whatever words get slung will have any lasting effect.

"And what are you going to do for work? How do you plan to buy this land?"

"I'm not an idiot. I can find a job."

Not that I've gotten to that point yet because I've been busy serving out my sentence, but I'll figure it out. I got my degree while I was in the navy, and while dairy farming isn't really what I want to do, I could probably do fine with a smaller herd.

Maybe.

"You're not thinking."

"No, you're not listening. I called to tell you about your niece, who is wonderful, and that I'm actually doing well and am happy, but you're too much of a selfish dick to hear that."

"This is just like you, you think only about you. What about Sean and Jacob? What are we all going to make you pay for a part of the land that you were going to inherit? Come on. I don't want that damn farm or any of the land, but we all made a promise never to move back!"

That promise had been the one thing that kept me from talking to him about this. My brothers were the only things in this world that mattered to me, and I love them, but I can't live my life like this.

"You of all people should know that things change, Dec. We aren't the same boys we were."

He doesn't say anything right away, and I look down at my phone to see if he hung up. "No," his voice breaks the silence, "I guess we're not. Tell me about Hadley . . ."

Then I remember that my brother isn't a bad guy. He's just protective.

Hadley comes running to the barn, brown hair up in a ponytail and her nose is bright red from the chill. "Where's Mom?"

"She went to see Sydney. I'm sure they'll be talking for hours. Hand me the wrench," I instruct her while I work on this stupid tractor.

No matter what I fix, replace, or tinker with, the damn thing won't start. While I would love nothing more than to set it on fire and get a new one, it's only three years old and should work. It's a test of wills at this point, and I refuse to give up.

"Do the brown cows make chocolate milk?" Hadley randomly asks.

"Uhh, no."

"Really because hippopotamuses have pink milk, which is weird. I wonder if it's strawberry flavored. I used to like strawberries, but one time, I ate too many and got sick."

These stories might have seemed stupid before, but now, I want to know everything. I've worked really fucking hard not to look at Hadley any differently or hug her too tightly. All I want to do is tell her the truth, pull her close, and promise her the world.

I want to make up for the time we've lost, which isn't possible.

"Yeah, I love strawberries."

"I could love them again," she says quickly.

I smile. I really love this kid. "What else don't you like?"

"Ducks."

My head whips around to stare at her. "Ducks?"

She nods. "Sydney said that we both have anatidaephobia. It's a big word, I know."

Sydney is in on this? Great. "And what exactly did Sydney say?"

"Well, she asked me if I liked ducks, and I said, they're okay but they have weird eyes. And she agreed and told me that you don't like ducks either, which means I decided that ducks really are dumb. When I told Sydney, she said that you have anatidaephobia. I looked it up, and decided we both have it because I don't like when they look at me and neither do you. We have a lot in common."

I'm not sure whether I should laugh or drive to Sydney's house and leave a hundred fake spiders in her bed and see who laughs then. But then I look at my daughter, who looks like our hatred of ducks has solidified her place in my world, and I don't care.

"We really do."

Her beaming smile grows brighter. "Do you know what else I'm afraid of?"

"No, what?"

"The Tooth Fairy."

I chuckle. "Really?"

"She's so creepy! Who comes into your room when you're sleeping and takes teeth? If I could be anything cool, it wouldn't be that. I'd probably want to be Santa Clause because he gives presents and makes people happy. I like to make people happy. Do I make you happy, Connor?"

I put my wrench down and move to sit beside her, grabbing us each our water bottles that Ellie makes us before we come out to the barn to work. "You definitely make me happy, Squirt. Finding you up in that tree house was the best thing that happened to me in a long time."

"Really?" Her green eyes brighten.

"Really."

"I love you!" she says and then wraps her arms around me, leaving me stunned.

I wrap my arm around her and pull her tight, not caring about the rules I've created. "I love you too, kid. I love you too."

twenty-seven

"Do you want to watch a movie?" I ask as I come back into the living room.

I just got Hadley to sleep and am doing anything I can to stop my mind from going to what happened today. I'm exhausted, on edge, and need a distraction.

"Yup, I already have it ready to go."

"You picked it already?"

He nods. "I sure did."

"I'm worried."

"As you should be, Angel, but since you asked me for a date tonight, it's only fair I get to pick."

I'm not sure about his logic, but I'm willing to give him this win because I don't have the energy to fight. "Then I get to pick the snacks."

Connor eats healthy for the most part. His breakfast and lunches are all about macros and some other term, and his idea of a good snack is carrots or peppers. I'm feeling Oreos and milk are needed tonight.

There's mirth dancing in his eyes, as though he can read my mind and knows he's in trouble. "I'm not sure I want to take that compromise."

"What can I do to persuade you?"

"You could kiss me."

I move closer, standing in front of where he's sitting on the edge of the couch. I like this position over him. "I think I could oblige."

I lean down, my hair creating a curtain around us, and while Connor may have asked me to kiss him, it's him who takes over when our lips touch. His hand slips into my hair, holding me where he wants me, but I want to be closer to him, so I push him back against the couch and straddle him.

The look of surprise in his eyes causes me to grin, but it doesn't last long because I need his kiss.

I want to be lost in his touch, warmth, and affection.

His arms snake around my back, and I kiss him with everything I am. Our tongues move together, my fingers run through his hair, and I grind down on him. I don't know if it's everything that happened today that has me so desperate for him, but I want to forget it all. I want the world to fade away in the way that only Connor can do for me.

"Easy, Angel," he murmurs as I kiss him again.

"I need you."

He holds my face in his hands, studying me. "I'm right here."

Guilt assaults me because it's not right to use him this way. I had no plans to tell him I went to see Kevin. I didn't plan to tell anyone, but he deserves the truth, no matter what.

"I went to the jail today."

"Please tell me it's because you had some distant relative incarcerated."

"I talked to Kevin."

His body goes tight, and I flinch, waiting for the anger and not expecting the horror I get. "Did you think I was going to hurt you?" I start to get up, needing space, but Connor grabs my hips, forcing me to stay. "Ellie, I will never hurt you in anger."

"I know . . ."

"I'll tell you until you believe it. Was I upset just now? Yes. Not because you went but because I hate the idea of that asshole anywhere near you. I would've gone with you if you had asked. All I want—all I will ever want—is to keep you and Hadley safe, and anything that puts you in danger has me on edge."

"I was safe. He can't hurt me there."

Connor releases a breath through his nose. "Then why are you on edge? What did he say to you?"

This has to be the most uncomfortable conversation in the most uncomfortable position. I'm sitting on the lap of the guy I've sort of moved in with who I'm falling in love with and talking about the man I'm currently divorcing.

"He said I was worthless and that he signed the divorce papers. He wants out and wants my bastard of a child not to be his issue. He basically let me know that he's not at all upset about it and I'm a whore."

"I'll fucking kill him," Connor says through gritted teeth.

I place my hand on his cheek. "And then what? I'd lose you again? Hadley would lose you. He isn't worth it."

He closes his eyes and then takes a beat before opening them. "That man will never speak to you again, do you understand? I can't fucking handle it. He will never come near Hadley, and I swear to God, Ellie, you can't be alone with him."

"I have no intention of it."

After today, there's nothing left to say. We'll be divorced since he signed the papers. And considering the charges and judge's notes on what happened, they'll sign off on it instead of making us go through mediation. Sydney provided a lot of notes and evidence to support the claim of abuse, including photos. Now that it's clear he wants nothing to do with Hadley, it's simpler.

"Just thinking of you being near him . . ."

I can see how distressed he is and I hate that I caused it. "It was something I needed to do. Even though it only confirmed what I already knew . . ."

His eyes, which are full of understanding, meet mine. "I get it."

"Your father?" I guess.

He blows out a breath and then tucks a strand of hair behind my ear. It's such a simple gesture, but the tenderness he's showing even in his anger speaks more than any words can. He isn't calling me names or yelling. He's showing me understanding.

"I confronted him more times than I care to count. I could never get through to him, and he felt no remorse for what he put us through, which is why when I left, I never returned. You can't make monsters see the light, Angel. You can't show them a better way because the darkness is what calls to them."

I shift in his lap again, feeling slightly self-conscious that the first time we're like this, I did it to forget. "Connor," I say softly, running my hands through his hair.

"Yes?"

"Can we start tonight over? Can I kiss you because you gave me something tonight I didn't know I needed? Can I lie in your arms as we watch a movie and enjoy that it's even possible to do?"

He moves his hands to my face, gingerly grips my cheeks, and then brings my mouth to his. This kiss is his and only his. My head swims with the sensations and emotions that he seems to be infusing into his lips. I feel his love, and more than that . . . I feel cherished.

We both deepen the kiss, not knowing where one begins and one ends. My fingers move to his chest, and I revel in the way his muscles flex under my touch.

Then his hands drift down my neck and to my back, grazing the sides of my breasts before landing on my ass. He grips me, pulling me a little higher until I can feel his erection growing.

"Connor." His name is a prayer.

"I want you so much."

"I want you too." And I do, even more when we're kissing. When I can taste, smell, and breathe all that is glorious and perfect about him. "You make me feel so good."

"You lead this, Ellie. I won't do anything you don't ask me to." He kisses me again and then pulls back, causing me to whimper. "Tell me, baby. Whatever you want."

My heart pounds so loudly it makes me dizzy. "Kiss me."

He does. He kisses me as though it's the only thing he was made to do. Our tongues clash over and over, driving me crazy. I need more. I want more. I want him to touch me and love me.

"Touch me." I barely get the words out before I go back to his lips.

He's the only man who has ever made me feel like this. Never in my life has someone kissed as thoroughly as Connor does. It's a full-bodied experience, and right now, my body wants more.

I've been loved by him before.

I've felt him inside me.

And I want to feel it all over again.

Connor's hands glide up my back and then back down. He breaks the kiss, and we watch each other as his hands move to my chest. Knowing he's measuring my response, I tear my shirt off, revealing my breasts to him, and then I grip his wrists so I can guide him there.

The heat in his gaze is enough to melt me, and my head falls back as he rubs his thumbs against my nipples and kneads my breasts. I swear that I could come just like this. I bring my head back up, and his touch, his eyes, and the power he's giving me is too much.

"You're so perfect. You're everything, Ellie. Tell me what you want."

"More."

He smirks but shakes his head, warm breath caressing my bare skin. "Be specific. Do you want my mouth on your gorgeous breasts? Do you want me to kiss your lips again? What do you want, Angel?"

I've never been vocal. In fact, I've always been forced to be quiet and obey. I don't know how to do this, but here is this big, strong man, surrendering himself to me, which is something I don't think he's ever done for anyone else. I want to be brave for him.

"I want your mouth on my breasts."

Heat flashes in his green eyes, and then, without breaking our connection, his tongue circles my nipple, which is the hottest thing I've ever seen. My fingers slide into his hair as he worships me. He kisses, sucks, and caresses my skin before going to the other side.

It's heaven and hell all at the same time. I start to move my hips, needing more.

"That's it, Angel, take what you want. Use me. Ride me and take what you need."

His words should embarrass me, but they don't, and I do as he says, giving myself the friction I so desperately need. We go at it like teenagers who don't know any better, but it's perfect.

I start to build as Connor's mouth is on my breasts and his cock strains against his jeans at the exact angle I need. My heart is pounding, body tense as I search for my release.

"Let go, Ellie. Let go, I'll catch you. I've got you in my arms, and I won't let you fall."

I push harder, moving faster as he groans. His tongue rolls my nipple around and then I feel his teeth bite down just enough and then . . . I fly.

My eyes close, head falling back, and he's right there, kissing my skin as I have what might be the best orgasm of my life.

My breathing starts to come back as embarrassment washes over me.

Connor looks up at me. "That was the sexiest thing I've ever seen. Watching you let go, it was beautiful."

I shift, and he winces. "But you . . ."

He takes my face in his hands and kisses me tenderly before bringing my forehead to rest on his. "I got everything I wanted, but I do need to"—he shifts—"go to the bathroom for a minute. When I come back, I'm going to hold you and force you to watch a movie. Don't go anywhere, okay?"

I don't know that my legs would even work if I tried. "Okay."

"Thank you."

"For what?"

Connor gives me a smile that melts my bashfulness away. "For trusting me."

I kiss him again. "Thank you for being a man I can trust. I . . ." I stop myself, knowing that's it's too soon to tell him that I'm falling in love with him.

I'm not even sure if I should love him, but here I am, hopelessly feeling as if I don't have a choice in it. I love him. I think I might've fallen in love with him that night eight years ago and I'm only just now allowing myself to acknowledge it.

"You?"

"I wanted to say that it means a lot to me."

"You mean a lot to me, Ellie."

"And I feel the same about you."

He brings my palm to his mouth and kisses it. "I'll be right back."

I get up and watch him walk toward the bathroom, feeling guilty that he was left unsatisfied, but then he turns and winks. He's truly the best man in the world, and for now, he's mine.

After a few minutes, he returns, and I'm sated and full of contentment as Connor wraps his arms around me and we snuggle on the couch. He pushes play, and I burst out laughing at his movie choice. Only Connor would pick *Beauty and the Beast*.

twenty-eight

It's the most beautiful fall day I've ever seen. The cool air is clean and crisp, and the sun is bright, illuminating every gorgeous color in the leaves. I stand on the porch with a cup of coffee, staring out at the cornucopia of reds and oranges that seem to soothe my soul.

Connor, Hadley, and I are going out for an adventure today. I have no idea what we're doing, but I was told to dress warm because we'll be outside.

Surprises used to be unwelcome, but with Connor, I never worry. He is beyond thoughtful, and each day I'm around him, I fall further in love with him.

Since the night on the couch a week ago, we haven't fooled around a bit, and it's all I seem to think about. When he brushes by me in the hall, I want to grab him and kiss him. He finds these little ways to touch me without really *touching* me. It's driving me nuts.

"Mommy! Where do you think we're going?" Hadley

asks, breaking the calm of the early morning I was savoring.

"I'm not sure, peanut. What do you think?"

"I think he's taking us horseback riding."

I tilt my head and narrow my eyes. "Does he have a horse?"

To be honest, I have no idea what Connor has on this farm other than a lot of work. He's been working on the barn and all the equipment in it since we got here. When he fixed the tractor yesterday, you would've thought he won the lottery. He was so overjoyed it was comical to watch.

"No . . ." I see the wheels turning. "You don't think he thinks we can ride the cows, do you?"

I chuckle and shake my head. "I think he knows better."

"Are you sure? He's not really good with the cows."

She isn't wrong. Thankfully, the foreman, Joe, and the workers on what was my farm love me and came here to help Connor. They hated Kevin and were all too happy to leave him, especially after they found out he beat me.

We've moved the Walcott cows onto Arrowood land to ensure nothing happened to them, but Kevin's farm is no longer functioning.

"I guess we could let him know if he tries it," I say conspiratorially. "But he seemed really excited."

"Mommy, is it okay if I love Connor?"

Her question knocks the air from my lungs. She and Connor have become very close, and he's made it very clear he wants Hadley and me in his life. "Yes, baby, it's very okay that you love him."

"Good, because I do."

"I'm glad. He loves you too."

She beams. "I know, he told me. Do you think Daddy will be mad?"

Shit. I don't know what to tell her, but I don't want to lie either. She hasn't said anything about Kevin recently. In fact, she's been completely avoiding anything that even remotely pertains to him. We haven't told her that Kevin isn't her biological father yet, and I know that Connor wants her to find out in a special way.

I don't want to take that from her.

"Hadley," I squat and take her wrists in my hands, "do you remember what I told you about love?"

She purses her lips and shrugs. "No."

Typical kid. "Well, I told you that when you love someone, it's a gift and that the person on the other end should always be grateful for it. How do you think you would feel if Connor was a part of our life? Would you want him to always be around?"

"Like a dad?"

I nod. "Yeah, like that. If we spent time with him and maybe loved him with all our hearts."

I'm on very shaky ground, but I'd like to gauge her receptiveness a bit. She's a huge part of my decision-making process. If the idea scares her, I will back off. I will never again put her in a position where she's filled with fear.

"Do you love Connor?"

"I do."

She smiles so wide I worry she'll break her face. "I think he loves you too, Mommy." Her voice is just a whisper.

"Why do you think that?"

"He watches you."

"Watches me?"

Hadley nods. "He stares at you, and I think he loves you and wants to kiss you."

Oh, she would be very right on the kissing part, but Connor and I are clearly not doing very good at hiding our feelings.

Just then, he comes striding up to the house like straight

out of an Austen novel. He strides through the thick grass as though he's Mr. Darcy with the sun streaming from behind him. He's so damn gorgeous that if I weren't holding Hadley's hand I'd be running toward him.

"See," Hadley's voice is quiet, "he's watching you."

I look down at her with a grin. "Yeah, I guess he is."

"I want to stay with Connor."

I don't say anything, but I squeeze her hand a little.

"There are my girls. How about we go on our adventure."

I'd go anywhere with him.

Hadley releases my hand and jumps off the porch toward him without warning. I almost scream, but he catches her without missing a beat. "Where are we going?" she asks as she wraps her arms around his neck.

"It's a surprise."

"Let's go!" Hadley exclaims.

We grab our jackets and get into his car. Hadley has her headphones on and is watching a show, oblivious to where we're going. Throughout the ride, I keep sneaking looks at him, and each time he catches me, he grins. Subtly, he places his hand on the center console and inches it closer to mine. Following his lead, I do the same until the tips of our fingers hook together.

I glance back at Hadley, who is engrossed in her show.

"She asked about you and us today."

He glances up in the mirror and then back to me. "And?"

"I think we should tell her."

"You know what that means?"

I do. It means that this thing we're doing is real. It means that he wants us to be a family and he wants us to move in with him and commit to something more.

As much as fear is a very relevant feeling, when I look at him, I still can't imagine any other outcome. Walking away from him isn't possible. I love him. It might be fast, but it's what I feel in my heart.

Connor is selfless and I've never had that before.

"I want it all, but I need to go slow."

"I know."

"As long as you understand that."

His hand shifts, and he weaves our hands a bit tighter together. "We can tell her and the rest is at your pace. Just know that when it comes to her, I may not be able to pump the brakes."

That part is perfectly fine. I want her to love him, and I want her to be the one thing he loves more than anything. He and I can pace ourselves a bit and don't need to work on a timeline, but I won't rob them of any more time together.

"Be gentle with her . . . if she'll let you."

He smiles. "I don't think you know how happy you made me."

My cheeks burn. That's all I want to do, and he has no clue what he does for me. Every minute with Connor is a gift.

"You do the same for me." I glance back again to make sure she isn't listening. "I just hope she doesn't hate us after this."

"We'll tread carefully."

I can't help but be nervous and anxious about this. While she loves Connor, she gets him as this friend. When he steps into the role as parent, her relationship with him will change. It won't be all fun and games—he'll be her father, and the first time he has to discipline her will be a challenge.

That isn't even taking into consideration how she will feel about the things I'd done. She will know that I lied, and I hope that doesn't diminish her trust in me.

Hopefully, we will transition without a lot of bumps, but then again, that doesn't really seem to be the theme of my life.

We make a turn onto a dirt road, and my curiosity spikes. Where the hell is he taking us?

Hadley pulls her headphones out and her face is glued to the window. "Are we there?"

"We are," Connor says as he continues down the path.

"Are there cows here?"

I burst out laughing, and Connor looks over like I'm crazy. "She thinks you're taking us cow riding because you seem so inept when it comes to the livestock you raise."

"Hey! I know you don't put saddles on cows unless you're in a rodeo!" he protests with a joking tone.

"Those are bulls!" she yells at him before covering her eyes with her hands.

"Same thing. I know things."

Her hand drops and she shakes her head. "You also didn't think you had to milk the cows."

"You know, you *were* my favorite, now I'm reconsidering giving you Betsy the new calf that was born."

"Apples!" Hadley yells instead of responding, her attention wholly focused out her window. "You brought us apple picking!"

I glance back at Connor as he nods. "Well, we both love apple pie, I figured maybe we should get some and try to convince your mom to bake it."

She giggles as her feet kick wildly. "Best day ever!"

I take Hadley pumpkin and apple picking each year, but Kevin never came with us. He was always too busy—or too angry—to do things with us. Connor is not only here but also has planned it. He wanted to spend time with us. He put thought and effort into something that he couldn't know we enjoyed doing, and yet, somehow, he did know.

The man managed to take a flippant comment about apple pies—a comment I'd made on the worst night of my life—and turn it into a joyful moment.

He parks the car, and Hadley is out.

I turn to him, and before I can stop myself, my lips part. "I love you."

Connor's beautiful green eyes fill with emotion. "I've loved you since the first moment I ever saw you."

"I think I have too, but it's so soon and there is so much we still need to figure out."

He grins and takes my hand in his. "We also have nothing but time. Now, let's go pick apples, and maybe tonight, we can start to make a plan on how to make this dysfunctional trio into a family."

And with that, he exits the car, and I wonder how I can ever thank his horrible father for forcing Connor Arrowood to come back so he could find me.

twenty-nine

"How many apples do we really need?" I ask as Hadley puts another two in the wagon. Yes, we have a wagon because the kid picked half the orchard.

"I like apples. They're good for you."

Okay, she has a point, but . . . we don't need fifty. "Fair, but I think we have enough."

Hadley stops, turns toward me, and puts her hands on her hips. "If we don't have enough apples, Mommy can't make pies."

I'm not really sure how to argue with that, but I can divert her attention to something else. "Do you like pumpkin pie?"

She scrunches her nose. "Ewww."

Now I'm not sure if she's my kid. How can she not like pumpkin pie? "Have you ever had it?"

"No, because it's gross. Pumpkins are like a vegetable."

Ellie sighs beside me. "You have no idea how much fun

this can be."

I don't think she understands that I couldn't care less about these arguments. I *want* to have a million of them. I'll debate whatever the little girl beside me wants to debate so long as I'm spending time with her.

"I'm not sure she can do anything I don't find interesting."

Ellie shakes her head. "Oh, I can't wait to see if you say that in a month."

I can't either. I hope that it never gets old, although, I know better. My brothers probably thought I was cute and interesting at some point. By the time I was two, I'd become their bargaining tool and scapegoat. Being the youngest meant I was stupid and listened to them.

"I'm sure it'll wear off in about five years."

"Connor, Connor! Look, they have a huge pumpkin!" She points at what has to be the biggest thing I've ever seen. "Can we get it?"

"I'm strong, but I'm not that strong."

Ellie snorts beside me. "Hadley, we can't fit it in the car."

Hadley's eyes find another that is only marginally smaller than the other one. "Can we get a big one like this?"

"Did you bring the tractor?" I ask.

"Does it work?" Ellie says with a snort.

My eyes narrow. "Not yet. It apparently needs another part."

Hadley grabs my hand and pulls me closer to it. "Then we can't bring it because it is *still* broken."

How does a seven-year-old master this level of sarcasm already?

"And we can't get a pumpkin the size of the car."

Hadley gives a dramatic sigh. "Fine. Can we get a pony?"

"Uhh," I say, not understanding how we went from a pumpkin to a pony.

Ellie stands there with a grin as though this is the funniest thing, and an expression that says *I can't wait to see how Connor will handle the question.* "I can't promise that, Squirt. I can barely manage the cows."

She looks off to the side, seeming to ponder that. "Okay."

That was easy.

"Maybe soon," she adds before taking my hand, stopping me from saying anything more. "Let's go look at the pumpkins—you know, the ones that Connor *can* lift without a crane."

We walk over to where there is a row of pumpkins, and she studies each one intently.

"Can you lift this one?" Hadley asks as she picks up one that's the size of her hand.

I give her a pointed stare, and she giggles. "You're just messing with me."

"I think you could lift all the pumpkins."

"You must really think I'm strong."

She nods. "You have big muscles, doesn't he, Mommy?"

I look to Ellie with a sly grin. "Yeah, Mommy, do I have big muscles?"

"You have a big ego."

Hadley scratches her head. "What's an ego?"

Ellie sighs. "It's what you think about yourself. And it seems Connor thinks he's super strong and handsome."

"He is handsome. You told Sydney you thought he was," Hadley informs us.

Ellie's lips part, and I can't avoid teasing her a bit. It's way too fun. "You did, huh?"

"I might have mentioned it—once."

Hadley puts her pumpkin down and comes over to take both our hands in hers. "I think you're handsome."

"Well thank you, Squirt," I say as I squeeze her hand. "I think your mommy is very pretty."

"Do you think I'm pretty?"

"I think you're beautiful," I tell her. "The most beautiful girl in all of the world."

Hadley beams under my praise and then releases Ellie's hand. Her arms wrap around my legs and she holds on tight. She gives the best hugs. They come from the center of her body, and it's like tentacles wrapping around you.

"You don't have to get me a pony, Connor."

I laugh because her mind just bounces on a whim. "That's good."

"I'll take a puppy instead."

Ellie snorts. "Let's start with a pumpkin and go from there."

thirty

Today was perfect. Everything went even better than I could've planned. Hadley had fun, we got a ton of apples, pumpkins, and some weird-looking things that Ellie called gourds.

Ellie is currently putting away the apples, and Hadley is waiting to head out to the tree house. Not only did we get pumpkins for the house but we also got them for the tree house because she explained that all places need decorations.

I may turn one of the cow pastures into a pumpkin patch to keep this kid happy.

"You ready?" Ellie asks as she comes out with the two pumpkins and a tablecloth.

"What's that for?"

"Curtains."

"Curtains?"

"Hadley needs to make the place a little homier, and curtains make a house a home."

I never knew they were so important. I look back at the house, which is curtain-less. I think my father was drunk once and ripped all the curtain rods out of the walls. Not that I think curtains would've made *this* house a home. The only thing that did that was my father dying and no longer being here.

"I think the people inside it do that," I tell her as I pull her to my chest. "You made this house a home."

Ellie smiles softly and gives me a quick kiss. "I think we should tell her now."

"Now?"

My heart begins to race and nerves hit me. I'm not a guy who feels fear. After my time in the military, I learned to breathe through it and not allow it in. In this moment, I can't stop it. Once we tell Hadley, her world will change. Mine has already been tilted on its axis, but I'm an adult. She's a child, and I worry about how she'll handle the news.

"The longer we wait, the more I feel like we're taking this from her. She should know that her father cared enough about her to give her a day like this. I want to give her this—you as her father."

My mouth opens, but words don't come. I can feel my palms start to sweat, and I feel like a kid again, not the grown man I am.

It's nerves and excitement and adrenaline and anticipation.

"Are you not ready?"

"No, I am," I say quickly. It has nothing to do with being ready. I've never been more ready for anything. "I'm sure, and I want to tell her. I just didn't think you were."

"It's time."

She's right. It is time. "Let's head out to the tree house."

Hadley comes running outside, carrying a basket and her doll. "I brought cider, cups, and cookies."

"Where did you get the cookies?" Ellie asks.

"The kitchen."

"I asked for that."

I hold in a chuckle because Hadley has great timing for a seven-year-old. The three of us make the trek out to the tree that has come to mean more to me than I ever could've known. Here is where I hid when I was scared and found what I had lost.

Now, hopefully, it's where yet another piece of my life will fall into place.

We walk quietly, well, Ellie and I are quiet, Hadley chatters about puppies and pumpkins until she spots the tree house. Then she's off like an arrow and climbs the staircase I built for her. It's nothing like any tree house I would've ever had. It has a roof, two windows, and a small porch on the back, which was my addition to it this week.

I don't want this place to be somewhere she hides, I want it to mean something else for her. The tree house should bring her joy and be a place where memories are formed. So, I'm probably going to end up giving her a bathroom, kitchen, electricity, and plumbing by the time I'm done.

"You put a deck on?" Ellie asks.

"I have no idea how that got here."

She rolls her eyes. "You know she was happy with just the piece of plywood as a floor as long as you came out here with her."

That is exactly why I've gone above and beyond with building this place. "I do, but she should have everything I can give her. That kid has been through hell, and if this is the one thing I can do that makes her smile, I'll do it."

Ellie takes both my hands and stares up at me. The words she said to me earlier still echo in my heart, and I am anxious to hear them again.

Both of us are oblivious until we hear Hadley's voice from beside us. "Are you going to marry my mom?"

No one can ever say this kid is subtle.

"Maybe someday, but right now, we're taking it one day at a time." I hope that's the right answer.

"Would you like Connor to be in your life forever?" Ellie asks, and it's clear where she's planning to transition this conversation to.

I choke back my nerves. If Ellie thought telling her that I'm her biological father would upset her, we wouldn't be out here right now.

"Yes! I love him, and he's my best friend. Plus, he's funny and handsome, and he is going to get me a puppy."

"I never said that."

"You will, you love me and I'm adorable." She bats her eyelashes and her lips are a tight line. She is adorable, and I have a feeling she's probably right. I'm a sucker when it comes to her, hence the deck on a tree house.

"Well, be that as it may," Ellie says swiftly, clearly unimpressed with her charm. "What if I told you that a long time ago, before you were born, I met Connor."

"You knew each other?" Hadley looks back and forth between us, and I nod.

"We did."

"We met once, and it was . . . well, it was very special," Ellie continues. "You see, your grandma and grandpa had died not too long before that, and I was very sad. Connor made me feel happy and helped my heart that day."

She looks to me and smiles. "Like he did for me?"

"Exactly," I cut in. "I happen to like making you two happy."

Ellie releases a shaky breath. "What I want to tell you is

that . . . well, that night, God gave me a baby."

"Me?"

She bobs her head quickly with a smile. "Yes, you. My beautiful, perfect, sweet little girl. Connor and I got a test that told us he is actually your real dad."

"But . . . I already have a dad."

I squat beside her. "You do, but you and I have the same blood."

Ellie gets to her knees and takes Hadley's hands in hers. "We didn't know until a few days ago, and your dad and I got married right after I met Connor. But Connor *is* your father, not Kevin."

We both are still as stone as we wait for Hadley to say something. She stands there, processing what she just found out.

"Daddy isn't my daddy?" she asks, her voice quivers a bit.

Fuck, this is breaking my heart. I love her, and I don't want to cause her pain, but at the same time, I'm glad we're telling her.

"No, baby, but you don't have to stop loving him. I don't know when you'll see him again, but he can always be in your heart."

I think about what he said to Ellie and have to force back my demand that Hadley not even give him that much.

She's kindness and everything good in this world, and he is nothing but poison.

I'm glad he was so willing to give them away because I'm more than willing to keep them.

"Hadley," I say with my heart in my throat, "I don't want to confuse you or make you sad. You don't have to call me dad or anything until you want to, and if you never do, I'll always be Connor to you. If I had known you were mine, I would've found you right away, but I will be as much a part of your life as you want me to be, and nothing has to change for us until you're ready for it."

She looks up at me, her eyes filled with confusion. "You're my dad?"

"I am, and I really am happy that you're my daughter."

Hadley drops Ellie's hold and walks over to me. Her little hands frame my face, and she smiles. "I wanted you to be my daddy too."

With that, my entire world shifts, and I swear that I could fucking cry.

"I'm not tired," Hadley complains.

"If you don't go to bed now, you'll never get up for school." Ellie doesn't allow her any room to negotiate. "Go brush your teeth."

There's a part of me that wants to ask Ellie to let her stay home. After a day like we had, surely, we can pretend the world around us doesn't exist for just a bit longer.

"Go on, Squirt," I say, backing up Ellie because I may want to keep Hadley home, but I'm not a fool.

The look of appreciation on her face tells me I did well, and I want to do well. I want to be the partner who supports her, which means I can't always be the good guy.

If Dempsey and Miller could see me now . . .

Here I am, Mr. Domestic and happy as fuck dealing with it. I never understood it before—how a kid could change your whole world. I watched Liam literally go from bachelor of the year to a family man in just a few months. I thought maybe Natalie had some kind of golden pussy or something, but I was a fucking tool. It was love.

It was finding that another human was so important that you were willing to forget all your stupid rules. Ellie is the piece of my heart I didn't know was missing. She's brought me to my knees, and I don't care if I can't ever stand again. For her, I'd stay here, at her feet as long as I have her here.

Hadley mopes to the bathroom, and a second later, I hear the water run as she starts her bedtime routine.

"What are you thinking?" Ellie asks as she comes up to me, wrapping her arms around my waist in a display of affection she usually only leaves for once Hadley is asleep.

"That I love you."

She smiles at that, her eyes filling with love and a little bit of apprehension. I can't wait for the day when I don't see the second part. "Say it again."

"I love you."

I say it without pause, and I'll say it a million times over again until she believes it. She'll never know what it means that she said it to me without prompt.

Ellie leans up on her toes and gives me a soft kiss. "I love you too, Connor, and today was . . . well, it was everything. She took it better than I could've ever imagined, and it feels as if the world is smiling down on us."

"Because it is. We deserve to be happy, and I think we've both had enough shit to last us a lifetime."

"I agree, and hopefully"—she kisses me again, and her eyes darken just a bit—"we have some more happy tonight."

"How happy?"

Ellie shrugs. "We'll see."

God, this woman is trying to kill me. I would like to be very, very happy, but I'll take whatever I can get with her. I may be patient, but I'm a man who is very much in love with the woman in my arms, and I'd like to show her.

She disentangles herself and tucks her hair behind her ear right as Hadley bursts into the living room.

"Can Connor read to me tonight?"

Ellie looks to me. That's normally something she does for Hadley, so I wait for her to give me the go ahead.

"Of course," Ellie says with a smile that I can't read.

"Are you sure?"

"I'm one hundred percent sure."

"Thank you, Mommy!" Hadley runs over to her, hugs her tight, and then rushes to me. "Ready?"

"Ready."

Then Hadley practically drags me into the bedroom that has become hers. The bed has been moved away from the window since she was afraid of something outside it, and the sheets are pink instead of the deep blue that used to be on Sean's bed.

It was strange to me that my father hated us enough to beat us but hadn't thrown away anything that would've reminded him of us after we left.

Everything was as it was when we lived here.

Like how my mother left it. Until we cleaned it out and got rid of the baggage.

Over the last few months, things have just . . . shown up. There's a plant in the living room, flowers on the table, and those mats on the floor in the bathroom.

Day by day, Ellie has made this house into more. Now, we're becoming a family.

And that makes me happy.

"So, how does your mom usually do this?"

Hadley sits on the bed and pats the blanket. "First you have to pick a book. I like those over there."

"Okay, pick the book." I feel like a total idiot. I should've known that much. I walk over to the stack and look for one that looks more worn. I'm assuming she has a favorite. "Any of them you like more?"

She shrugs. "I love *all* of those."

"*Green Eggs and Ham?*" I ask. Who doesn't love Dr. Seuss? My brothers and I loved *Go Dogs Go*. No surprise. It was all about going fast and not liking hats.

Hadley's eyes brighten. "I do not like green eggs and ham . . ."

"I do not like them, but Hadley can." I wink at her and come to the bed, not really sure where to sit.

Hadley scoots over, and I take her cue. I rest with my back on the wall and then she mimics my position, but instead of her head lying back, she rests it on my arm. Her little hands grip my bicep, and I'd swear, she's holding my heart instead.

I look down at her, wondering what God ever thought I was worthy enough to be a father. After all the bad things I've done, I don't deserve her.

Still, she's mine, and I vow a new promise right now. I will never do anything to shame her. I will be honest, devoted, and dependable.

"Will you read it?" she asks staring up at me.

"I will," I answer, but not to the question, but to my own silent vow.

"How did you meet my mom?" she asks after I read the first page.

Crap.

I can't not answer, so I'm going to be vague. It's a good plan—I think.

"We met at a restaurant." It isn't a lie. They serve food there, and I actually took Ellie there for a date last week. It qualifies.

"Did you kiss her?"

Oh, God. Where is Ellie? "I kissed her, yes."

Hadley mulls that over. "Did you love her?"

"Your mom is very loveable."

In my head, I just keep hearing the word: evade. I want to evade all possible questions and get the story read. So, I open the book back up and start, but Hadley isn't having it.

"Do you think you'll marry her?"

Maybe answering a question with a question is the best bet? "Do you want me to marry her?"

She nods. "Then you'll really be my dad."

Here's where I'm treading again. I don't want to scare her with the reality of what this all means for her, but at the same time, I want to reassure her that when it comes to me, I'm here for good. I will never abandon her.

"I'm really your dad now. I will always be your father, Hadley. Always. You and I are family in blood and in our hearts."

She smiles at that. "So, no matter what, I will always be your daughter?"

"Always."

"Even if you and Mommy don't get married."

"Even if that never happens."

Hadley's eyes brighten before she drops her head on my arm. "I'm glad."

"Me too, Squirt. Me too."

"You can read now."

And so I do. After twenty minutes and two more books, because I can't seem to deny her anything, I head out to the living room where I'm hoping to find a happy Ellie.

I find her reading a book on the couch, and I lean against

the doorframe to look at her. She's so beautiful. Her dark brown hair is pulled up on the top of her head, and she has her glasses on. There's no effort in her beauty, it just is. She chews on her bottom lip and then turns the page.

I want to pull her into my arms and kiss her senseless.

"Reading anything good?" I ask, unable to stay away from her a minute longer.

She jumps a little and then smiles. "A romance about two people who found each other again. They were apart for a while, both of them wondered about the other but obstacles kept them apart."

"So, it's an autobiography?"

"It seems a little like us, only less drama."

I grin and move toward her. "I could do with less drama."

Ellie puts the book down and then snuggles herself in my arms after I sit. "The drama is what keeps it real, though. Life is filled with ups and downs. It's the pain that allows us to feel the good parts. If I'd never known the sadness of being with the wrong man, when you came back to Sugarloaf, I don't know that it would've been the same."

Maybe that is the case, but that doesn't mean I like the idea of Ellie ever having felt that kind of sadness.

"I would've rather found you happy with him than in the hell you were. Even if that meant I could never have you."

She settles against my side. "I would rather have you. I don't think my heart was ever really anyone else's. I'm where I belong."

"I hate that you went through so much in the time it took for me to find you again."

Ellie tilts her face so she's looking up at me and gives me a soft smile. "It's all over now. My divorce will be final soon and Hadley is ours. We can figure the rest out and move on from our pasts."

I start to say more, but there's a pounding on the door. "Stay here," I command.

No one ever drops by here. I go to the shelf that houses a hidden gun safe. It takes a second to scan my finger, but then the front drops open, and I grab the gun.

Ellie's eyes widen, but she doesn't move. I probably should've mentioned the house has many things like this. When I promised to protect her, I meant it.

I hold the gun down at my side, ready to eliminate any threat.

There's another knock.

"What can I do for you?" I say, hand ready to react.

"You can open the fucking door before I freeze my ass off."

Fuck. I really didn't need this tonight.

I put the gun down on the side table, open the door, and release a sigh while glaring at the asshole standing on the porch. Declan has come for a visit, I wonder why.

"What? Not happy to see me? No welcome home, brother . . . it's nice to see you?"

"Unexpected to see you, Dec, didn't know you'd be coming by."

"Yeah, I talked to Jacob and Sean and drew the short straw to come check on things, make sure the conversation we had wasn't because of some head injury, and meet your girl."

Good for him, but I don't want him here. I was about to have a happy night, and that has just disappeared.

"Go find a hotel," I say and try to shut the door.

"Connor?" Ellie says from the other side. "Is everything okay?"

My brother pushes through the door, his smile as wide and as charming as ever. "You must be Ellie, I'm Declan, this ingrates older and more dashing brother." His hand slaps on my shoulder. "I didn't mean to intrude on your night, but I had a few days with no meetings and wanted to come out."

"Oh!" She rushes forward with her hand out. "It's so nice to meet you. I'm Ellie, which you knew, and well, I've heard so much about you." Ellie's voice is soft, and then she looks down. "I'm a mess. Please don't judge me on this."

"Of course not, it's late, and I dropped by unexpected. Please don't judge me on whatever manners my brother doesn't have, and we'll call it even."

She laughs, and I shoot daggers at the back of his head. Such a fucking tool. "Dec was going to find a hotel."

I make my way to stand beside Ellie. I have no idea what exactly my brother's motives are for coming here. I don't think it's just for a friendly visit, though. If I had to guess, he's here to make sure Ellie is real and that my request for land isn't because I'm being run around by my cock. God forbid I be happy. Just because he's too chicken shit to go for what he wants, doesn't mean I am.

"A hotel?" Ellie asks.

Declan looks back to me and then to Ellie. "Is there even a hotel in Sugarloaf? I figured you'd offer me a room at least."

Ellie slaps my chest. "You can't make him go to a hotel!"

"Yes, I can."

"I wasn't interrupting an important evening, was I?" Declan's grin makes me want to punch him.

"Yes."

"No," Ellie answers at the same time.

He smirks at me as though he knows what he spoiled tonight. That's fine, he isn't the only one who has something to use against the other. Declan forgets that this town is small, and we're not in the days of no cell phones and where we have to sneak out to see someone. I can get a message to a girl he's avoiding very quickly.

"We just got Hadley . . . our . . . my . . ."

"Our daughter," I answer, saving her from trying to figure out if I'd told him or not.

Her smile is warm, face shining with joy. "Our daughter to bed. I'm sure you guys have a lot to catch up on, and it's getting late, so I'm going to head to bed."

"Please, don't feel you have to run off on my account." Declan tries to stop her.

"No, no, it's not that. I have work in the morning, and I really am beat."

I want to choke my brother.

"Dec, why don't you go to bed, I'm sure you're tired after your long, uninvited drive out here. Ellie and I were going to talk."

"Connor, it's really okay, we can talk anytime. You and your brother probably want to catch up." She walks over to me, places a kiss on my cheek. "Good night."

"I really wanted us to be happy." I know I sound like a petulant kid, but I don't care.

She smiles. "We can be happy tomorrow."

Declan laughs but covers it with a cough.

He's dead.

Ellie blushes and then takes a step backward. "Good night, and it was nice to meet you."

"You too, Ellie."

When she's out of sight, I turn to my brother. "What the hell are you doing here, Declan?"

"We have to talk, and I thought it was best to do it in person."

He turns and heads outside, giving me no other option than to follow.

thirty-one

eclan and I walk in silence, and I can feel the tension rolling off him.

He keeps going, and as much as I want to stop him and demand he spill it, I know my brother. Sean and Jacob can be pushed, Dec can't. He works through things in his mind, weighing each possibility before attacking. It's why he's successful in his business. He sees the field before making a play.

When we get to the barn that I've busted my ass in getting fixed up, he finally stops. "She's pretty."

At first, I'm not sure if he means the barn or Ellie, but then he looks back toward the house. "She's more than just pretty."

"Is that what this is? A crush or whatever you want to call it?"

"Fuck you for even asking me that," I spit back at him. "I have a kid, Dec. A fucking kid. I love that woman, and I love my daughter."

He raises both hands. "Easy! I'm asking because the last time I saw you, it was *fuck this place* and *burn it down*. Now you're asking to buy some of the land on the very farm we swore we'd never come back to. I don't know how the hell you thought any of us weren't going to come see if aliens abducted you or whatever. For all we knew, she found out who I was and was extorting money from you."

I clench my fists and release them at least three times before deciding I need to walk away for a minute. There has never been a time where I've actually wanted to raise my fists in anger toward my brothers. I may be willing to break my other promises, but that is one I never will. Declan must know how pissed I am because he stays silent as I work through it.

Once I'm calm enough, I turn and face him. "You may be willing to walk away from what you want, but this isn't an option. If you three don't want to sell me the land, that's fine. I'll take the money from the sale and buy my own. You don't have to understand or agree with me, but I thought you'd at least respect my decision."

"I do respect it! That's why I'm fucking here! I called Sean and Jacob, who think you're insane, but they also want you to be happy. How much do you know about Ellie?"

I swear that he's trying to piss me off on purpose. "I know enough."

"I don't think you do, Connor." There is a small stretch of silence where I want to demand he tell me what the fuck is going on, but I force myself to wait him out. "I came because you need to know something, and like I said, I wasn't going to do this over the phone."

"If it's so important, just tell me already." I'm tired, and my brother ruined what was looking like a good night. I have no patience for listening to him talk in circles.

Declan sighs, and in an uncharacteristic move, he runs his hand down his face. I've seen Declan upset, angry, disappointed, and proud, but this emotion I don't know. He looks almost . . . sad.

"What do you remember about that night?"

My body locks because of all the things we talk about in our past, that night isn't one. We never bring it up, content to pretend it didn't happen. It was when I knew that, no matter what, I could never forgive my father. It was the night he made four boys deal with something they never should've. He forced us all into a lifetime of regret and anger.

Declan tried to shield the three of us, but there was no way he could. Dad made sure that if one went down, we all did. He wanted to be sure that through our guilt, we would protect him because we always protect each other.

"I remember everything."

"Me too. As hard as I try to forget, I can't."

"Why are you bringing this up, Dec?"

He sighs and then sits on the bale of hay. "I need you to hear me out before you go ape-shit and act like I did something you wouldn't have done if the roles were reversed."

"Okay."

I say it, but I don't mean it. If he did something to jeopardize my relationship with Ellie and Hadley, my brother will not like the results.

"Right. Well, I'm going to get it all out, and you're going to listen because whether you want to believe it or not, this family is all I care about, and anyone who threatens it is my problem. I worked way too fucking hard to keep the four of us out of jail or turning into degenerate drunks like our father."

"The point, Dec."

I can now add that stalling is something my brother isn't good at. It's going to come out, so he might as well get it over with.

However, Declan seems to be struggling with whatever it is that he drove four hours to come tell me.

"After our call, I had my security team check Ellie out."

Now I'm going to lose it. "Excuse me?"

"Jesus Christ, I did what any one of us would, Connor. I had her investigated."

My lips flatten, and I focus on breathing through my nose. "You crossed a line, Declan. You had no right to do that."

He throws his hands up. "I had no right? I'm your fucking brother who has stood by your side, protected you, given up everything, just like you did! I'm not playing games, Connor. I didn't take some great joy in this. The last thing I wanted to do was come here and have to show you this!"

"Show me what?" I keep my voice even. It's clear that Declan is upset, which has me on edge.

He runs his hands through his hair and shakes his head. "First, let me explain what I found."

I motion for him to go ahead.

"I didn't have much to go on other than she was in Sugarloaf and had to live close. After some digging, they found Ellie Walcott, who was married to a Kevin Walcott, who was recently arrested, and they had a daughter."

I roll my eyes and huff. "I know all this."

"Just shut up and let me get this out."

"Fine." My patience is wearing thin.

"They had a hard time finding any history on Ellie. She wasn't from the area as I had . . . assumed because, who the fuck moves to Sugarloaf? So, they dug deeper and that's when we discovered her history."

"Is she some kind of drug dealer and her parents died in some nefarious way?" I taunt him because this is a bit melodramatic.

Then he extends an envelope. "Not exactly, but, you're not that far off."

"Far off about what?"

"In that envelope is her birth certificate, marriage license, and a police report. All of which you'll piece together."

I'm still not following. "What does any of this have to do with anything?"

Declan waits, his hesitation almost cloyingly thick. "Open the file, Connor."

I blow a deep breath through my nose and do as he asks. I lift the documents, first seeing her birth certificate, and then marriage license, showing she did marry Kevin, and then the police report. The one with the date I will never forget.

I look to him, the blood draining from my face. "No."

"Her last name," he says the name at the same time I read it again.

It must be true. My brother wouldn't drive four hours to come see me just to lie to me. He wouldn't have this look of dread in his eyes if it weren't the one name that could destroy everything. "Cody."

And then the perfection of the day is gone.

Because my father is the one who killed Ellie's parents, and I helped cover it up.

Declan shakes his head. "I'm sorry."

I grip my hair and groan. "No! Fucking hell! This can't be my goddamn life! Jesus, she's never going to understand."

"Look, I know that this is a lot, but you can't tell her, Connor. You *have* to protect all of us. This isn't just about you—this could fuck all of us."

I look at my brother like he has ten heads. He can't possibly mean I need to keep this from her. "You can't ask that of me."

"Do you think I do it easily?"

I don't care. "I fucking love her, Dec! You can't ask me to

lie to her."

"You want to see us all in jail? You'll be there too, right next to your brothers." His hand grips my shoulders. "We're family. We're all each other has, and we have to protect each other."

I take a step back. "Then why fucking tell me?" I scream and shove him. Declan stumbles back slightly but catches himself. "Why would you put this on me, you son of a bitch? How could you think I would be able to go on with my life after you told me? Do you not see what this means? Hadley's grandfather killed her grandparents. I mean—Jesus fucking Christ, how the hell do I keep this secret?"

Pity fills my brother's eyes, and he sighs. "I don't know, but until I talk to Sean and Jacob, this isn't your secret to tell yet. I told you because if you'd learned it from Ellie, you would've done exactly this."

Until now, I'd always admired my brother's ability to think clearly. In this moment, he doesn't understand. He can't. Ellie isn't just some piece of ass I'm willing to walk away from. She's my future.

"I don't know how long I can hold it in," I admit. "I'm not going to lose her, Dec. If she figures it out on her own, that would be it. I'd lose her and Hadley, and I'm sorry, I love you and Sean and Jake, but . . . I choose her. And if you, of all people, don't understand that, well then, to hell with you."

Declan made a choice eight years ago, and it cost him everything he loved.

Sydney.

"I need a few days. Let me talk to them, and . . . we'll figure it out. I'm sorry, brother. I really am. Believe me, I made them check the information three times and then pull the police report because I didn't want it to be true. I know you think we're all pissed that you found someone, but we're happy for you. We don't want you to walk away from it. Just . . . give me a few days, and then the chips can fall where they may."

A few days of lying and pretending . . . God help me.

thirty-two

I'm sitting in the teacher's lounge, trying to focus on work. Today, my boss is going to observe me, and all I can think about is Connor.

I need to get it together.

He and his brother were already out when I got up this morning and I missed having coffee with Connor on the front porch. It's become our morning ritual, and now my day feels off because we missed it.

Hadley was a whole other derailment this morning. Getting her up was almost impossible. She was slower than normal and had to ask a question every three seconds. It was a miracle I was able to get to work on time today.

The door opens, and Mrs. Symonds walks in. "Ready for today?"

No.

"Of course," I answer instead.

"You don't have to lie, I know my teachers dread me coming in, but this is an exciting observation, Ellie."

It's my last one. If I get through today with good remarks, it's most likely they'll offer me the permanent position. I'm really hoping that's the case.

I've never had anything that allowed me choices. Having this job gives me an income that provides an independence I need. While Connor and Kevin may be nothing alike, it doesn't mean I will ever be beholden to another man.

I want to love and be equal with Connor.

"I'm actually really ready for it and very hopeful that the outcome suits us both."

She sits at that table and rests her hands on mine. "The last few months you've really blossomed. You've not only been smiling more than I think I've ever seen you do before but also your students are thriving. I never wanted to pry into your personal life, I make an effort not to do so with any of my teachers, but I want you to know that I'm relieved that you're in a better place."

"I am too. It's sad it had to happen the way it did, but I'm happy now."

"You know, Connor was one of my students," she says with a wistful smile. "He was the sweetest of the Arrowood boys. That Jacob was a thorn in my side, but Connor was always the kindhearted one, even if he didn't think he was."

It isn't hard to imagine what he was like back then. He was just eighteen years old, and I was too. We were barely adults, kids who had been forced to grow up rather quickly.

"He's a good man."

"It's sad how those boys grew up. I knew their mom, she was such a wonderful woman, and their father loved her with a ferocity that was unparalleled to anything I'd ever seen before. When she died, he lost it. I remember trying to drop by once, and he was so drunk, I don't think he knew his own name, let alone mine."

I stay quiet, feeding on any information she's willing to share. Connor and I talk about things, but asking him to go back in time is not something I want to do.

"Anyway . . ." She seems to remember herself. "I wish I had stepped in. We all saw the bruises, but back then, it wasn't something teachers reported that often. At least not in a small town like this. So, we all kept quiet, remarked to each other about the tragedy that was the Arrowood brothers, and I've lived with the regrets ever since. It also taught me not to stay quiet when I see things."

"More people need to speak up for those who can't," I say and hope she understands that she's part of what forced me to wake up. "If it weren't for the people who cared about me and Hadley, I don't know that I'd be sitting here today."

Mrs. Symonds wrings her hands together and sighs. "And that would've been a loss I never would have recovered from. I'm hoping today goes well, Ellie. I'd like for us to have more talks in the future."

Her not-so-subtle hint makes me smile. It's one more thing to be grateful about in my life.

"Me too."

"I'll see you in a bit, I need to go grab a cup of coffee."

As soon as Mrs. Symonds leaves, I grab my phone and see a message from Sydney.

Sydney: Hey! I spoke with the judge and your divorce paperwork is being signed today! I should have a copy of the decree very soon.

My back hits the chair and a puff of air expels. It feels like it all happened so fast. Sydney appeared in court today for me, and since the divorce was uncontested and I didn't want any of Kevin's assets, the judge must've signed it.

I'm going to be divorced today.

I thought I would feel different, maybe even just a little sad. Not because I loved him and wanted things to work but because I failed to make the marriage work. In some recess of my mind, I had this belief I'd be like my parents were. Happy, in love, and wanting to raise a family, and I think that's part of why I stayed even when things were so bad.

I wanted to be like them.

My mother married a man who was not like Kevin, though. She wasn't plagued by anger, fists, and the never-ending feeling of not being good enough.

Sometimes, I wonder if she would've stayed if she were in my shoes. I like to think that she wouldn't have.

I send Sydney a text back.

Me: I'm in shock, but there is also a huge sense of relief. Thank you. Thank you for everything.

Sydney: You're welcome. Thank you for trusting me.

I almost tell her that Declan is in town, but I'm pretty sure that wouldn't be welcome news. Plus, I don't know how long he's staying. The note that Connor left this morning explained that they had business to deal with but that *he'd* see me later— not they would see me later.

I did tell Hadley about him being here in case she sees some really tall guy who kind of looks like Connor walking around.

Me: You're a great friend, Syd.

I suddenly don't feel like one.

The last thing I want is for her to be blindsided, so maybe I should at least warn her there is a possibility of her running into him. As I start to type out the text message, the bell rings, and I have to get back to my class.

"Shit," I say looking at the phone. If I send this now, I won't be able to reply to her inevitable questions, which will probably leave her freaking out for the next hour.

I'll just have to tell her later.

Right now, I have a job to secure.

"I got the job!" I yell as I enter the door to find Connor, Hadley, and Declan all in the living room.

"You did?" he asks with a smile that doesn't quite reach his eyes.

I nod. "I did. Mrs. Symonds said I nailed it and then offered me a full-time position! It means benefits and time off. I'm so excited!"

Hadley runs over and wraps her arms around my legs. "Good job, Mommy!"

"Congratulations," Connor says and then he kisses my cheek before retreating quickly.

I don't know why he's being weird, but I'm going to assume it's because his brother is sitting here.

"It's a day of a lot of great news."

"What else?"

I hold up my finger, asking him to give me a minute. This last part I don't want Hadley here for. Regardless of how great she seems to be taking everything, I'd rather not say it like this. She knows I'm divorcing who she's always known as her father, but she doesn't need to know all the details.

I look down at Hadley. "Did you finish all your homework?"

"Yup."

"And did you do your chores?"

"Yes."

Of course, the one day she's on top of her life is the day I need her to have something else to do for a minute or two. I look to Connor for a little help.

He puts his hand on her shoulders. "Why don't you show my brother the tree house?"

Her eyes widen, and she turns her smile to Declan. "Do you want to see it?"

He looks over at Connor and tries to match her enthusiasm, but it looks almost painful. "Uhh, sure."

Clearly, he isn't a kid guy, and if I didn't want to tell Connor about my news from Sydney, I would follow Hadley and Declan out to the tree house just to watch the man climb it in his expensive-looking suit.

Connor grins. "Oh, you'll love it, Dec. You can climb a tree again and hopefully not fall out."

"Great. It sounds like a ton of fun."

"Take your time with him, Hadley. He's old, and it's probably going to be hard for him to move quickly," Connor says with a laugh.

Declan glares at him. "I'll show you old."

"You could try, but you might break a hip. If you're hurt, I'm not coming to help you."

There's a teasing edge to his voice, but then there's an undercurrent of something else. Almost like he's angry at him, which I don't understand. Declan has been really nice since he's been here. I hope to meet the rest of his brothers soon, and that one day, they'll accept Hadley and me. Since she is their niece.

That thought sobers me.

She's gained an entire family. Where before it was Kevin and me, now she has Connor and his entire family.

"I won't be gone too long, but then again, you don't need all that much time anyway," Declan says as he claps him on the back. "You were always a finish-too-fast kind of guy."

Now I can't hold back, I burst out laughing.

"See?" Declan's voice dances with mirth. "Even Ellie knows it."

"Oh, no. I didn't say anything," I defend quickly.

"Hadley, make sure you have a tea party up there. Declan loves talking to and playing with dolls."

"Okay!" she says with all the joy that she can muster.

The two of them head out of the house, and before I can say a word, Connor hauls me into his arms and gives me the hottest, most intense kiss he's ever given me. He isn't normally this aggressive, but it feels as though something else is driving him.

I hold on to him and give it back, pouring myself into it. Last night, I had plans for something very similar to this. I wanted to give myself to him—at least give as much as I could.

His mouth is warm and soft against mine, and I want more. My lips part, and we both move at the same time. With my back against the wall and his strong body pressing against me, I'm trapped in the best way.

My fingers move up his arms to the back of his neck, and he deepens the kiss. His hands move down my body and then hook under my thighs, lifting me off the floor.

Instinctually, I wrap my legs around his waist as he carries me.

"Connor," I say breathlessly.

"God, you drive me crazy. I want you so bad."

"I need you."

And I do. I need him, and I need us, and I don't care that it isn't like I planned. Nothing in my life ever goes that way anyway. If it had, I wouldn't be in this man's arms at all, which would be a sin.

"Ellie," he murmurs and then brings his lips back to me. "My beautiful angel."

We kiss continuously—each one bleeding into the next and causing my lips to plump under the assault. I want it to go on forever. Minutes go by, and I swear that I want to rip my clothes off and take him now.

I don't even know if I'm breathing since what exists in this world is Connor and his perfect mouth on mine.

He pushes me higher against the wall, using his thighs as leverage to hold me up, and then his hands are on my breasts. I moan, head falling back as he touches me.

I know I had something to say to him, but I can't remember.

Something big.

Something about . . .

"I'm divorced," I say the words, knowing I need to get them out while I remember my name.

His hands stop and he watches me. "You're . . ."

"Divorced. As of today."

"That means . . ." He pauses.

"That means that you and I, well, I'm hoping it means that what we were just doing here can be something we do when we're not trying to steal a few minutes."

He looks down at our situation and curses. "Fuck!"

"Hey," I say quickly, touching his cheek. "What's wrong?"

"This is not how . . . Jesus, Ellie, I'm sorry. I was like a madman a second ago."

He slowly puts my feet back on the floor and then cups my face in his warm hands, which I really liked on my breasts a moment ago. "I wanted you just as badly."

"There's stuff we need to talk about, and I lost my mind for a minute."

"It's fine," I reassure him. "I promise, we have plenty of time to talk."

His eyes flash with something I don't quite catch. "Just . . . I don't want to do this now or here. Not when Hadley and Declan can come walking back in. You and I, we need some time."

I nod. "I agree. We have a lot to talk about."

"Yeah." He breathes the word.

"Okay, when is your brother leaving?"

He looks out the door and runs his fingers through his hair. "Tonight. He has to get back to New York."

That gives me some relief from the guilt of not calling Sydney when I got out of work to talk about him being here. "Okay, so maybe I can ask Syd to keep Hadley tomorrow?"

I plan to have Connor all to myself.

His smile doesn't quite touch his eyes. "Tomorrow then."

"Tomorrow."

thirty-three

I pull up to the house and check my face in the mirror. I really wish I had some time to change into something sexy or really do any primping at all. Thankfully, I spent a good extra twenty minutes in the shower shaving and scrubbing areas I sort of have let go the last few months.

Tonight, I need everything to be perfect.

Hadley is at Sydney's house, where they have a whole girls' night planned with nails, hair, and movies. I'd let my daughter go on and on about everything she was going to do until my friend shooed me out the door with a comment about making good choices and wiggling her brows with a grin.

Yes, we all know what is going to happen tonight.

Nerves hit me like a ton of bricks, cementing me in place. I know that I love him, and I want this. I know that if we hadn't been worried about Declan and Hadley coming back last night, I would've let him strip me down right there in the hallway.

Desire and trust aren't the issue—it's fear that I'm not going to be what he wants.

I'd only ever been with him that one night, and then I was with Kevin. If you ask my now ex-husband, he'd tell you I was terrible in bed.

I worry that Connor will feel the same.

My head drops to the steering wheel as I fret over a whole new set of things for a few long minutes until I hear a knock on the window beside me and scream.

"What the—"

Connor is standing there, looking at me with concern in his eyes. "You planning on staying here?"

"I'm planning on trying to remember how to breathe first."

He gives me a soft smile and opens the door. "I heard the car and waited, but you didn't come into the house."

"I was having a sort of freak out, but I'm okay now."

I get out of the car and take his hand. When we get to the front door, he turns to me. "Ellie, I don't want you to be nervous. I want to talk, and hopefully, we can—"

My hand presses against his lips, silencing him. We've talked and talked and talked. I'm not up for more of that tonight.

No, tonight, I'm done with words.

"I'm not nervous, Connor." And then I stop myself. I don't want to lie to him. "Okay, I am, but not for the reasons you think. I'm nervous because, for the first time in my life, I feel like things are good. You're everything, and I want us right now—"

Connor's lips are on mine before I can say anything else. They are soft, sweet, and nothing like they were last night.

We aren't worried about time or anyone else tonight. We have nothing to stop us from loving one another now.

I pull back, needing to say what's in my heart. "I love you."

"You have no idea how much I love you, Ellie. There's no way I could ever explain it."

I lift my hand, brushing my fingers against his stubble. "Then show me. We can talk after."

He hesitates for a second before leaning down and scooping me up into his arms. We don't say anything else because, sometimes, more words aren't needed.

We reach his bedroom, and he pushes the door open. My head rests on his chest, and I can hear the steady thrum of his heart. I want to memorize this sound. Each second of this night, I want embedded in my brain.

To be loved, truly loved, is all I've ever wanted.

He sets me on the bed and then takes a step back.

"What's wrong?"

"Wrong?" he asks.

"You . . . you're well, you're over there."

Connor closes his eyes and breathes through his nose. "I have things I need to say."

I get to my feet and go to him. "We've talked a lot the last few months, and right now, I want to feel. Will you let me feel?"

He wants me to ask for what I want, and I'm doing it. I don't want to talk about our pasts or our future. I want the present.

"I'll give you everything you want."

I shake my head. "All I want is you."

I lean up on my toes and bring our lips together. He has no idea how frantically my heart is pounding in my chest or how him saying those words was enough to bring me to my knees, but it did. The trust I have in us is staggering.

Never before did I think I would be able to do that. Being vulnerable is scary and raw. Too many times, I've tried to avoid it because I learned that, when you allow another person to have the power to hurt you, they will.

However, I don't think he will.

He would never hurt me—not intentionally.

Connor's hands move from my arms up to my neck so he can tilt my face and deepen the kiss. He walks us backward, our mouths still together until I hit the bed.

"Lie down," he instructs.

I do as he asks and slide onto my back. He doesn't follow, though. He stands back, looking down at me. "Please don't make me beg," I say with a shaky breath.

I need him. No matter what tonight proves in regards to how we are together now, I need him.

"Never. I will never make you beg."

"Then love me."

"Always. Even though I don't deserve you, I want you to know that you own my heart."

"And you own mine."

"God, I hope so."

Before I can think too much about that, he moves to me and lifts my shirt from my body. I also made sure I wore matching underwear, so Connor finds a deep purple bra with lace that barely covers anything.

"Jesus Christ," he says under his breath and then his mouth is on my neck.

He kisses his way down but doesn't move the fabric. His warm mouth covers my very hard nipple through the lace, giving me so many different sensations all at once.

There's the scrape of the lace against my overly sensitive nipple mixed with the wetness from his tongue finding my skin the fabric doesn't cover. My fingers are in his hair, and my eyes are closed as I allow myself to get lost to him.

He moves to the other side, and his fingers tuck under the strap as he slowly pulls it down. The feel of his callused hands on my skin is overwhelming.

"You want more, Angel?" he asks as his mouth moves back up to my ear.

"Yes, I want it all."

His groan is husky as he drags his lips down the column of my neck. "Then you'll get all I have. Every-fucking-thing that I am will be yours."

He pulls the other side of my bra down, exposing my breasts to him. His tongue darts out, circling around my nipple, and then he takes it into his mouth, lavishing it with heat.

I could die. I thought what we did the last time was hot, but being in his bed, where everything around me is his, is almost too much.

I can't breathe without smelling his cologne. I can't open my eyes without seeing something that's his. And I feel him. Everywhere.

His hand moves down the front of my body to my jeans. Slowly, he undoes the button, and the sound of the zipper is loud, but it's nothing compared to the sound of my breathing. I'm so turned on.

Connor watches me, and I nod, letting him know I still want this. He glides my pants down, removing my underwear too, and I've never felt more exposed and liberated at the same time.

He looks at me as though I'm a priceless piece of art that he's won. Lips parted and eyes warm as his gaze caresses my bare body.

"You humble me, Ellie." His voice is thick with emotion.

I don't say anything for fear of breaking out in tears, and wouldn't that be the most embarrassing thing ever? So, I sit up and brush my fingertips along the slope of his jaw before dropping them to the hem of his shirt and lifting it.

The last time we fooled around, I didn't get this part. He wouldn't let me touch him, and this time, we're going to be equals. It's only fair to have him naked too.

We both move slowly, savoring the seconds that we have. I don't need to rush tonight, in fact, if I could, I'd put it in slow motion, allowing every single moment to last a little longer.

Connor is absolutely breathtaking without a shirt on. I know it isn't a manly word, but that's all I have. My brain is scrambled as I look over the finest male specimen I could ever dream of.

Each muscle is firm, and the skin strains against them. His stomach is all ridges and valleys that my fingers itch to explore. The muscles on his arms are thick, and even though they've been wrapped around my body as they held me, I didn't fully grasp how powerful they were.

I trace the tips of my fingers from his forearm up to his shoulders and then down his stomach, enjoying the flexing of the muscles as I touch him. He's holding perfectly still, allowing me to explore, so I move to his other arm and look at the tattoo on his shoulder. "What does this mean?"

It's a series of what look like Celtic knots in the shape of a triangle. "It's the symbol of brotherhood."

"It looks like the spear of an arrow and is beautiful."

His smile is soft. "Each of us has one."

I lean forward and press my lips to it. Then I get up on my knees and go around to his back, needing to see every inch of skin he has on display. I find another tattoo right below his shoulder blade. "And this?"

My fingers trace the black ink of the skeleton of a frog holding a trident of some sort. "That's a tattoo that SEALs get when we lose someone in the line of duty. It's a bone frog because we are frogmen."

"I'm sorry you lost someone."

Connor's hand wraps around my wrist, and he pulls me back to his front. "I've lost a lot of people in my life, and God, I pray I never lose you."

"You never will."

His eyes close as his forehead rests on mine. "I'm trying to be patient, but you're killing me, love. I need to touch your perfect skin," he says as his hand roams down my side. "I need to kiss every inch of you." His lips find purchase on my upper chest, right above where I really want his mouth again. "I want to feel myself inside you." I make an incoherent sound of pleasure as he lays me back down. "But right now, I really want to make you come on my tongue."

And then I'm pretty sure I melt into oblivion. "Connor," I say, not really sure what I'm asking for. I want him, but God, it's been so long since anyone has cared about me or my pleasure.

I don't even know what I like or want.

"What, love?"

"I just . . . it's been . . . I don't know."

"Shh," he coos. "Just tell me if I do something you don't like."

I release a deep breath and try to relax. He will never hurt or force me to do something I don't want or like. I have to trust him, and I do.

He parts my legs, and then kisses the insides of my thighs. I relax as much as I can with equal amounts of nerves and desire swirling around. Then I feel his mouth move down toward the juncture of my legs, and my breathing is so heavy my head is swimming.

"Relax, Ellie, I'm going to make you feel good."

And then he does. His tongue swipes against my opening, drawing pleasure from me in a way I haven't felt since . . .

him. He licks, sucks, and teases my clit, pushing me higher and higher and then easing me back down. He does this a few times, which makes me want to scream, cry, and beg him to never stop. It feels so good I almost can't take it.

I'm panting and holding the sheets in a death grip as an orgasm sits on the brink of exploding. I call out his name, and he sucks harder and then flicks his tongue. Then I'm gone.

Everything is light and perfect and I never want to come down.

He crawls up the length of my body, and I stare at him, wondering how the hell we ever found each other again and what a stroke of luck it was. I take advantage of this position and move to his jeans, needing to touch him.

He helps me get them off and then my breathing catches. He's magnificent. His cock is thick and long, and everything I remember and have fantasized over. My fingers wrap around him and start to move. Connor's eyes close, and I need him to talk. The silence is deafening.

"Am I doing it right?"

"Oh, love, you couldn't do it wrong. You touch me, and I'm in fucking heaven."

He shifts a little, lying on his side and this angle is much better. Our lips meet again as I continue to stroke him. "I want you to make love to me," I say. "Now, Connor. I need you."

He kisses me harder and then moves so he's on top of me.

His lips are back on mine as he settles himself between us. We look at each other, and I have to get out all that's inside me. It's too much. The emotion, the pleasure, the feelings that I can't contain. "I love you. I love you because you make me happy. You give without want, and I have never had that. I love you because you loved Hadley and me before you knew we were truly yours, but I am yours, Connor. I think in some way, I always have been. Please, take me and love me."

He doesn't say anything, but he doesn't have to. I see everything in his heart in those gorgeous green eyes. I feel what his soul is saying as his lips claim mine and he slowly slides into me, changing my own soul irrevocably.

thirty-four

I'm going to hell.

I can't seem to care enough about the descent to get there to stop. My entire plan was thrown out the door when she begged. Denying her was impossible, and I had to have her just once.

I know I'm a bastard. There isn't a doubt in my mind that she'll hate me for this, but at least I can hold this night with me when she's gone.

"That was . . ." Ellie says, trying to catch her breath.

It was every fantasy I've ever had.

It was every fantasy I never knew to have.

It was everything I hoped and feared, and it'll be the last time.

"Yeah," I say, lying on my back, staring up at the ceiling, and wishing to God I could have more time. "It was."

She curls against my side, her arm resting on my chest,

and I hold her tighter. I keep telling myself to say the words, to tell her what I know and give her the truth, but then I bargain for another moment. I would go back in time, do anything to undo the past, but I can't, and I hate myself more than I can ever express.

All I want is to make her happy, and now, something that happened eight years ago—something that changed both of our lives but was neither of our doing—is going to force me to break her heart. In turn, it will destroy mine.

I always thought that if I ever told someone about what happened, the weight would be lifted from me. For so long, I've held it in, pushed it from my mind so that I could live with myself. How wrong I was. I would do anything to keep it inside until the end of time.

It was why I worked so hard in the military, because I needed to be a better person and try to save someone.

I knew that coming back here would resurrect a lot of ghosts from my past, I never thought it would collide with my future. A future I want more than the very breath in my lungs or heart in my chest.

Fuck my father.

Fuck Declan.

Fuck everyone who knew they'd be the sole source of pain for the person they loved and were too selfish to walk away.

My brothers and I are ready for whatever the consequences may be. They're willing to take the fall because they know I can't be a father to Hadley or the man Ellie needs with this secret between us.

I can't do this to her, and yet, I have to.

How am I going to say the words? I try to concoct a plan that could mitigate the damage, but there is none.

"Connor?"

I look down at the very sated Ellie who doesn't seem to

have a worry in the world. "Yes?"

I wonder if she can see my guilt. If she can feel the angst that's rolling around inside me, the self-resentment that is growing with each passing minute. Does she know that I love her? Does she know I was willing to fight my brothers for her? Will it matter?

"I love you."

And that's my undoing. She loves me, a man whose father stole two lives from her. She told me about how hard it was losing her parents. All these years her mystery has gone unsolved and now my father can't even pay for the pain he caused her.

Why did it have to be her?

Why couldn't it be anyone else?

"I love you, Ellie. I fucking love you with my entire fucking world and . . ." I have to say it. It has to be now. Here, in the bed, naked after loving her with all that I am, I have to break her.

When she sits up, her eyes are filled with a million questions. "What's wrong?"

"I have to tell you something."

"Okay." Her voice shakes a little.

I shift so that we're facing each other. I have to be a goddamn man and own up to what happened when I was basically a kid.

What I'm not ready for is to lose her.

"Eight years ago, the night we met, do you remember I said that my father and I went at it?"

She seems to visibly relax and nods. "Yes, of course."

"We were arguing about something that happened the night of my high school graduation, which was the week before. My brothers were home for my ceremony. They knew I had joined the navy and wanted to be here for my swearing-in ceremony."

Her fingers link with mine, and I swallow hard. Jesus, she's fucking comforting me. The knot in my stomach is so tight it hurts.

"We don't have to talk about this . . ."

"Yes, we do. That night, Ellie, the night of my high school graduation was a fucking nightmare. My father had been drinking, like always, and he was out of control. He was yelling at everyone, calling my brothers and I names. He tried to take a swing at Sean, but he wasn't a kid anymore, so they ended up fighting. It was . . . well, another fun night for the Arrowood brothers. The four of us took off for the barn, like we always did when we wanted to get away. And that's where mistake number one happened."

"I don't understand."

"We left."

She shakes her head. "I still don't get it."

"He never had access to the car keys. He wasn't a fun or silly drunk. He was belligerent and thought he was better and smarter than any of us. Good ole Dad thought he could do what he wanted because no one tells an Arrowood how to live."

She starts to fidget her hands. "He drove?"

There's no going back now. Here is where I have to say the words.

"Yes, he drove, but he didn't drive his truck. He wanted to teach Sean a lesson so he took his car. Declan saw the headlights pulling away from the house, and we ran. We got into the back of Jacob's truck and took off. But we didn't have a plan. I mean . . . how do you get a drunk driver to pull over?"

"Connor . . . I don't understand."

Of course, she doesn't. She has a good heart and wouldn't put two and two together. Or maybe she will. The look in her eyes tells me that she knows where this horrible story is going.

"We followed him through three towns, trying to figure out a way to get him to stop. The entire time, we argued over what to do. I wanted to run him off the road, let him kill himself because it would be a gift, but Jacob refused. We were still arguing when we saw another car coming. I swear, Ellie, all four of our hearts stopped beating. We were screaming, flashing the lights to get the oncoming car to stop. They didn't see that my father was swerving so badly he probably didn't even know what lane he was in. Jake tried, he bumped the back of Sean's car, hoping that it would send him into a ditch, but . . ."

"But it sent him into oncoming traffic." She barely gets the words out.

"Into the other car."

Her eyes close, and a tear falls down her beautiful cheek. "Into my parents."

I wait until she looks at me, praying she sees the regret and sorrow in my eyes. "Yes."

thirty-five

I sit here, replaying the words in my head over and over. His father was responsible.

My body feels as though thousands of ice shards are poking me. I keep shaking my hands, hoping the feeling comes back. I struggle to draw air into my lungs, and it's as though the walls are caving in. I can't stay here. I can't just . . . sit here.

I jump to my feet, pulling the sheet with me and wrapping it around my body, my stomach roiling and saliva flooding my mouth. I'm going to be sick if I sit still a second longer.

He was there. He saw my parents be killed. By his father.

He knew. He fucking knew what happened, and all this time, he's kept this from me.

"Ellie," he says from behind me.

"No! No! Don't say another word."

My mind is going in circles as I look at him. Connor, the man who I am so in love with that I gave myself to him wholly, the man who held me after I had been beaten, had been lying to me. He vowed to protect me, built a tree house for Hadley, made me believe in him, and all for what? All so he . . . could . . . break my fucking heart?

His chest rises and falls as he extends his hand toward me. "Ellie, let me explain."

There's no way he can. He used me, just like Kevin. Anger churns in my gut, and I explode. "You knew!" I scream. "You knew, and you, what? You came and rescued me so that you could ease your conscience? Was I some game? Was this fun for you? Save the girl whose parents you killed?"

His eyes widen. "No! What happened with us had nothing to do with any of this."

"Right." I laugh. "The hell it didn't. You were there, Connor! You were there, and you kept your big secret, and now you tell me? After all of *this*!" I point to the bed where I let him love me. I felt his love all the way through my bones, and now I want to break every last one of them.

How could he do this to me? How could he use me like this?

"I didn't know until the other day."

Please. "I'm not a fool. Sure, I've acted like one, and I was the dumb girl who stayed in an abusive marriage, but I wasn't lying about any of it. I gave you everything! I gave you my heart, my love, our *daughter*!" I scream the last word through a sob. "God, you let me tell her! You fucking asshole! How could you do this to her?"

My tears fall easily while my heart breaks into a million pieces. I trusted him. I thought that he wouldn't lie to me, but he did. He has been all along.

I wipe my face, feeling angry and broken.

"I didn't know until Declan came. He pieced it together, and I swear that's the truth. I love you, and I love Hadley, I would never hurt you on purpose."

Well, he's a little late for that. It's exactly what he did. He used me to get what he wanted.

"If that's true, then you still knew before you let us share a night together. Why? So you could get laid before you told me you saw who killed my parents?" I can't stop yelling at him. I feel so betrayed. He was supposed to be different.

Connor was the man who would never do this to me, and yet he is.

"I didn't plan this, Ellie. I had every intention of telling you! Hell, I tried when you got here!"

"Don't you dare put this on me! You had plenty of opportunity, but you didn't."

He grips the side of his head before his shoulders slump. "I'm not putting any blame on you. I should've told you, you're right."

"Then why didn't you?"

He watches me, his breaths coming in short bursts and then he looks to the ceiling. "Because I didn't want to say it. I didn't want to ever say the words, least of all to you. Maybe I'm a bastard, but I need you. The idea of hurting you was fucking killing me, but you deserved to know more than I wanted to protect myself."

"There's no maybe about your being a bastard, Connor. You lied to me. You used me, and you used the fact that I love you to gain what you wanted."

I'm such a fool. Always the damn fool with her hand in the jar, hoping to find a cookie and then getting bit by something.

That's what I am.

"I didn't use you. I made love to you because I knew this would be all I got. I knew that, once I told you the truth, you'd leave me, and I love you more than anything in the world."

I shake my head, tears falling as I stare at the man I no longer know. "Love? Love doesn't take. Love doesn't rob someone of choice. Love gives, and love cares. You took something from me, not just that night, but right now."

His eyes are filled with regret and sadness as I tear through him. "I fell in love with you not knowing who you were. I have lived with the guilt of what happened for eight years. I didn't know, Ellie. Hurting you goes against every fiber in my being. I would take a bullet, cut my arm off, or anything to avoid it."

He may think that's what he means, but I don't believe him. He shot the bullet, right through my fucking heart. "Go back to where you say you didn't know. When didn't you know?"

Connor licks his lips and then closes his eyes. "Ever since the day I met you . . ."

"When we met at the bar where my parents were last," I say with new knowledge dawning on me. "I want to know everything. I want you to tell me every detail on how it happened." He . . . he knows what happened, knows how broken I've been because of it, and he never told me. "After their car flipped and they were left for dead, what happened then?"

Connor swallows, his Adam's apple bobbing before he speaks. "We pulled over immediately, and Declan and I jumped out to help your parents while Jake and Sean went after my father, who kept driving as though it didn't happen. We tried to help them, but . . . they were . . ."

"The coroner told me that they died instantly." My voice sounds detached.

"When I got to their car, they weren't breathing."

It's as they said. "So, you didn't . . . try? You just ran and left them?"

"I'm not proud of what we did. You know me, Ellie." Connor takes a step closer, but I retreat. He cannot touch me. I will lose it, and I'm barely holding on. "I'm not a monster. I was a fucking wreck, and it took my three brothers to literally pull me into the truck. I wanted to go to the cops, but we were fucking kids. We didn't know what to do or what any of it meant.

We had a plan to get him home, call the cops, and have him arrested."

I shake my head in disgust. "Then why didn't you?"

None of these answers do anything to quell the storm inside me. All I can focus on is that the man I love was somewhat responsible for my parents' deaths. This entire time, I've thought about how much they'd love him. I hoped they'd be proud of the man I found and grew to love. How could they ever feel that way now?

"When he woke the next day, the four of us told him what he'd done. He laughed and called us fools for thinking we could get away with turning him in. It was Sean's car that caused the accident, after all, and he said someone most likely saw Sean driving the car back to the farm around the time of the accident. We were all known troublemakers, so he threatened to tell everyone it was Sean driving the entire time."

What a horrific man his father was. "And Sean's car?"

The one thing that has always eluded me was what happened to the car that ran them off the road. It was the only clue we hoped to find. All we pieced together was it was a red car due to the paint transfer.

He moves toward me and then stops himself. I can see how much pain he's in, but I need to know. "It's in one of the storage garages on the property."

The entire time I'd been searching, it was right next door.

"Did your father know who I was?" I barely get the words out. My heart is pounding, and it actually hurts to breathe.

"I hadn't seen or spoken to him since the night I left. None of us had. My brothers and I left town and swore we'd never see him again. He was a manipulative piece of shit who broke everything he touched. We made a pact that we would never marry, never have children, and never be like him."

I don't really give a shit about his pact. Not when I feel dead inside. My fingers tremble so hard I'm worried they'll break, but I've been beaten down before and I can take a punch. "Answer my question."

"If I had to guess based on the fact that he managed to force his sons back to the one place they never wanted to step foot in again, then yes, I think he probably knew who you were."

Unreal. What a horrific man he had to have been to use his kids to cover up a hit and run, only to turn around and be nice to Hadley and me. It's too much. I hate him for what he's taken from me, yet again.

"How can this be happening?" I ask aloud.

Connor steps forward again before stopping. "If I could bring him back to life to kill him myself I would. I hate him, Ellie. I would fight him over and over again, but I can't change any of it. If we hadn't fought that night, I would've never met you, and even if I lose you, God help me, you would still be the best thing in my life."

I wipe my eyes, wondering one more thing. "That night we met, what did you *really* fight with your father about—the whole thing?"

He sits on the bed, head falling down as his eyes lift to mine. "I was the only brother still living here, but he found out I was leaving for boot camp in the morning. He threatened me, demanding I stay because my brothers and I were under his thumb. He told me that he had power and the ability to fuck all our lives and that I wouldn't go to the military if I was arrested. Sean was playing college ball, Jacob just got his first acting gig on a sitcom, and Declan was already on his way with his startup. All of us had something to lose, but he didn't. He'd already lost it all. There were only two things he cared about: my mother and this farm. I told him if he ever breathed a word about it, I would ruin his business. I'd tell every farmer, supplier, and buyer that he was an abusive drunk who killed two people and blamed his sons. We would ruin him as much as he ruined us. He told me to get out and never come back.

So, I left, and I met you . . ."

My stomach plummets, and my head is fuzzy from the on-slaught of information. Before I can catch my breath, I start to crumble, and then Connor's arms are around me. I bury my face against his chest. I cry for my parents, who lost their lives on the side of the road. I cry for the four boys, whose father was so heinous he used his sons to get away with murder. And I cry for myself and everything I'd lost.

For what I am still going to lose when I walk out of this room.

I cry because I've never loved another the way I love him and I can't stay. I let it all out in the comfort of his arms be-cause I'm not strong enough to do it any other way.

"I'm so sorry, Ellie. You have no idea. I hate myself. I wish I could go back in time, but I can't. Please don't fucking leave me. I love you and will spend the rest of my life proving that to you. Please, say you won't leave me."

I wish I didn't have to. But that is not a promise I can keep. Maybe I could have if they hadn't left my parents on the side of the road alone, if they had waited for paramedics to show up. If they had, I would have at least had answers.

He has no idea what I went through afterward, the weeks I spent doing nothing but searching for clues. I called every body shop, gas station, and junkyard looking for a red car that had been dropped off with unexplained damage. I called the cops sometimes three times a day, asking them if there were any leads. I was desperate for answers, hoping that I could just . . . know.

That night changed the trajectory of my life, and maybe if I had answers I wouldn't have been so emotionally broken that I married a man like Kevin.

Chasing that thought is that, had I gotten my answers back then, I never would have met Connor in that bar. Hadley wouldn't exist.

That is unbearable for me to consider, and I refuse to walk down that path of what-if.

God, I want so desperately to believe that he didn't know any of this until his brother showed up. I really do. But the trust is gone, and I don't know if I'll ever believe him again.

I made that mistake with Kevin each time he told me he would never hit me again, and I won't blindly follow a man, regardless of the love I have for him. After everything I've endured, I'd rather take the loss now than later when I'm in far too deep.

Not that I think I haven't already hit that place. The love I have for Connor is unlike anything I've ever felt before. Losing him . . . well, that might destroy me.

The sobs continue until my body is empty. I'm hollow and broken. I don't remember how I got back into the bed. I have no memories of wrapping my limbs around him as though, if I only held on tightly enough, I wouldn't have to let go, but here I am.

I lean back, waiting for him to tell me this was a bad dream, but the look in his eyes tells me it isn't.

"I have to go," I say, my voice raw and hoarse.

"No," he says quickly.

I lift myself off him, my heart breaking with the loss of his touch.

"You had to know this was going to be the outcome."

"What do you want me to do? Turn myself in? I'll do it. I'll go right now and see Sheriff Mendoza and confess."

I shake my head, a new wave of tears coming. "I don't want or need that, Connor. I sure as hell don't want another one of Hadley's fathers in jail."

He takes my face in his hands. "Tell me what I can do."

That's the thing, there's nothing. He didn't actually drive the car that killed them, none of them did. If he were to go to the sheriff, all it would do is hurt people who have already paid for the sins of their father.

"You can make this as easy as possible for me. You can show me that you love me by allowing me to get off this bed and walk out the door without having this be any harder than it already will be."

His jaw clenches as if he wants to argue, but then he sits up and moves to the side of the bed. He's doing exactly what I asked, and yet, it feels like another betrayal. I don't want to lose him. The idea of walking away is killing me, but I have to get my head straight.

I can't make the same mistakes.

I slide off the bed, grab my clothes, and head for the bathroom.

Once dressed, I look at myself in the mirror. Who is this woman? It's been months since I've cried. Months of feeling strong, beautiful, and smart. All of that gone in one instant. I think about Hadley and the lessons I've fought to teach her.

She is going to be crushed—more so than she ever was about Kevin. She loves Connor. She loves living here and had hopes that will dissipate like mist when I tell her.

Once again, I've chosen wrong.

I exit the bathroom and find him leaning against the wall. Our eyes meet, and I have to look away. He is my weakness, and right now, I need strength.

"Where will you go?" he finally asks, breaking the silence.

"I'll go to Sydney's for tonight. Then I don't know. I guess I'll look for a place."

"Stay here."

"Here?"

He pushes off the wall, coming close but not touching me. "Yes, this is where Hadley is happy and comfortable. You can stay here, and I'll find somewhere else."

"You want me to stay in this house?"

"I want you to stay with me, but I'm trying to make this easier and let you go."

Nothing about this is easy.

"I need some time. I can't pretend that none of this happened. I want to believe that you didn't know and that your brother just filled you in, but it's all very . . ."

"You don't have to say more. If you need time, I'll give it to you."

I want to throw myself at him, beg him to hold me, and refuse to allow any space or time to separate us. But wants are dreams, and I have both feet in reality now.

"Hadley will want to see you."

A deep sigh comes from his throat as his face pales. "I'll be here. Anytime . . . for either of you."

I head to the front door, not caring about clothes or anything because nothing matters. I grab my purse off the front table and pause with my hand on the door.

Just open it, Ellie. Walk away because you know you have to.

But my hand is frozen because I can feel him at my back. "Ellie . . ."

As I close my eyes, another tear falls and a sob lodges in my throat. Nothing has ever hurt so much.

Nothing.

I'd take a thousand more beatings if it meant that I never had to endure this moment.

I push a breath out, straighten my shoulders, and dig for whatever strength I might have to push forward. "Goodbye, Connor."

And then I walk out the door and make it to my car.

Once I'm halfway down the drive and the house is no longer in view, I put the car in park and cry harder than I've ever cried before.

thirty-six

It's been two days.

Two days of complete and utter misery. I can't eat. I can't sleep. I manage to be strong when Hadley is around, but even that is half-hearted.

"Mommy, where is Connor?"

The eyes I'm trying to avoid stare back at me. Her lip quivers, and I reach my hand out to stop the trembling. "He's at his house."

"Why are we still at Sydney's?"

Because we don't have anywhere else to go.

Lying to her goes against everything, but I can't tell her the truth. "He's not feeling well, so we're going to stay here until he is."

She tilts her head to the side. "Shouldn't we be there for him?"

My heart feels as though it's about to rip out of my chest. I want to be there with him, but how can I?

How can I forgive him after all that happened? He lied to me. All this time, I've been giving my soul to him, only to have it crushed.

"Not now."

"When can we go home?" she asks.

I sit up, taking her hands in mine and attempt to smile. She's been through so much and I feel as though I've failed her again. I put my faith, once again, in a man who didn't deserve it. All these years my life has gone down a path because of the choices his family made.

Now I have to prepare our daughter for the new path. The one where a family we were building falls apart.

"Hadley, Connor and I . . . we're . . . well, we are taking some time apart."

"But!" She rips her hands from mine. "I love him."

"I love him too, but sometimes it's not that simple."

Hadley's head moves side to side in denial. "We have to go back, Mommy! We have to. Connor loves us, and he makes you happy. You don't cry anymore, and Connor doesn't hit you!"

There are wounds that aren't physical. "I know that, honey, but we had a fight and we agreed that we needed to take a break."

Her eyes widen and then she touches my face with her hand. "He's my best friend."

"And he's your father and will always be a part of your life. I will never take that away from you."

Tears leak from her eyes, and everything inside me is tightening. Breath by breath, it constricts as I watch my baby grapple with what I'm saying.

Surely, this can't be how it should feel. When I left Kevin, it was freeing. This doesn't feel free. It feels like agony.

"Please, Mommy! Please! We have to go back. I have a treehouse, and he doesn't know what to do with the animals! We have to help him. He needs us and . . . and . . . he never makes us sad. Connor takes us to get pumpkins and apples. *Please!*"

Please make this stop.

I can't stop the tears that fall down my face. Watching her fall apart this way is bound to destroy me.

My fingers graze her cheek, wiping the tear that falls. "You will always have Connor, Hadley. Always. I know this is hard for you to understand, but sometimes, we have to walk away from someone we care about, even when they take us for pumpkins and apples. Sometimes, it doesn't work."

And sometimes, you want to die in the process.

Her chest rises and falls fast, breaths coming out in loud puffs. "I want to go back to Connor!"

I do too.

"I know, and I'm sorry. You have no idea how much I love you, Hadley, and I would do anything for you, but I can't give you this."

"You always forgave Daddy." Her voice quivers. "I don't know why you can't forgive Connor."

And with that, a sob breaks from her chest as she runs down the hall. When the door slams, I jump and another part of me shatters.

"Ellie, I'm worried," Sydney says at four in the morning.

I've cried non-stop since my talk with Hadley. If it wasn't

hysterical tears where she was holding me, it was a constant stream.

I haven't been able to recount what happened because it's too painful, and I'm not one hundred percent sure of what Sydney's legal responsibilities would be. I have no idea if she has to report it. Hell, she might already know since she and Declan used to date.

Everything is a mess.

"I'll be fine."

"Will you? Because I've never seen anyone cry this much. What happened?"

I want to talk to someone, but I'm not sure the words will come. "I learned a lot that night. Things that Connor probably hoped I'd never know, and . . . I can't be with him."

"Did he hurt you? Because, I swear to God, I'll kill him."

"No, not like that. Not . . . physically or anything. It's just some things about the night we met."

"Oh," she says as she rubs my back. "Well, that was eight years ago, right?"

"Yeah, but it's complicated."

"I'm sure it is, but you guys have come such a long way. I hate to see you fall apart over something that happened when you were still practically kids."

If she knew what it was, I'm sure she wouldn't think that. In the end, the only two people whose opinions would matter aren't here to give them.

"I'm not sure there's a way to fix it. Hell, I don't know how I could overlook it even if I wanted to."

She shakes her head. "I wish you would tell me so I could help you."

"The details don't matter." Well, they do, but not in regards to her.

"Okay, then tell me without the details."

I lean back on the couch, clutching the pillow to my chest. "Connor knew what happened to my parents."

Her eyes widen. Sydney is aware of how my parents died and that their case had gone cold years ago. "He knew?"

"Yes, he did. He claims he didn't know who I was when we met and that he really didn't figure it out until four days ago, but he knew what happened that night."

That's the part that has me the most confused. How could he not put it together? Had I known that his father was involved in a hit and run on the same night my parents died, I would have put it together.

He didn't.

"And do you believe him?"

"I don't know."

Sydney leans back, tucking her legs under her butt. "I've known Connor since we were kids, and he's many things, but deceitful isn't one. That boy couldn't lie if a gun was held to his head. We used to have to sneak around to make sure he didn't see us and tattle. I'm not saying he hasn't grown up and changed, but he's also fiercely loyal and protective. Do you think he has it in him to purposely hurt you?"

No . . . at least, I didn't think so.

"How do you explain it then?"

"I don't know, Ellie. I really don't. I've dealt with some crazy shit in my job and then volunteering. I like to believe I'm a pretty good judge of character, and I don't believe he could hurt you. Not ever. I've seen the way he looks at you, and I swear . . . it's like nothing I've ever encountered before. There's a fierceness in his love."

I saw all of that too. He was always on guard, willing to do anything that would make me happy. He was patient at a time when most men probably wouldn't have been. When he was angry, he never took it out on me or even raised his voice.

The other part of me goes to his loyalty. He was protecting the people he loved, worried that he and his brothers would take the fall for something they didn't even do. And then I remember all he said about turning himself in. He was willing to take whatever the consequences were if it gave me peace.

I blow out a heavy breath. "Maybe it wasn't that way. I don't know. Either way, it doesn't make it any easier."

"No, I guess not. And Hadley isn't taking it well, I guess."

"No." I wipe a tear. "Neither of us are. She loves him so much, and God, Syd, I do too. I love him so much, and that's what's killing me. How can I get past this? How do we move on from it? It doesn't seem possible."

She lifts her shoulders slightly before they fall. "I don't know. Did you guys talk?"

"I lost it when I found out, and then we . . . I don't know, it was very tense."

She shifts a little, and there's a faint smile on her lips.

"What?"

"You say that you don't trust him, and I understand that you both have some issues right now, but answer me this— honestly—would you have lost it with Kevin?"

I jerk back because there's no way in hell I would've. "No, he would've hit me. I never lost my temper. I don't think I had emotions."

When Sydney sits back, there's a sort of smugness coming from her that I don't understand. "I got all night . . ."

What the hell is her point?

So what if I got angry with Connor and I never could with . . .

"I was able to be angry," I say as it hits me.

She grins. "If you didn't trust him, you never could've

yelled. You would've run or shut down, but you didn't. I know that you're angry, and you have every right in the world to be, but ask yourself if you want to spend the rest of your life trying to find a man even half as wonderful as Connor. You have a chance at a real family with him. He loved Hadley before he knew she was his blood. I don't know many men like him, Ellie. I'm not saying you don't have a right to be hurt, but be hurt together and find a way through it."

"And what if he doesn't want me back because I left him?"

"Then he isn't the man I think we both know him to be."

thirty-seven

"Can you watch Hadley until I get back?" I ask already getting to my feet.

"Of course, but where are you going at four in the morning?"

I force a mangled smile and rise to my feet. "I'm going to go see the two people who I need to talk to and hope they're listening."

I know that I will never find anyone like him again. He is my once in a lifetime. The problem isn't whether I love him or not, because I will love him for the rest of my life. It's finding a way to let it go.

And there's only one place I can think to go.

Sydney pulls me into her arms. "I'm so sorry you're hurting, Ellie. No one in this world deserves it less than you. But I want you to know that, while it's no excuse for Connor to lie to you, those kids had it rough growing up and it screwed with their heads. I also want you to remember that I know how you feel right now, and that, even after eight years, there isn't a day that goes by I don't wish I could go back and make Declan mine again."

And that's what I worry about. The regret that letting him go will leave a gaping hole in my heart forever.

"I appreciate that."

She smiles, a look of understanding fills her eyes. "Go, I'll watch Hadley."

"Thank you, Syd."

"Anytime. Go find your answers, and then ask yourself if your life is better or worse without Connor Arrowood? Chances are you already know the answer."

I lean in and kiss her cheek. "I always wanted a best friend. Thank you for being that."

I rush out of the house and get in the car. The last few days have been hell. My eyes are puffy, my hair is a mess, and my heart is mangled. I think about the question she asked, and I know the answer. My life is worse.

My world is sad and lonely.

He brought richness, love, and understanding into our life.

Connor showed Hadley and I what tenderness is.

All I want is his arms around me.

At night, I've clutched the pillow, wishing I could feel his warmth. I know what it feels like to leave someone and it be the right choice, this isn't that.

I park the car and walk through the cemetery gates with my legs shaking. I'm tired. I've been up all night, my nerves are shot, and I feel broken inside.

And I miss him.

If this is what two days feels like, a lifetime without him will be unbearable.

I lower to kneeling in front of my parents' headstones and

place one hand on each of them. "I found it all out, and I feel worse than before. How could I love the man who knew all along what happened to you? How can I have a life with someone who was there and didn't tell anyone? Whose father is the person who took you from me?"

I sit back on my heels and wipe away a tear. "I'm so confused, and I have no one. The last few months, I've had him, but—" I look up at the sky, wishing I could see her, and take a gulping breath. "But then I think about how he must've felt, and it just makes my guilt worse. Am I betraying you and everything I promised? His father is dead, and I can't make him pay, but you deserved so much more than what you got. You and Daddy shouldn't be in this cold ground."

"It should be me," Connor's deep voice says from behind me. I freeze, unable to think let alone move. "Your family was whole, and my father broke it. And then I did a bang-up job of hurting you."

"What are you doing here?" I ask, still not looking back.

"I felt like I should pay my respects and explain myself to them. I've come here once a month since I've been back." His voice is getting closer, and my breathing accelerates. "I was going to go when I saw you, but I was worried."

"I'm not okay," I tell him the truth.

"I'm not either. I can't sleep, Ellie. I can't breathe without you." I turn to give him some remark, but when I see him, no amount of preparation could've prevented my heart from lurching to a stop. His eyes glistening with unshed tears as he drops to his knees in front of me. "I can't let you go. I can't watch you walk away without knowing how I feel." His voice cracks. "I have hated myself for years because of what happened. I thought that, if I remembered, it would kill me, so I pushed it away. I was wrong, and I am so sorry."

Everything inside me is at war. Seeing him this way, sad, alone, and hurting because of sins committed by his father causes me to want to wrap my arms around him, but I don't. I intertwine my fingers to stop myself from taking his. "I don't know what to say."

"Then tell me you'll come back to me. I need you, Ellie. I don't want to live in a world without you, damn it. I've done it before, and I don't want to do it again. I want our family."

My chest heaves as my crying continues. Everything inside me is a mess. His head falls forward, and I want to tell him to look at me, to launch myself at him and tell him that I won't leave him, but I am still as a statue.

"I've told them the story about it all before. I came the day after I met you and left flowers. I know you don't believe me, but Ellie, I swear, I didn't know who you were."

Now that the initial shock has worn off, I believe him. "I'm not sure that part matters."

"You know I was just eighteen years old. I wasn't a man, even though I thought I was. Imagine if it were Hadley, what would she think if her father was threatening to have her thrown in jail. For years, he'd manipulated us into doing whatever he wanted. It wasn't an easy decision, and then we were older, and we . . . I don't know, we did what we could to survive and be good people."

I drop my head toward the ground, eyes closed, wishing I could hear my mother's voice. She was the kindest person I'd ever known, and I want to think she would forgive the boys. I don't know about my dad, but she would.

They weren't driving the car. They didn't urge their father to drink and drive.

All Connor is searching for is redemption, and he needs my forgiveness just as much as I came to seek my parents'. He and his brothers did what they had to in order to survive, as we all do. Was it right? No. But they were protecting each other.

Suddenly, it's imperative that I give it to him. He shouldn't carry around guilt over something that wasn't his fault or for not telling me sooner. I don't think he knew who I was when he met me in that bar or when he walked up my driveway that day. If he had, that would be a level of cruelty that he isn't capable of. I close my eyes and turn to face the first rays of the morning sun as they break over the horizon.

"Did you know that my mother didn't drink?"

"I don't know anything about them other than what you've told me."

"My mother was raised by an alcoholic father. I've always imagined him to be a lot like how you describe your father." I turn to him. "She wanted better for me. Even though my dad liked to drink each night, she married a man who doted on her like she was the sun, and everyone thought they were perfect."

"The way I see you."

My heart sputters. "I'm far from perfect, and they were too. As much as I've tried to idolize them, the truth is that my mother was never taught to use her voice when she thought he was wrong, and he had a tendency to make bad choices."

I glance back at my father's grave. He wasn't a drunk, by any means, but he liked his beer each night. Mom didn't care as long as it was just one.

"I don't want you to ever quiet your voice. I want us to talk. We're going to fight, and I'm going to piss you off. Things will happen, but I love you, and I meant what I said about fixing this. I could've lied to you, Ellie. I could've pretended that I didn't know anything about your parents' death, but I wouldn't do that. Not only because I love you but also because I don't want secrets between us. We've both been through hell, but when I'm with you, it's like heaven."

My eyes mist over, and I nod because I feel the same. "I know you weren't responsible. I knew that before I ever left your house, but I needed time to process everything, but . . ."

He leans forward, hope in his eyes. "I can wait."

While I'm sure that's true, I don't want that. He was willing to do whatever I needed to be at peace, had risked my walking away just so I knew the truth, and had offered to turn himself in even though it put his brothers at risk. He faced something that he'd been running from for years because he didn't want me to live another day with my own demons.

I love him.

I love him in a way that defies all logic, and while some may not understand it, I don't care.

I bring my hand to rest right over his thundering heart. "I can't."

"You can't, what?"

"Wait. I've seen monsters, and I've lived in nightmares. You aren't either. While what happened is tragic, it isn't your fault, and it is unfair of me to ever put that on you. Your father was driving that car, not you or your brothers." As I say it the sun starts to rise higher above through the clouds. "I can't imagine what I would have done if my parents were threatening me. I was angry, and more so when I thought all we had was a lie."

"None of it was a lie."

"I know that now."

"When you walked out that door, I thought I would fucking lose it. I wanted to get on my knees and beg you to see what we have."

I shake my head, bringing my fingers up to his cheek. "I don't want you to beg. I forgive you, Connor. I forgive all of you, and I think my parents would too." The sun warms my face and I look up with a smile.

"I hated that I had to hurt you."

"And that's why I think it's so easy to forgive. Because you, Connor Arrowood, are a good man." I hold his face in my hands. "You are a wonderful father. You're sweet . . ." I kiss his lips. "You're generous . . ." I repeat it again. "You're the only person who has ever made me feel safe."

His hands glide up my back, holding me tight against his body. He kisses me deeper—but not in a lustful way. In a way that allows me to feel it in my soul. His lips drift away from mine, and then I rest my head on his shoulder, allowing the warmth of the sun and the strength of his embrace to heal me just a little.

"I don't deserve you."

I release a deep breath and nestle in closer. "I deserve you. Take me home."

"I'll take you anywhere, as long as I'm beside you."

thirty-eight

"It's just my brothers," Connor tells me for the one hundred millionth time today.

"It's not just anything. It's the day I meet your brothers and they meet their niece and it's her birthday and . . ."

"And it is all going to be fine. It's a family barbeque where you are going to meet them and everyone can put their fears to rest."

Easy for him to say. He isn't the one who's about to meet the three most important people in his life.

I'm freaking the hell out.

At least Hadley is over at her friend's house for a few hours so we could set up and I can, hopefully, get the initial introductions out of the way. Not that it would change anything if she were here, but I feel like the five of us need a little time first.

"What fears do they have?"

"That you really haven't forgiven them."

I sigh. "Clearly, I have. I mean, I planned the party and invited them."

"I know this, you know this, but they're idiots who also want to alleviate their guilt a bit."

I guess I get that, but it isn't making my anxiety any better.

"Well, there are things to be done, and I need to do them."

I can't stand here, or I'll freak out. I head into the living room, straightening up a little more and moving the balloons—again. There really is no place to put them that doesn't seem strange. I go to the window, fluff the curtains a bit before trying to make them sit perfectly on the floor. I hear him chuckle behind me.

"It's not funny," I say with a tinge of hostility in my voice.

He walks up, wrapping his arms around me from behind and swaying gently. "It kind of is."

"You being charming isn't going to work."

"If I had more time, I bet it would."

I shake my head as I lean it back against his solid chest and exhale.

"Do you have to go see Nate this week?" Connor asks.

"Yup." Every-freaking-day it seems I have to go in. The court date is coming up, and it's been non-stop going over details and mock cross-examinations. "I can't wait for this to be over."

He kisses the top of my head. "Me too. But it's almost over and then we can move forward."

I like that idea. "Yeah, if I don't have a heart attack after meeting your brothers."

Connor's chest vibrates, and before I can turn to chastise him for laughing at me, I see dirt start to kick up on the driveway. Immediately, I jerk out of his arms.

"Ellie, relax, I promise, my brothers are going to love you."

It isn't just that, which is a huge part, it's that they know I know. They are here to talk to me about it, and that's . . . a lot of pressure. I want them to like me. I want this family to maybe start to repair itself a little.

Connor takes my hand and squeezes it. "I wish it didn't have to be this nerve-wracking. I mean, I've met Declan, but your other brothers are famous. It might have been better had you not told them all how I reacted when you told me."

"I know, and I'm sorry for that, but I also told them that you have a huge heart and clearly love me. The sooner we get this over with, the sooner they'll let you in on every fucking secret that I never wanted you to know about me."

"Like your irrational fear of ducks?"

His brows furrow. "Ducks are weird and have eyes on the sides of their heads. Not to mention, they just stare . . . out of the side."

That gets me to laugh, and I know it was meant to, but it's a slight relief.

We walk out onto the porch as three men exit a jeep.

"Well, well, if Duckie hasn't fixed the place up," one of the Arrowood brothers says.

Connor ignores him and guides us to where they're all starting to congregate.

"Jackass, I mean, Jacob, this is Ellie."

Jacob removes his sunglasses and smiles at me warmly. "Ellie, I'm very glad to meet you. I want to tell you how sorry we all are."

Well, that was quick.

"Jacob, geez, give her a second." Connor slaps his brother's arm.

"No, I appreciate getting it out of the way now. Thank

you," I say and look away.

Other than the shaved head, Jacob is almost identical to Connor in appearance. I can see why he does so well in Hollywood.

"This is Sean." Connor motions. Sean looks nothing like Connor, other than the eyes. Sydney wasn't kidding when she said it was a trait. Still, his hair is a bit longer and a shade or two lighter but he's no less good-looking.

Sean moves toward me and pulls me into his arms. "I'm so sorry, Ellie. I wish we were meeting you when apologies weren't in order, but it really is nice to meet you."

I hug him back and fight against the new wave of emotions that hit me. These guys are all amazing. How they can come here and welcome me and be so honorable is beyond me.

"I'm honestly happy to meet you," I say as I rub his back.

He disentangles himself from around me and then Connor looks to his oldest brother. "And you know Declan already."

"I'm sorry I didn't tell you when I was here before. I'm sorry about all of it. You have no idea how glad we are that Connor found you and Hadley."

And now I can't stop myself. I burst out in tears, overcome by it all. The anxiety leading up to this was almost too much, but now that the moment is here, I feel like I can breathe.

Connor immediately takes me into his arms. "What the hell did you do, Dec?"

"I don't know!"

"He always makes the girls cry," Sean or Jacob says. I can't tell because my face is buried against Connor's chest as I let everything go.

"It's because she realized that he's the ugly one of us."

"True story."

They joke back and forth, and I feel Connor's chest rumble. "Ellie, baby, why are you crying?"

"Because they're so nice!"

They all laugh, and I grip his shirt and tuck tighter against him so I can hide how bright red my face must be.

"They're not nice at all, but you'll learn to love them in time."

"Come on, Ellie, we have a lot more to say, and we'd like to get to know you," one of them says and then touches my back.

I sigh and step away from Connor because I can't hide against his chest forever and, well, crying rarely leaves a girl looking beautiful, they all probably know that.

Connor and I turn to head up the first few steps, but the three brothers stare at the house as if it might grow teeth and eat them.

"What's wrong?" I ask.

"This house . . . it's not easy for any of us," Connor answers.

I can only imagine. "Well, I promise that I will protect you all."

They all smile the same lazy and attractive grin. I am so glad I wasn't a teenage girl growing up around them. They are all insanely hot, and I would bet they are all good at getting what they want.

Declan is the first to take a step to me. "On that note, what could we possibly have to fear?"

Connor beams at me, and I can feel the fresh blush painting my cheeks.

We all walk in, and I hear a whistle from behind me.

"Nothing like it was the last time we were here."

"Yes, and it feels nothing like it either," Connor adds on.

Connor spent months fixing the house, barn, and equipment on the property. While he's worked on the outside, I've done my part to help by cleaning the whole house from top to bottom and adding plants and curtains.

"I'm sorry that we've sort of taken over the house," I say sheepishly.

"Sean, you're sleeping in the barn or you can snuggle with Jacob," Connor says with a laugh. "It's Hadley's bedroom until we move."

My eyes widen. "Move?"

"We'll discuss it later. First, let's all go and talk."

I don't like the sound of it, but I'm not about to argue in front of his brothers.

I grab a pitcher of lemonade and cookies I baked before joining them at the table. I really did go above and beyond because, while they may be here to apologize, I don't need it from them. The more Connor shared about his life inside this house, the less I cared about anything. I may have married an abusive man, but at least I could leave.

They couldn't.

"I'd like to say something first, if that's okay with you?"

They share a look, but then Declan nods. "Of course."

"I've never really had a family. I was an only child, and when my parents were killed, I was young and made bad choices—well, mostly bad choices." I sigh and shoot a small smile to Connor. "I just thought you should know that when I was eighteen, I was stupid. When I was nineteen, I was still stupid. And honestly, until Connor came back here, I was still stupid, only this time I was making stupid choices that affected my daughter as well. My point is, what you all did was wrong, but I don't have the right to judge you. Your father, from all I've heard, was a horrible man, and he took advantage of the love you four share to get himself out of trouble. And he's doing it even now by forcing you to be in a place that causes you grief, and for that, I'm sorry."

"Ellie . . ."

I put my hand up to stop Declan. "No, I'm sorry for what you endured. While my adult life has been pretty horrific, my childhood wasn't. So, I'd like to make a deal."

Sean leans back in his seat with a smile. "A deal?"

Then I remember what Connor told me about their word to each other. "No, I take that back, I want to make a vow."

Declan's eyes shoot to Connors, and he grins. "You know an Arrowood vow is unbreakable."

"So I've been told."

"Well," Jacob interrupts, "it is for some of us."

"I hope you'll forgive him for breaking the one about love and kids. I'm really okay with that one going to the shitter."

They all chuckle. Connor takes my hand and lifts it to his lips, kissing the back of my knuckles. "I am too."

God, I love this man. I look into his eyes, and I get lost. He loves me so deeply that it hurts to imagine what life would have been like had he stuck to that vow. I wouldn't have him, and that would be a tragic thing.

Someone clears their throat. "The vow?"

Crap. "Yes. The vow. I'd like for you all to give me your word that you will forgive me for all that I've done in the last eight years, and in turn, you'll get mine that I will forgive you for all that happened eight years ago."

Declan clasps his hands in front of him. "While I appreciate that, I think our debt is a little greater."

"Why is that?"

"Because you lost parents who were good people. You've made the choices you probably wouldn't have made because of that night."

"And so have you. All of you. This is my only request. I'd like the five of us to be a family. I want Hadley to know her uncles and . . . I hope you'll love her."

Sean smiles, sits forward, and puts his hand on my and Connor's hands. "I vow to forgive."

Jacob follows, his hand covering his brother's. "I vow to protect this family, as insane as it is."

Connor's other hand goes to the top. "I vow to love you."

Sean makes a choking noise.

Declan is the only one who still sits back. He watches Connor, and the two of them seem to speak without opening their mouths. Finally, Declan leans forward. "I vow to move forward—as a family."

This moment, this fragment in time, is something I will never forget. Here, holding hands with these men I just met, I feel at home.

They all did what I asked, and I pray that we can all find our way through the next however long with nothing hanging over us.

A tear pricks, not from sadness but from the beauty that this all is.

All four Arrowood brothers turn their gazes to me. "Oh, I'm supposed to vow?" Connor winks at me with a grin. "Okay then. I vow to let go of all the past sins and do everything you already said."

After a second, they all remove their hands, and then Sean releases a heavy breath. "You know, you better marry that girl, Connor, or I just might."

My heart accelerates at even the suggestion, so I pretend I didn't hear it and decide I will get through the trial before I allow myself to even consider it as a possibility.

Connor laughs once and then shrugs. "One day, I'll break the bow."

I smile at him. "And then maybe your shot will hit the target."

"I think it already has."

"I think so too."

Just then, the door flies open, loud footsteps echo down the hall, and in comes Hadley, skidding to a stop when she sees everyone at the table. I watch her take in the scene and before I can do anything, Connor handles it. "Hey, Squirt, you're here a little early. We have a special surprise for your birthday. Remember how I told you that I have three brothers?"

She nods.

"Well, they were so excited that they're your uncles and wanted to meet you."

"Uncles?"

Connor heads over toward her. "Yes, you already met Declan. He's my oldest brother."

He winks at her. "He loves the tree house," Hadley mentions.

"You should definitely show it to him again," Connor encourages.

Then the other brothers walk over to where we stand.

"The tall one with the ugly hair is your uncle Jacob." Connor drops his voice to a whisper. "He thinks he's super special because he's on television."

"No way!" she yells and then waves at him.

Before Connor can introduce Sean to her, he squats down and hands her a cookie. "I'm your uncle Sean. And I'm the best one out of all of them."

Her eyes narrow on the sugary goodness in his hand before she grins. "I like you."

Connor wraps his arm around my shoulders and chuckles. "You like him now, but don't let him know your fears."

Hadley nestles herself against Connor's side, her shyness is something I rarely see. "Are you all here for my birthday?"

"We are," Jacob says. "In the car, I have the biggest present for you."

Hadley looks to us and then to her uncles. "I really like your brothers, Daddy."

And I think it's Connor who got the best present of all.

thirty-nine

I hold Ellie's hand as we sit in the courtroom. The hearing is over, and we are waiting for the verdict. Nate did an exceptional job painting Kevin as a cruel husband who abused his wife and threatened Hadley.

It was incredibly hard to listen to Ellie recount the times he hit her, how he used her, and how he tore her down emotionally. It took everything in me not go over the rail and choke him myself.

Of course, it was even harder to hear his attorney paint Ellie as a whore who was having an affair with me, even though that isn't even remotely close to the truth. Hadley being my daughter, though, did little to help our case.

However, all of us spoke the truth, and thankfully, Nate was able to have Hadley speak to the judge in chambers instead of subjecting her to the actual trial.

"Are you ready?" Nate asks from his desk.

Ellie does her best to smile. "I'm . . . not sure, but regardless there will be a restraining order, right?"

"Yes, a permanent restraining order has already been granted for both you and Hadley."

She looks to me, and I give her a reassuring smile. It's little comfort to her, I know this, but I will never let that motherfucker near her. If he wants to break it, I'll be happy to break his face. Though, there is already a for sale sign up on his property, so I doubt we'll ever see him again regardless.

The trial took a lot out of us. We were stressed, but at home, I did everything I could to ease her worries. I hated seeing her nervous and unsure, hated seeing that Kevin had the ability to keep hurting her while he was locked up.

Nate's lips form into a thin line. "I wish I knew a little better which way the jury was leaning, but I feel as though we did the best possible job presenting our case."

Ellie nods. "You did great, Nate. Thank you."

"If I had known about what was going on earlier, Ellie. I would've done something."

He said as much a few weeks ago when Ellie was really delving into her past with him. The horror in his eyes at how long it had gone on was clear. She spoke of times they were together and the bruises she hid and how much a simple hug could cause her to almost faint. I thought Nate was going to lose it when he found out that the reason Ellie and Kevin had canceled a dinner party was because she had a black eye.

I was proud of her for not protecting him any longer.

She was cold and distant after that, seeming to retreat into herself, but that was nothing compared to how she was in the days leading up to the trial. She couldn't eat or sleep, and if she managed to close her eyes for a few hours, she had nightmares that had her screaming in her sleep.

It wasn't until Hadley broke down in tears that Ellie admitted it was an issue. Sydney referred her to a counselor, and it's helped a lot. She urged me to go as well, to deal with my past, but right now . . . I'm not there. I'm happy for the first time in my life, and I'm not ready to dig up things I've buried.

I am glad she's getting help, though, because it has allowed her to sit here, strong, solid, and unafraid. It's a sight to behold, that's for sure.

Ellie looks around. "Where's Sydney?"

She's signing paperwork that I was waiting for, hopefully, she'll be carrying in a deed for me, but I don't tell her that. I plan to surprise her tonight. "No idea."

I hate lying to her, but this is more of a fib because of a present. Surely, she'll understand.

"I figured she'd be here for this at least."

"I'm sure she will be here."

Then, as if us talking about her had summoned her, she strolls through the courtroom doors. Her face is stoic as she approaches. She looks every part of an esteemed lawyer and nothing like the girl who would chase Sean around the lake with snakes because he was—and still is—terrified of them.

Then I think about how the next seven or so months are going to be for her. Declan comes back in a little over a month, and Sydney has basically demanded we not talk or mention it.

"Hey, sorry, I got tied up at the office."

"No worries." Ellie tries for upbeat, but it comes out a little nervous because Kevin is staring at her.

I want to knock his head off his neck. Instead, I smile because, in the end, I won. I have my daughter and Ellie, and if all goes well, he's going to jail.

A few seconds later, the judge enters, and we all rise. He takes his seat and everyone waits.

"Has the jury reached a verdict?"

Ellie squeezes my hand so tight I wonder if she breaks bones, but I let her hold on to me.

"We have."

I hold on to my restraint, knowing that whatever happens will in no doubt affect our family. Ellie told me that if he's released, she's going to pack a bag and we leave with Hadley. I'm on the other side and would like to stay and stand our ground. However, those two girls are my world. If they want to leave, we will be packing three bags, not two. Sure, I came to an agreement with my brothers to buy a huge plot of my family's farm, but I could always sell it back to my brothers—hopefully.

The judge reads the paper and then hands it back to the bailiff. "What say you?"

The foreman of the jury stands and looks at the judge. "We, the jury, find the defendant, Kevin Walcott, 'guilty.'"

And just like that, Ellie relaxes and lets out a sob of relief.

He can never hurt her again.

"What do you think, Daddy?" Hadley asks as she holds up a drawing of a four-story house with a steeple, a gate, and a moat around it. I'm not sure who the hell she thinks is living there, but it's nice. "It's a bit small."

She beams. "I know, it should be bigger! We could have horses and pigs and goats and chickens all over here." She points to the other large building, which I'm assuming is a barn.

"I was thinking something like this." I show her my drawing. It's a lot simpler, a modest house with a porch, much like this one.

"That's boring."

"Boring?"

Hadley shrugs. "We should have a palace."

"Because you're a princess?"

"Exactly!"

Oh Lord, I'm in so much trouble. "Well, Princess Hadley, we're going to have to compromise."

Each day, Hadley and I have drawn different houses. She has no idea why and for good reason. The kid is the worst secret keeper in the world. She loves knowing things and can't wait to tell everyone else who will listen.

Therefore, I've just made it something we do. I have seven drawings from Hadley and seven from me.

"What are you two doing?" Ellie asks from the doorway.

Her hair falls down around her shoulders, barely brushing the swell of her perfect breasts, and her soft lips are turned up. Basically, she's nothing short of breathtaking.

"We're drawing houses!"

Worst. Secret keeper. Ever.

"Houses? For what?"

This wasn't how I wanted to tell her my grand plan, but I'm learning that life doesn't ever really go according to how we think it will anyway. Life with Ellie and Hadley has taken a lot of turns, but all of them have led me to this moment.

I want to propose, and if I thought for one second that she was ready, I would marry her tomorrow. I'm finding that it doesn't much matter that she isn't ready.

What does matter is having a home that is wholly ours and free of the ghosts of bad memories.

I'd like to tear this one down, but that'll be my brothers' issue, not mine.

I get up off the floor where Hadley and I were coloring and grab the papers. "Which do you like? I think mine are better, but Hadley likes this one."

Ellie takes them and seems to ponder each one carefully. "I see."

"You like mine, right, Mommy?"

"Hmmm." Ellie's noise is thoughtful as she moves to the next.

"Mine is better than Daddy's!"

"Hey!" I grumble at my daughter playfully. "I think I did good."

She nods and then pats my back. "You did okay, for an adult."

"Gee, thanks. Here I thought I was your favorite."

She giggles. "You are! But I'm going to win!"

I scoop her up into my arms and kiss her cheeks. "No way, Squirt. I'm going to win."

Ellie clears her throat. "I have made my decision."

"Put me down, Daddy." Hadley kicks her feet while laughing.

"Yes, we must be very official."

She mimics me when I stand at attention as though Ellie is my commander and I am receiving orders.

"At ease, soldiers." Ellie gives a salute, and I groan.

"We aren't soldiers, we're in the navy."

"Okay, whatever, sailors, people who can't draw." She winks, and Hadley and I both blanch in mock indignation. "I've decided which house is my favorite."

She lifts the drawing that Hadley did with the moat and entire farm. "I knew it! You owe me ice cream!"

I don't remember making that bet. "When did I say that?"

"You didn't," Hadley informs me. "I think I should get some since I'm the winner."

I think we're going to win something else.

"I have another idea . . ." I walk over to my jacket and tug out the papers hidden in the inside pocket. "What if we did something else for a prize? Something we all might want?"

Hadley's attention is piqued, and so is Ellie's. "What are you up to, Arrowood?"

I grin as I walk to Ellie. "I was thinking that this family has one big flaw."

"What's that?"

"We don't have a house of our own."

Ellie shakes her head with her lips pursed. "We are living in one now."

"Yeah, but my brother is going to be coming soon, and that got me thinking, we should have somewhere that's just for the three of us. A few months ago, I approached Declan about this," I extend the paperwork.

"What did you do?"

"Just open it."

She does so slowly, and her eyes go wide as she reads the agreement. "You're buying land?"

"I'm buying *us* land. My brothers agreed to sell me part of the Arrowood farm once it's able to be sold, and I'd like us to build on it. The good part is that we can actually start to build before it's sold. We can stay here while it's being built, but everything is ready to go if you are."

Hadley makes a squeal as she holds on to my arm. "Can we have goats?"

Her and the animals. "Let's see if Mom goes for the house first."

Then she looks at the paper behind it, taking a minute to examine the architect's sketch of the house I'd had designed. "That's what I had drawn up. I was thinking that, even though it doesn't have a steeple or gates, it would be great for us."

"Connor . . ."

"It has four bedrooms, the porch goes all the way around, and there's an office where you can work when you need to. I was thinking we could put—"

Ellie grips my face, pressing her lips to mine, effectively silencing me.

"Eww," Hadley complains, and we both smile against the other's lips.

"What do you think?"

"I think I love you and this is perfect."

I lean down and pull Hadley up into my arms and then grab ahold of Ellie. "This is what's perfect."

Ellie gives us each a kiss. "What do you think, Hadley?"

She grabs both our necks and pulls us close. "I love our family."

"Me too, Squirt."

"Me three."

And everything I have in my arms is everything I need.

epilogue

Two months later

"Dealing with these contractors is driving us crazy. But it's a huge relief that the Walcott farm sold and now I don't have to worry about Kevin living next door."

"Yeah."

"Connor took me out for dinner last night, and I swear, Syd, I thought he was going to propose."

"Uh-huh."

"I don't know if I'm ready, but then I wonder about what more I need to be ready."

"Right."

It's been an hour of us sitting here in the farmhouse. We're supposed to be having a girl's lunch since Connor is at the build site and Hadley is at riding camp, but Syd is being a grump. Instead of eating, she keeps moving the food around the plate and giving one-word answers.

I pick up my napkin and toss it at her. "What is up with you?"

"I'm fine."

I know she isn't, and I have a feeling I know what is bothering her. "Declan comes this week."

Sydney's eyes light up for the first time. "I don't want to talk about it."

"You never do, but I think you should."

I can't imagine this is going to be easy on her, and she's been doing her best to pretend, but time is up. Declan has cleared the next six months so he can do his time on the farm.

The brothers decided that when the conditions of the will were met, they were going to split up the land into quarters and if one wanted their portion, they could have it, but they forfeited all rights to any proceeds for the other three. When Declan, Sean, and Jacob go to sell, they'll split it three ways since Connor is keeping his.

The section we're building on is perfect. It's Connor's favorite spot and where Hadley's ridiculous tree-mansion sits.

Still, we're nowhere near done with building since they broke ground only a month ago. Instead of taking Declan in as a roommate, which he refused to even consider, he had a sort of tiny home built out by the barn, which is now completely finished and functional.

"I'm sorry, I have a lot on my mind."

"Okay . . . like, Declan?"

She gives me a pointed stare, which I'm sure intimidates some people—just not me. "I need to figure some things out."

I hate that she's clearly upset. "Syd, you know you can tell me anything."

She releases a deep breath and then looks away. "I made a

mistake."

"Okay . . ."

"I . . . screwed up the weekend of Hadley's birthday."

Oh God. I have a bad feeling about this.

"And?"

"And I was an idiot. I left the party, because I didn't want to be anywhere around Declan. I was a mess. I kept crying because our stupid song came on the radio, and so I went out to the pond because that's what dumb girls who are still in love with their exes do. I stood out there, thinking of him, wanting for things to be different."

"Syd . . ."

She lifts her hand. "It gets worse. Apparently, he was feeling the same way . . . nostalgic and he came out there as well."

My chest aches for her because I know how much she still loves him. He's been *the* guy. The one who she can't seem to get over and yet doesn't want back in her life.

He hurt her more than she'll ever admit.

"Please tell me you didn't . . ."

"Okay, I won't tell you."

Yeah, it's bad. "And now?"

Her eyes lift to mine and a tear falls down her cheek. "Now, I need to take a test."

I take her hand, and decide to confess my own fear. "I do too."

"You're?"

"I don't know," I say quickly. "But I'm late, and Connor and I have been pretty . . . busy not caring."

I had my IUD removed, and we both sort of figured if it happens, then it's meant to be. I've always wanted more kids, and he's the only man I want to have a family with.

"Do you have a test?" she asks.

I picked up one of those value packs because I'm one of those crazy people who will need at least four tests to confirm what test one says.

I nod, and we head into the bathroom. I hand her the one, letting her go first, and then, it's my turn.

We have three minutes.

I set the timer, and we sit in the dining room.

"Not how you thought lunch would go, huh?"

I shake my head. "No, but . . . I get it."

"What am I going to do if it's positive?"

I remember all too well how it felt when I found out I was pregnant with Hadley. It was terrifying. I wasn't ready to be a mother, but there I was.

"I know you're scared, probably more so because you're alone, but Declan is a good man. He's not going to make you do this alone."

"He can't know."

Now, it's my turn to be taken aback. "You have to tell him."

"When I'm ready. Not now. Promise me, Ellie. You have to promise you won't tell him or Connor."

"I can't lie to Connor."

She shakes her head and grabs my hands. "You don't un-derstand—"

The timer goes off and both of us freeze. "I won't say any-thing unless he asks."

Sydney releases a heavy sigh and then nods. "I guess that's the most I can ask for. Hopefully, it'll be negative and this will all be a bad dream."

I hope so for her too.

We both get up and head toward the bathroom to see the

results.

Again, I stand outside, waiting for Sydney to come out, and I say a prayer, asking for this to go the way we both want it to.

But before I can go see the results, Connor comes through the door.

"Hey, baby." He walks over and gives me a kiss.

"Hi."

"What's wrong?" he asks because it's clear I'm distracted.

I shake my legs back and forth and then bite my lip. "Wrong? Nothing's wrong, just need to use the bathroom."

Then the door opens and Sydney comes out holding both tests. She looks at me and shakes her head, but I'm not sure what that means. Then she kisses my cheek and holds out what I assume to be my test to me.

Connor's eyes drop to the unmistakable object in my hand.

Then she turns to him and smiles. "I'll see you guys tomorrow. I need to go."

"Syd?"

There are tears in her eyes, but she doesn't say anything. She touches my arm and then walks away.

I stand here, watching her go while holding my test. I'm worried about her.

"Ellie?" Connor says. "Is that?"

My pulse spikes because if this is positive, everything will change. Not that our life hasn't been constantly evolving, but a baby will amplify it. Then I think, what does it matter? He and I love each other and knew this was a definite possibility. I can't imagine my life with anyone else.

He's already an amazing father, and this time, it won't be scary. I'll have him with me each step of the way.

"I'm late," I explain. "I thought that maybe I could be

pregnant."

He smiles wide, and now I really hope the test is positive.

I lift the test, and my entire world becomes just a bit brighter. "We're pregnant," I say with tears in my eyes.

He wraps his arms around me and kisses the side of my neck. "We're having another baby."

"It seems we are," I say as a tear rolls down my face. "Are you happy?"

He pulls back. "Am I happy? I'm fucking beyond happy! We're having another baby, and God help me, Ellie, I'm going to marry you. I know you wanted to wait, but—"

"I don't want to wait."

"What?"

I take his face in my hands. "I love you, Connor. I love you more than any woman has ever loved a man. I don't need to wait to marry you. I don't *want* more time. We've wasted enough of it. I want us to have our family whole, and I want to be your wife."

He kisses me, and I forget how to breathe. I have no idea how long it goes on but we both start to strip each other.

His hands move down my body, soft and sensual. Connor kisses me deeply as he walks us back into our bedroom.

Slowly, he pulls the straps of my dress down, watching me as he does it. My hands go to his shirt, and I lift it off. I love his body. I love how my body reacts to his touch too.

We both explore each other with our hands. He brushes his thumb across my nipple, causing it to pebble before his mouth is lowering and he's sucking it into his warm mouth. I moan, relishing how good it feels and pregnancy only amplifies it.

He continues to drive me crazy with his mouth and then his hand is at my clit. He flicks it back and forth, causing my back to bow. "You feel so good," I tell him.

"I always want to make you feel good."

And he does. He uses his hands to pleasure or show me affection, never in anger. It's so different being with him. Sex is unbelievable, and I truly don't know if I ever really had an orgasm after being with him.

It was as though my body rejected anything that Kevin did.

When you love and trust your partner, it's a different experience. One that I'm glad I can share now.

He pushes me higher, licking my nipple, and moving his finger faster. I start to pant, my orgasm building with each passing second.

My head thrashes from side to side as I build even more. I call his name, begging for more and also for him to stop. I can't take it. It's too much.

"Connor."

"You're so beautiful. I love you so much."

He puts his thumb on my clit and pushes down, and I'm done. Wave after wave of pleasure laps over me. It's so good that I never want it to end. He pulls every ounce of pleasure out of me that my body will give. Then he's above me.

In one swift move, Connor pushes into me, both of us moaning at the sensations. My body welcomes him, loving how well we fit together. I slide my fingers down his back, and he surges forward again.

We make love. It's soft and hard at the same time. He flips us so I'm on top, and his hands hold on to my hips.

I ride him while he guides the pace.

"Ellie, I can't hold back."

I love when I make him lose it. There's something powerful about being able to do that to him.

"Then don't," I tell him as I grind down harder.

"I love you."

I swirl my hips and then drop down, bringing my lips to his. And then he finishes.

We're both sweaty, lying beside each other, neither really moving. That was intense and fantastic and emotional all at the same time. He props himself up on his elbow, looking down at me with a wry grin.

"What?"

"I love you," Connor says as his hand moves to my belly. "And I love you."

"We love you more."

"Not possible."

We clean up and then head back to bed, where we tangle together. We've both been just lying here, enjoying the quiet and warmth of each other.

"What was up with Syd?" Connor asks, breaking the silence.

I think about my friend and what her head shake meant. "I think she has a lot on her mind."

"My brother was weird on the phone today when I mentioned her."

Yeah, well, they both might have a lot more weirdness if that test was positive. However, I don't know if it was or wasn't, so my not telling him isn't exactly lying.

"Thank you," I say after a moment.

"For what?"

"For loving me. For giving me a family. For giving me a life I only dreamed of."

Connor's lips press against the top of my head. "I'll give you the world, Ellie."

And I know he will because he already has.

Thank you for reading Connor and Ellie's story. I hope you love them and the rest of the Arrowood Brothers as much as I do. Declan and Sydney's story is coming next and has so much heart and emotion in their second chance love story!

Fight for Me is available at all retailers

Sign up for my newsletter and receive exclusive content that is only for subscribers. Plus, you'll get freebies and a chance to catch up with your favorite characters!

www.corinnemichaels.com/subscribe

acknowledgments

To my husband and children. You sacrifice so much for me to continue to live out my dream. Days and nights of me being absent even when I'm here. I'm working on it. I promise. I love you more than my own life.

My readers. There's no way I can thank you enough. It still blows me away that you read my words. You guys have become a part of my heart and soul.

Bloggers: I don't think you guys understand what you do for the book world. It's not a job you get paid for. It's something you love and you do because of that. Thank you from the bottom of my heart.

My beta reader Melissa Saneholtz: Dear God, I don't know how you still talk to me after all the hell I put you through. Your input and ability to understand my mind when even I don't blows me away. If it weren't for our phone calls, I can't imagine where this book would've been. Thank you for helping me untangle the web of my brain.

My assistant, Christy Peckham: How many times can one person be fired and keep coming back? I think we're running out of times. No, but for real, I couldn't imagine my life without you. You're a pain in my ass but it's because of you that I haven't fallen apart.

Sommer Stein for once again making these covers perfect and still loving me after we fight because I change my mind a bajillion times.

Melanie Harlow, thank you for being the good witch in our duo or Ethel to my Lucy. Your friendship means the world to me and I love writing with you. I feel so blessed to have you in my life.

Bait, Stabby, and Corinne Michaels Books—I love you more than you'll ever know.

My agent, Kimberly Brower, I am so happy to have you on my team. Thank you for your guidance and support.

Melissa Erickson, you're amazing. I love your face. Thank you for always talking me off the ledge that is mighty high.

To my narrators, Andi Arndt and Zachary Webber who bring these characters to life and always manage to make the most magical audiobooks. Andi, your friendship over these last few years has only grown and I love your heart so much. Thank you for always having my back. To many more concerts and snow sleepovers.

Vi, Claire, Mandi, Amy, Kristy, Penelope, Kyla, Rachel, Tijan, Alessandra, Meghan, Laurelin, Kristen, Devney, Jessica, Carrie Ann, Kennedy, Lauren, Susan, Sarina, Beth, Julia, and Natasha (meh)—Thank you for keeping me striving to be better and loving me unconditionally. There are no better sister authors than you all.

about the author

Corinne Michaels is a *New York Times*, *USA Today*, and *Wall Street Journal* bestselling author of romance novels. Her stories are chock full of emotion, humor, and unrelenting love, and she enjoys putting her characters through intense heartbreak before finding a way to heal them through their struggles.

Corinne is a former Navy wife and happily married to the man of her dreams. She began her writing career after spending months away from her husband while he was deployed—reading and writing were her escapes from the loneliness. Corinne now lives in Virginia with her husband and is the emotional, witty, sarcastic, and fun-loving mom of two beautiful children.

books by corinne

The Salvation Series
Beloved
Beholden
Consolation
Conviction
Defenseless
Evermore: A 1001 Dark Night Novella
Indefinite
Infinite

Return to Me Series
Say You'll Stay
Say You Want Me
Say I'm Yours
Say You Won't Let Go

Second Time Around Series
We Own Tonight
One Last Time
Not Until You
If I Only Knew

The Arrowood Brothers
Come Back for Me
Fight for Me
The One for Me
Lie for Me

Co-Write with Melanie Harlow
Hold You Close
Imperfect Match

Standalone Novels
All I Ask